INHERIT EARTH

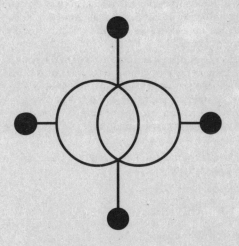

Editor:	Stewart Wieck
Cover Artist:	Pauline Benney
Copyeditor:	Melissa Thorpe
Graphic Designer:	Pauline Benney
Art Director:	Richard Thomas

INHERIT the EARTH

TABLE OF CONTENTS

One
The Treatment of Dr. Eberhardt

by Stefan Petrucha

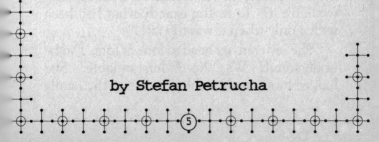

"No one suspects the days to be gods."
— Emerson

Half-way through the session, she tiredly mumbled "shining moment", then pressed back into the headrest of the leather couch and stretched her thin neck against the curls of her black hair. As she released, she began to tell, with the certainty that comes only after long internal deliberation, of her final conclusions.

"For as long as I can remember, I've believed there would come a moment when I could finally take a clear step back from my life and really see the pieces. It would be like this filthy glass had been removed from between my eyes and the world. Things would be clear, unambiguous. I'd finally understand why things happened to me, absolutely know what was in my control, what wasn't. And then, with the knowledge in my grasp, I could just rearrange the pieces, put them in some kind of order, make this response to that, feel this about that. Finally, finally, finally."

"Go on."

"I guess I've always been afraid the moment would come when I was dying. That's what kept me from killing myself. Because it would be silly, wouldn't it? To realize exactly what had been wrong only when it was too late?"

She lowered her head to look at him. Did he understand? Was she understandable? She looked away, at the table, the lamp, the family photo and some sort of glass knick-knack that seemed to glow from an inner light.

She was just about to ask what it was when he said, "And now?"

"Now I know, beyond words, that this depression is the only clarity I'll ever experience. Even you've run out of tricks to keep me going." she said. She paused, then added, "Haven't you?"

When there was no immediate answer, a tear welled in her eye. It grew to the limit of surface tension, then trickled down the side of her cheek. Quietly, Dr. Stuart Eberhardt breached his own etiquette and glided out of his chair to sit next to her. Weakly, she leaned towards him. Knowing he shouldn't, he pet her shoulder. She pressed her head into his chest and nuzzled against him.

He really was out of tricks. They'd tried Paxil, Prozac, Zoloft, even a few special brews, not to mention the years of therapy that only seemed to uncover layer upon layer of sadness. There was no effect, no improvement. And only one thing left to try.

He touched his index finger to her forehead and gently pushed her head back, exposing her face and neck. Staring into her helpless eyes, he parted his lips as if to speak or kiss, but instead drove the sharp points of his canines deep into her jugular.

She started a bit as the cutting tingle spread through her body, but then, with a sigh, her beleaguered mind began to relax. Tension slipped from her muscles. Her life had suddenly morphed

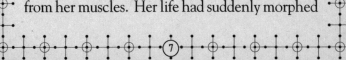

into a surreal, cliché, horror-show dream and she, having no reason to do otherwise, gave in to it. The blood flowed sweet and easy.

But just as the sanguine warmth spread along his stomach, some tick, some slight sense of happiness or contentment, or perhaps just a glimmer of pride at having existed at all, surged and surfaced. Her body stiffened, her eyes opened wide. She tried to scream but only gurgled. Ready to fight, she tried to pull away. She wanted to live. She really did. In spite of it all, she wanted to live.

"Too late for that," Eberhardt thought, folding his arm around her. Helpless against him, she struggled, pulled and moaned for what seemed a terribly long time. As her strength drained in waves, unable to see the clock from his current position, he guessed it might have been as long as ten minutes. Then, the little spark in her eyes, that some might have likened to her soul, diminished and died.

"Well, that was annoying!" Eberhardt said, letting go. "You try to do someone a favor and look what happens."

The body listed to the side. Unbalanced, its limp, hanging arm pivoted freely in the shoulder and swept the end table, sending both photo and knick-knack towards the floor. The photo was little more than a prop, but the orb was a gift from the Giovanni. It was a trophy for his research on Hunters, the so-called "imbued" humans who actively sought to exterminate the Kindred, and were forever increasing in number. Through knowledge, Eberhardt had made himself invaluable among the ranks of the night's children. The orb contained, so they said, the soul of the first of two Hunters he'd "treated."

In half a second, well before it hit the floor, it was safely in his hands. As an after-thought, he caught the photo, inches from the ground, between the thumb and forefinger.

After gently setting the orb back on its stand, he glanced at the photo, the shadow of a shadow-life, a sunny day on the beach, playing in the sand. He did not miss his wife, having always resented the fact that, since they were two people, there were gaps between them he could never bridge. The children, though, there was a time when he had felt at one with them. The memory sent a vague ripple through the crenellations of his undead mind. He tossed the frame back on the table.

Hissing, he swatted at the body as he would an errant shoe. It fell to the ground, achieving a position years of Yoga practice would never allow. He briefly told himself he'd been trying to do her a favor, but with fresh blood sating him, he knew it was a lie. The simple fact was that he should never see a patient while he was hungry. If he waited too long between feedings, everything started looking good. Thankfully, this had only happened twice during his three and a half years of night hours.

He looked at the time and gritted his teeth. His 7:30 would be arriving soon. A new patient. A special case. There were plenty of neurotic workaholics delighted by his evening hours, but they were inconvenient for a child. Her parents, upon hearing he was the city's pre-eminent specialist in delusional psychosis had sought him out as a House of Last Resort. It certainly wouldn't do to have the little one be greeted by a corpse on her first visit. There was time enough for that later. So he hefted the thing and thrust it into the supply closet. Glancing at the couch and the floor, he was pleased to see there was not so much as a drop of blood visible. Even before his Embrace, Dr. Eberhardt was nothing if not precise.

A few minutes later, the buzzer rang. Straightening his clothes, he walked across the office and through the small waiting room. He paused to straighten the Monet print (a final gift from his hurt, confused ex), pulled open the heavy white door and tried his best to smile the way he thought a human would.

It was no surprise when Mark and Sheila Simon, who'd been talking with hushed anxiety in the hall, fell silent when they saw him. They were, after all, terrified that their daughter was mad, and this was the place where that determination would be made. He could have looked like an angel and their reaction would have been the same. At 5'8", with an average build, curly black hair and blue eyes, he was paler than most, but didn't quite look like a vampire, either.

"Dr. Eberhardt," Mark said, offering his hand.

"Call me Stuart. Please," he said. To avoid contact, he waved them through the door. "Mark, Sheila, Jessica, come in, come in."

Bundled in a red over-size jacket, her arms nearly immobile in its puffy sleeves, the expressionless child turned her Yoda-like eyes up at him, then back to her parents before she followed them inside. She wanted to warn them, but knew what their response would be.

Coats met hooks. Small hands wriggled little arms to freedom. No one noticed the Monet.

"Well," Eberhardt said, clasping his own hands with a nonchalant little rub he imagined was a pleasant, reassuring gesture, "there's plenty of magazines and some cable TV here to keep mom and dad entertained."

Turning to the short creature, he smiled widely and said, "I'd like to speak with Jessica alone for a while now — if that's all right with you, Jessica?"

The answer was quick and simple — "No."

Mother smiled, but Eberhardt saw the fear in her eyes, "Go ahead honey, we'll be right out here…"

"You'll stay?"

Dad, pointing to the office door, jumped in with his own insincere grin, "Anytime you want, you can open that door and see us."

"I won't lock it," Eberhardt said.

As he held open the door, she toddled under his arm, careful not to make physical contact, and peered around inside. He nodded to Mark and Sheila then gently closed the door. At the click of the latch, she froze, terrified. Then a look of conscious control made its way along her features, and she bravely turned to face him. He motioned pleasantly to the couch. And as she clambered onto it, he wondered just how to begin.

A child, a child – how does one speak to a child? Especially one who can really see you? Too sharp, too adult, you frighten her. Too soft, too slow, she'll smell the lie. Children naturally know disingenuousness, he mused, a knack often lost to mortal adults as a consequence of engaging in their own. And in this one, that sense might be even more heightened. The two Hunters he'd examined previously enjoyed a general increase to their perception of 25% or more as compared to their previous life — most likely a result of actually having to pay attention to the world. Start simple. Let her set the pace.

"Do you know why you're here?"

"My mommy and daddy are worried about me."

"Yes. Yes they are. Do you know why?"

"They don't see the bad eyes."

Eyes. It was skin pallor, visible veins, or an aura that gave them away to the other two, coupled with a general sense that the being they confronted just was not alive. What was it about the eyes for this one? A reflection of her own?

"But you do see them?"

"Yes."

"Does anyone else?"

"They see each other," she said hesitantly, then added, bravely, "You know."

Eberhardt decided to reward her.

"Because I'm one of them?"

She scrunched up her brow.

"Yes."

"And you're afraid of them? Of me?"

"Yes."

"Why?"

"You hurt people."

"You're afraid we'll hurt you?"

A nod, then, "Or my mommy or my daddy."

"Well, what if I promised not to hurt you?"

She looked at him, full of suspicion.

"Why?"

"Because I really do want to help you."

"What about later? If you get angry or scared or hungry?"

He really did smile at that.

"Yes, well, we all get angry or scared or hungry sometimes. That can make us forget our promises. But you know, there's a special promise among some of us bad eyes that we can't ever break. It's called a Blood Oath."

"A Blood Oath?" she perked up, keenly interested. As a child, her experience was inherently limited. Here was an excellent opportunity to learn how much knowledge, even in a neo-linguistic, structural form, was given to Hunters in the moment they acquired their strange, predatory status, the so-called imbuing. Perhaps this was even a chance to determine if the imbuing was an outside force, as both of his previous subjects suspected, or something they were born with that simply, somehow, activated at some point in their life.

"What if I made a Blood Oath not to hurt you?"

She eyed him warily, so he added, "Just for tonight?"

"And my mommy and daddy?"

"Of course!" Eberhardt said. With that, he knew he'd won the first round.

"All right," she said solemnly.

"Then it's done."

"Don't you have to use blood?"

"Do you want me to?"

"No."

"Then I won't."

He had to be careful about what he said next. She could be a great ally in his quest for truth, if he kept things honest. So the answer was obvious, he said nothing.

Slapping his hands to his thighs, he stood, saying, "I think that's enough for tonight, Jessica. I do want to see you again in a few days, and I hope you'll feel a little more comfortable and we can talk some more."

"Will we have another Blood Oath?" she asked, climbing off the couch.

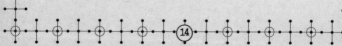

"Of course," he said. "Would you wait here a minute? I want to talk to your mommy and daddy for a second."

His words to them were quick and reassuring: "It's natural, to an extent, for a four year old to have, well I hesitate to call it trouble, but let's say a permeable boundary between reality and fantasy. Jessica may be going through little more than an extreme version of that. I would like to continue seeing her, a few times a week, to try to learn what emotions her fantasies are enabling her to play out. As part of the therapy, I'm playing along with her, so don't be surprised if she tells you I've admitted to being a 'bad eye.' It will help me determine what that means to her."

Mark Simon braced himself and asked the question foremost on their mind, "Stuart, we brought her here because you've been, well, pre-eminent in treating this sort of thing. We heard about the patient who attacked you. Is it the same?"

Eberhardt shrugged good-naturedly, "Oh, I wouldn't worry about it at this point. The full-blown psychoses I've treated are more closely related to a fairly common schizophrenic delusional structure, where the person believes a loved one has been replaced by some identical, yet somehow evil, entity. I don't think that's what we're dealing with here."

The Simons visibly relaxed.

"Then what are we dealing with?" Sheila asked, "Sometimes we'll be walking down the

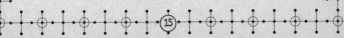

street and she'll just start screaming and pointing at someone, insisting they're some kind of horrible creature!"

"It's way too early for me to say, but we might just be dealing with, well, childhood," he answered. She seemed to accept this, and it was clear she desperately wanted to. The more of Jessica's behavior he could get them to accept as normal, the easier time he'd have studying her.

Further relieved that he didn't plan to offer any medication, Eberhardt noted with pleasure the first vague signs that they were beginning to trust him. He called Jessica in and they made ready to leave.

As her parents put on their coats, Jessica pulled Dr. Eberhardt down for a whisper.

"She forgives you."

"Who?" Eberhardt said, genuinely confused.

She leaned forward and spoke even more softly, "The lady in the closet."

A little taken aback, he nodded. She must have looked in the closet. Lightning-like, he rattled off the possibilities in his mind and concluded that even if she did tell her parents about it, they wouldn't believe her.

As Eberhardt watched from the open door, the small family passed through the pools of light shed from the hallway sconces and soon vanished into gray. Once satisfied they were gone, he returned to his office and spoke to an empty corner.

"You can come out now, Garth. I know you're here."

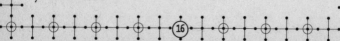

With a little laugh, some shadows in a corner of the room congealed into the long lean form of Garth Warburton, Eberhardt's liaison with the powers that be, of quite high standing himself. He was the city's Keeper, who answered directly to the prince. The fact that Garth visited Eberhardt personally was a great compliment to the psychiatrist's work, an honor in itself. Over time they'd become something akin to friends.

"How long?" Eberhardt asked.

"Just after you closed the door to the waiting room," he said.

As if continuing the same sentence, he pointed a long bony finger toward the orb on the end table. "You're keeping the saiwala, in plain site, where the humans can see it."

Eberhardt heard the implied criticism, but knew it would be silly to respond directly. Garth never gave an opinion, he simply described events in such a way that his opinion seemed a simple matter of fact.

"It amuses me," Eberhardt said, "to hide in plain sight. I find it liberating."

"I doubt the Giovanni would be so amused."

Eberhardt shrugged.

"What did she whisper to you, as she left?" Garth asked.

"That the lady in the closet forgave me. I had a uh.. lapse of judgement with my last patient," he answered, without hesitation. There was, after all, no way of knowing when the Keeper had really arrived.

"Yes, I know all about it!" Garth said, grinning. "I have to admit I'm pleased to see you indulging a bit! It's good to know you're not quite so tightly wrapped. But the interesting thing is that the child knew. Could she already have some hunter abilities, even be a sort of clan member?"

Eberhardt waved the thought off with a smile, "You've read my work too closely. I once suggested they might have something akin to the clans, with different capabilities based on breeding. But while we share blood, I haven't found any similar physical link among the Hunters. More likely she wants to be one of the Rugrats or Power Puff Girls."

Garth furrowed his brow, confused by the references. Then his mouth formed a small "o" as he recalled, "You were a father, yes?"

Eberhardt nodded, "Three girls. Did you... ever have children?"

"Once...," Garth began, almost sadly, "with a light cream sauce. Not unlike veal."

Eberhardt laughed, "Every single bit of available data, my studies combined with what we've heard, indicates that hunter abilities are predicated on the basis of adult preferences. They're not innate."

"But adult preferences could be innate, couldn't they?"

Dr. Eberhardt smiled, "Nature, nurture – let's not go there again, shall we?"

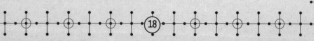

Garth gave a little bow.

"What would you like me to tell the primogen and the prince?"

"That we have here a wonderful opportunity to study a hunter without medication."

Garth raised an eyebrow, "Really? That's surprising. I know how much you enjoy the pills."

"Oh, absolutely, but she's barely four. She's no danger to us physically, and no one will believe her. Why not?"

"Well, what if someone does believe her? Or one of those dreadful abilities surfaces early?"

This part, Eberhardt knew, was just a game. Garth had already decided what recommendation he would make. Now he only wanted to hear the obvious.

"Well, of course, she'll have to be eliminated before she gets much older. I'll bring her to you if you like. You can try another cream sauce. Or perhaps a hunter sauce would be more appropriate?"

"An imbued child would be quite a prize. Thank you for the offer, but I'll defer to my prince. Or the current seneschal. Depending on which way the wind is blowing."

"Wise as always. You'll be seneschal yourself some day."

"Yes, I think you're right," Garth said with a smug little smile. Then, again proceeding as if it were the same thought, he added, "You have no interest in rising in the ranks, Dr. Eberhardt?"

Eberhardt gently shook his head and opened his palms towards his office, "I'm quite content with my lot."

"A man without ambition is simply a man whose ambitions remain unknown," Garth said, smiling. "Well, life is long and there is much to learn. At any rate, as long as these Hunters continue to grow in number and become more of a nuisance, your position is quite secure. I'm sure our prince will grant your permission. You have no other hunter-clients right now, so there's little danger of her being… affirmed, shall we say? Take your time. More than with the last, for heaven's sake!"

"Oh yes. Peterson. It's a shame the drugs destroyed his mind so quickly. I was getting close to isolating the mechanics of some of his abilities," Eberhardt said apologetically.

"Tut-tut. I didn't mean it as a reprimand. In science you learn as much from your mistakes as your successes, no?"

"Thank you."

"I know. I know," Garth waved off the gratitude. Then he began to vanish again. Watching him, Eberhardt, surprisingly, laughed.

"Is something funny?" the Keeper said.

"I just realized, to me, you're the visible face of the prince, yet you're usually invisible!" Eberhardt said.

"Quite right! I am fond of it," Garth said, chuckling himself. What little color he had faded. Then the black and grays of his form subsided into the wall.

Outside, a few blocks away, Garth re-materialized among the evening crowd. He had to check up on some drug deals the primogen were squabbling over – he was often the visible face in their dealings with humans as well. There were faster ways to reach the slums, but, feeling unusually cheerful, he instead made his way to the elevated trains, one of his favorite ways to travel. There was always someone interesting on board to talk to, or follow, or feed on there.

Overly distracted by his general sense of well being, he failed to notice that he was being watched. Across the street in a parked Honda Civic, James Padavano, police detective, followed the odd figure with his eyes as he punched a number on his cell phone.

"O'Malley," the voice at the other end said.

"This is Jim. Warburton just hit the trains."

"Did he see you?"

Annoyed, Padavano pushed some breath between his lips, "Like I said, this is Jim. All of a sudden you don't trust me? I've seen this guy talk to a score of dealers. Just because I haven't managed to connect him with any suppliers yet doesn't mean I'm going soft."

No answer, then: "You ever…" the voice trailed off.

"Ever what?"

"Nothing."

"What?"

"Did you ever notice anything strange about him?"

"Strange like what?"

"Like… anything?"

"You mean aside from the usual horrible narcotic crap? Needles, sadism, torpor, abandoned babies, vomit, blood?"

"Yeah. Aside from that."

Padavano thought about mentioning the fact that Warburton was able to slip through crowds like mercury, often disappearing in the time it took to blink. Then he figured he was just tired, that it was a trick of his eye, and rather than reinforce any doubts O'Malley may have about his abilities, he just said "No."

"Okay. Good. If you do, you lemme know. Not in an hour, not in a minute. Immediately."

Click.

• • • •

> As I was walking up the stair
> I met a man who wasn't there.
> He wasn't there again today.
> I wish, I wish he'd stay away!
> — **Hughes Mearns**, *The Psychoed*

"Let's play a game. Do you like games, Jessica?"

"Yes."

"You ask me a question, any question — and I'll answer it, as truthfully as I can. Then I'll ask you a question and you answer me as truthfully as you can. Does that sound fair to you?"

"Yes."

"Good. You go first. Ask a question."

Surprisingly, she didn't have to think about it and asked, rather quickly, "Do you like being a monster?"

Eberhardt, for his part, didn't have to think much about the answer.

"Yes, Jessica, yes I do. Very much. I'm strong, I can see and do things that humans can't, I never get sick and I believe I'll live forever."

He leaned back in his burgundy leather chair and let her mull his answer. He could almost see the wheels grinding in her small brain. The lines her facial muscles made were a much better match for her dark surroundings than the pink dress, light brown locks and fair skin. She seemed to almost glow against the heavy curtains and deep brown built-in bookshelves that lined the office walls. Some patients had commented that it always seemed slightly shadowed in here, no matter how many lights were on. He assured them they were projecting their own negativity.

Tonight, after two weeks and six halting, cautious sessions, Eberhardt was beginning relax and enjoy her small brain. To be sure, it was often simplistic and usually chaotic, but, on occasion it was capable of the sort of insight about things one only has when seeing them for the first time. He also enjoyed, albeit less consciously, telling her the things about himself he could never tell other patients, things which would bore other Kindred to tears.

"Don't you miss your family?"

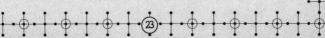

"Ah — my turn, Jessica. When did you see your first monster?"

"Under my bed. Only it wasn't real."

He shook his head.

"No. Truthfully. You know what I meant. Your first real monster. Like me."

"In the park. A long time ago. It was night. He was eating a hot dog, only it wasn't really a hot dog. I told mommy, but she wouldn't believe me. My turn."

She pointed a stubby finger at the orb on the end table.

"What's that?", she asked.

Eberhardt pursed his lips and exhaled. Noticing, her eyes twinkled. She was tickled by his discomfort as if it were a prize she'd unearthed at the bottom of a cereal box.

"It's a *saiwala*, a soul-trap. In it, as far as I know, is a man's soul. Do you know what a soul is?"

She shook her head.

"Well, some people might say it's the part of us that makes us who we are, and no one else."

Her eyes went wide. She pulled her knees up under her and moved towards the edge of the couch for a better look.

"And he can't get out of there?"

"My turn. How many kinds of bad-eyes have you seen?"

With great ceremony, she put her hand in front of her and counted her fingers: "One…

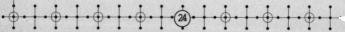

two... three... four... no, wait... One... two... three... four... five..., uh..."

Fearful she would spend the rest of the session trying to get past six, he shook his head for her to stop, "Just describe them for me."

"Okay. There's the bald ones, they're really scary, the dirty ones, the animal ones, the crazy ones, the ones with nice clothes, the ones who wear like... like... daddy when he goes to work, only funny and black," she said.

"Suits?" Eberhardt offered.

"Yeah, suits. There's fancy ones, ones with dark skin and... and... the crazy ones... and the bald ones...," her voice trailed off.

"It's hard to tell which are which sometimes," she offered, trying to keep up her end of the deal.

He nodded. He recognized a few of the clans. The bald were Nosferatu. The crazy Malkavian. The dark skin could be Lasombra, but where would she see one in *this* city? Wherever, the fact remained that though her lexicon was highly personal, her catalog might well be complete. Was that part of the imbuing, too? The way a newborn rodent knows to be afraid of snakes?

"Which kind do you think *I* am?"

She shook her head, said, "My turn," and pointed to the orb again.

"Is he stuck in there forever?"

Eberhardt bobbed his head back and forth noncommittally.

"Pretty much, unless the glass breaks. My turn. Which kind do you think I am?"

She looked at him, scrunched her eyes and concentrated for a while. Finally, she shrugged.

"I dunno."

"Well, if that's the truth, then it's your turn," Eberhardt offered. He'd have been surprised if she had picked a clan for him. He was Caitiff, high generation, quite far removed from the famous, supposed biblical progenitor of the Kindred, so he had no inherited characteristics and hence no discernible clan. Though he was certain his nose had gotten sharper since his Embrace, Garth and others assured him this was vanity. He had no need for a clan, adopted, as he was, in a sense, by the primogen and the prince for his work.

He expected her to follow the question up and ask what kind of bad-eye he was, so he was busy figuring out how to couch his response, when she surprised him.

"If being a monster is so good, why didn't you change your family into monsters, too?"

Eberhardt stared at her, silent for so long she had to nod her head for him to answer. Recovering, he said, haltingly, "Well, when you become a monster you don't feel the same way about things or people anymore. I just don't care about them that much."

"But you still have their picture."

"For decoration. So people don't know I'm a bad-eye."

She stared at him, sensing some distance between himself and his words.

"Well?" he prodded.

"You said the truth. That's not the truth."

Eberhardt smiled. He was about to say something about how she'd understand when she was older, when he remembered she wouldn't be getting very much older at all.

A click of the outer door made them both turn.

"Your parents," Eberhardt said, relieved, "Time to go."

Wordless, perhaps still expecting an answer to her question, she followed his movements with her eyes as he rose, walked across the room and opened the door. Mark and Sheila were smiling, always happy to see him, comfortable there was progress being made. Their acceptance of Jessica's fantasies as normal had doubtless led to a lot less tension at home. Eberhardt, for once, was genuinely pleased to see them as well.

"How is she doing?" Mark said softly.

"It was a good session. I think I'm starting to get through to some of the underlying structures that compose her fantasy."

"That's good," Mark said, nodding. He turned to Sheila and repeated, "That's good."

He expected some confirmation from her, but she hadn't heard him. She was looking into the office, motherly consternation crossing her face.

"Jessica, put that down! That's not yours!"

Eberhardt whirled just in time to see Jessica holding the Saiwala high above the hard wood floor.

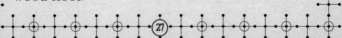

How could he not have heard her?

He visibly tensed. The parents noticed immediately.

"Honey, put that down right now," Sheila said.

Jessica, a look of fake innocence plastered on her angelic little face, moved to place the globe back on its stand. Eberhardt couldn't be sure if it was a childish lack of coordination or malevolent intent, but she missed the table by a half inch.

The thing that hurt most was that he could have caught it easily. In fact, he could have snapped her neck, pinched both parents on the cheek and caught it with time to spare, but that would mean having to explain how he happened to be faster and more agile than a cheetah. Instead, he braced himself, grinding his teeth as the precious bauble shattered and the soul within it, set free, melted, unseen, into the world.

The child's face registered joy for a moment, then tensed as she awaited punishment.

"Jessica! How could you! That was very, very bad!" Sheila said, running up and grabbing her arm.

"It was an accident!" she protested.

"It doesn't matter. It wasn't yours. You shouldn't have been playing with it to begin with."

"I'm sorry, Mommy!"

"Stuart, please," Mark said, reaching for his checkbook, "Let me pay for it."

Shaky, Eberhardt waved off the gesture, "That's all right. Really."

"Wait until I get you home young lady…" she said, yanking Jessica along by the arm. Just before they disappeared down the hall, the girl turned and gave Eberhardt a mischievous little smile.

He shut the door and listened to the silence at his back. Closing his eyes, he hoped he was alone.

"That was most unfortunate…" Garth said, melting in from the window.

They both stood there for a moment, staring sadly at the pieces. Eberhardt spoke first.

"Garth, even Bellini, the Giovanni who gave it to me, wasn't certain there was a real soul there. It was primarily symbolic."

"Still," Garth said, then repeated, "Still. It was a lovely gift."

Eberhardt slumped into his chair.

"Things are changing," Garth said.

"Oh? Why? Not the orb, I hope?"

"The orb, the fact that the child knows the clans. The fact that she was able to snatch your most precious object when your back was turned. The fact that she hurt you."

"And?" he asked, expecting there was more.

"She's one of these ridiculous predators. She's a hunter."

"She's a child," Eberhardt said, balking at the thought she might be some sort of threat.

Garth drummed his fingertips against one another and looked off through the window.

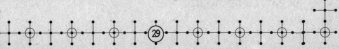

"A young lupine," he said, "lost, deranged, I suppose by that strain of rabies that seemed to be making its way through them then, stumbled its way here about ten years back. An unsuspecting Toreador cornered it, thinking to indulge his curiosity, never having seen one, and believing, as you, that it was only a child. It chewed straight down to the neck-bone before the three others traveling with him managed to pry her off."

"I take your point, Garth. Anything else?"

Garth sighed, hesitated, then spoke, "Yes. Her questions about your family rattled you."

Eberhardt smiled at that.

"I know how this has to end," he said, "I look forward to it."

Garth cocked his head to the side.

"Do you?"

"Do you underestimate me that much? Don't you understand how much I've learned so far from her? How far we can go?"

Garth smiled and shrugged pleasantly.

"I suggested no course of action. I still hope to leave that to you."

The sudden reminder of Eberhardt's "place" in the scheme of things riled him, but he knew expressing that emotion at this point might do him terrific damage. Eberhardt shook his head as if dislodging beads of anger from his brow. Regaining control, he vaguely pointed to the shards of glass that still covered the floor and began to apologize.

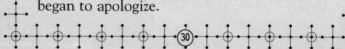

Garth already knew the excuses he was about to make, the apologies he was about to offer — being upset and so on over the destruction of his precious saiwala. Garth also wasn't convinced they'd be genuine.

"All right, all right," Garth said. Then he left.

Eberhardt cradled his head in his hand. That was a mistake. It had all been a mistake; the level of honesty, the game, turning his back on her after explaining how the soul could be freed. It all smelled of weakness, awkwardness at best, at worst... what? He should be done with it now, medicate her ego into oblivion, snap her sweet neck, or wrap her up as a gift to the prince, but he just couldn't shake the feeling that deeply rattled his old psychiatric bones, that he was on the verge of a major break-through. And what would that mean, if he reached it? What paths would the answers reveal? Could he help the clans be rid of the Hunters permanently? Would it bring him vindication?

Garth, meanwhile, slipped vertically down the side of the building, caressing the rough texture of the frayed brick walls like black mercury. The uncomfortable exchange with the good doctor had left him very tense. As such, he debated reporting the shattering of the saiwala, but decided against it. It was Giovanni business at best, little to do with the primogen or the prince. He would make a careful note of it, though, laying a paper trail in case it proved to foreshadow some later aberration. But even then, no one would blame his silence. Eberhardt was highly thought of and Garth, well, Garth, for the most part, was allowed.

As was his habit, he reformed in an alley three blocks away. After a few steps, a dull nagging made him stop short and thrust his nose in the air, as if literally smelling something amiss. He whirled a full half-circle, a straight ebon tree trunk pivoting on its center among the lesser pedestrians, before his eyes came to rest on a pock-marked, midnight blue Civic across the street. Making eye contact with the driver, Garth strode through the traffic and stopped at the window.

"Come with me," Garth said.

Nodding, James Padavano stepped out of his car.

∙   ∙   ∙   ∙

"We'll eat you up, we love you so!"
— **Maurice Sendak,** *Where the Wild Things Are*

Four weeks later, Eberhardt sat on a fire escape outside the fifth story window of the apartment building where Jessica's family lived, pondering the end of the game. As invisible as he could manage, though a piker compared to Garth, he watched Sheila read *Pierre*, a children's book about a boy who didn't care, while Jessica listened, rapt.

It was time, according to Garth, to get the lay of the land and make plans. The sessions, though dragging on, were moving, in fits and starts, towards what even Eberhardt had to concede was a natural conclusion. He tried to convince himself that watching her further growth would provide even more valuable insight into the hunter-psyche, but logic had mercilessly truncated that line of reason. Reports of hunter-attacks were rampant. It was only a matter of time before another hunter spotted her — and she became, full-fledged, full-blown — the enemy, not only to the Kindred in general, but likely to Eberhardt in specific. He did not kid himself that their odd little truce in the therapeutic bubble of his office would stand the test of harsh reality. What was to be done was not an issue. The question was how?

He could drug her into madness, as he had the rather dull-witted Avenger he'd treated previously, leaving him perpetually twitching, strapped to a hospital bed, with various tubes to feed and vacate him, but that seemed, on an aesthetic level at least, a waste. There were other options. He'd toyed with turning her, but really, how would that look? He was already under a cloud of suspicion, something he could not afford. As a Caitiff, he was given the protection of the clans by virtue of his usefulness. If he betrayed some sympathy, some preference for a hunter, even as a childe, his ability to continue his work would be imperiled. There was even the possibility, though he felt it slim, that they would reject him entirely. And that would rapidly mean his final death. Unprotected by the status quo, he would easily fall to the rogue elements that often dined on Kindred blood. Though the air that whipped around him was cold, the thought made him shiver.

Inside, Sheila tucked her daughter in and brushed the child's hair from her forehead. Leaning forward, she gently kissed the bare spot of skin her hand had revealed. As his eyes followed her out of the room, Eberhardt pensively stroked the tip of one of his canines with his tongue.

He already knew what he needed to — the number and location of the doors and windows, the security system and so on. Entering, taking her, or killing them all, could be accomplished in minutes. Not tonight, though. A few days, a week at most. Any further delay and there'd be direct pressure from Garth. And that, well, that would just look bad.

In any event, it was time to hunt for some sustenance — perhaps a bohemian from one of the local coffee shops — then return home to his notes and his books. For some reason, instead of moving, he kept watching the child.

Jessica was awake, but barely breathing, clutching some little stuffed animal to her chest, staring at the ceiling, eyes half-closed. He remained, a statue, indistinguishable to a casual observer, from the rest of the building. He was trying to understand his own instincts, to comprehend what it was he wanted from this child before he killed her. Shaking his head free of whatever spell kept him, he turned and was about to make his way back to the roof, when he noticed her lips moving.

His hearing was extraordinary, of course, but wind and traffic obscured the words. Shifting his weight, he pressed his ear to the glass.

She was singing, something soft, something familiar.

I will hold you
For as long as you like
I will love you
For the rest of my life[1]

Eberhardt swooned as a strange vertigo shook his core. At once enraged, he tore at the wall, hand over hand, until, at the top, he propelled himself through the air like a great black raven, briefly in flight before sprawling onto the tarpaper roof. He pulled himself onto his knees, but couldn't bring himself to stand. He was panting, pained as if a stake had been driven into his heart.

Could it be coincidence? Yes. No. Had he ever mentioned it to her? Ever? No. Never. Why would he? It would be madness. Even madder to forget. Could she, as Garth suggested, already have some hunter powers? According to the hearsay he'd studied, some could see things, know things. It might explain how she destroyed the saiwala.

Whatever the precise explanation, she may just as well have signed her own death warrant. Clearly she was too powerful. It was all he could do to keep from bursting through her window at that very moment and shredding her like paper.

The song she was mumbling to herself in the darkness with her high, sweet voice, was the same

he once sang to his own children, before putting them to sleep.

• • • •

Garth remained composed. If he was shocked, as Eberhardt suspected he must be, he didn't show it. He did wait for Eberhardt to repeat himself.

"I want more time with her," Eberhardt said again.

"To what purpose?" Garth said, enunciating each word carefully.

"This is a singular opportunity to chart the growth cycle of a hunter, from beginning to end," Eberhardt leaned back in his chair, trying to look calm.

"To end? Do you propose we adopt her?"

"No."

"Perhaps pay for her education?"

"As she grows, drugs can be provided … or she can be dominated… or …"

"They're breeding like rats. Others will find her."

"Not if we're careful," Ebrahrdt said, rising.

He walked over to the lean, taller creature and put his hand on his shoulder. The Keeper's eyes narrowed at the odd contact, but he allowed Eberhardt to continue.

"I know how it must sound, but I'm on the verge of a break-through. I honestly believe I can deliver some final answers, some solutions, information that could well lead to the salvation of the Kindred!"

Garth twisted his head to the side, genuinely confused. "The children of Caine stretch back through time, to all but the beginning of man. We *will* stretch ahead to his end. I don't believe the Kindred require salvation from you, Caitiff, nor do I think the prince will find the concept even remotely amusing. These Hunters are an irritation, a blip on the screen. What exactly do you think you can learn? We already know they can die. The rest is mere detail."

Eberhardt held his ground, "We also know *we* can die. And that they can kill us."

Garth relaxed a bit, as if remembering their friendship, "You put yourself in danger."

"I've dealt with Hunters before," Eberhardt said confidently.

"The girl is only your third. But, I don't mean that you're in danger from her, which, of course, you are. Remember, I like you. I will do for you what I can, but in the coming days I advise you not to deceive yourself about your importance to us."

Eberhardt turned away.

"You'll pass my message to the prince?" he said.

"Along with my impression of it," Garth said.

"Good."

"Good-bye, Stuart," Garth said.

In a clearly agitated state, not bothering to conceal himself Garth crawled out of the window and down into the street. In plain view he walked down the block, his mind ablaze with phrases and strategies, his goal shifting from protecting Eberhardt to protecting himself.

John O'Malley, police detective, hunter, sensed Garth coming before the creature even entered his field of vision. Feeling a dull tingling at the back of his neck, he put his newspaper down on the steering wheel. He glances up just in time to see the lean figure weave quickly through the crowd and pass a mere few yards from him. In an instant, he knew what Garth was.

Growling, he started the engine, thinking the traffic lean enough to let him follow, and knowing he'd finally gotten lucky. He'd been parking for hours, nearly every night for weeks now, in different spots, just a few blocks from where they'd found Padavano's head.

•   •   •   •

As Gregor Samsa awoke one morning from uneasy dreams, he found himself transformed in his bed into a gigantic insect.
— **Franz Kafka,** *The Metamorphosis*

Just what, Eberhardt wondered with his fine mind, as he slumped in his fine chair and scanned the fine walls and fine windows of his fine office, had brought him here, to this odd spot, where his future was as murky as the past? As a mortal, he'd dabbled in Jung, but ultimately became a Freudian. Why? He once thought it was out of spite, because Freud was out of vogue. Now he wondered if perhaps even then he was hewing to some deep psychological need to walk between worlds. Maybe that was the problem right there. A need to test his position. He was never a very good psychiatrist. The more familiar he became with the sort of problems his over-privileged clientele had, the more he found himself at first resenting, then utterly hating them. At least as a vampire he found them interesting, if only as a potential food source.

Towards the end of his mortal career he wasn't really treating anyone. Mostly, he enjoyed the process of tweaking the dosages of various psychotropic medications, and found the results often delightfully surprising — sometimes downright titillating. He could make them laugh, he could make them cry. He could give them dreams with colors they never even guessed existed. It was a joy he carried with him even when he was turned. The sole joy he could recall with any completeness from his time spent in the cycle of living and dying – before he looked into the abyss and found it looking back.

Three and a half years ago it found him and he knew. He knew at least something was watching. For weeks, at odd moments, alone, he felt a chill on his back that would slowly creep inside him and overwhelm him with its desolation. At first the sensation seemed invoked by his own through processes, which had grown increasingly dark, as if he had conjured the heavy elan himself. But, eventually, it came unbidden.

When it finally braved the safety of distance and came to him outright, even his terror was mitigated, on the one hand, by the satisfaction of knowing his intuition had been right and on the other, by relief that what had been haunting him was in fact external and not the projection of some disenfranchised insect corner of his psyche.

He was sitting in a coffee shop between sessions, reading a new translation of Kafka's Metamorphosis, hard cover, first edition, when it sidled up beside him trying to project the faint echo of human lust.

Eberhardt remembered the book well, even the texture of the paper page as it poked through the black ink. In it, a daring translation of certain phrases gave rise to the possible interpretation that Samsa's transformation had in some sense, freed him. As a creature of the fantastic, Samsa was no longer beholden to the pattern and form of his stale, old life, leaving the creation of an utterly new one, if he could just let go of the shadows of former habit, within his grasp. The tragedy, then, was not in what he became, but in clinging to what he remembered himself to be. The possibility tickled Eberhardt, feeling claustrophobic as he was, in his own senseless routine.

"You like books?" it asked, smiling.

"Some," he responded, barely looking up.

"Expressions of will chained in the vagaries of syntax and grammar. Do you really think they matter much?" it wanted to know.

Eberhardt looked up into what he could see of its eyes, shaded as they were by the rose-colored spectacles made briefly popular by Coppola's co-opted Dracula.

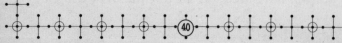

"Nothing has more power than an idea whose time has come," he said, rattling off the quote as if ordering a usual meal.

It laughed freely, like the lively she its form recalled, then draped a white hand on his shoulder and whispered in a language that wrapped around his world-weary mind like dream. It promised tingling without consequence. It promised to shatter the wall between will and action, to free an ancient longing from the mind's cage of word and image. It promised an end to decay, to the descending spiral of natural change. It promised to leave only the grand momentum of existence, the ebb and flow of desire and fulfillment.

Eberhardt put the book down. The sound the hardcover made as he laid it on the table burned into his head, blurred though it was by the murmur of lesser conversations and the nearby hiss of milk being steamed with the machine-like precision of well-trained vendors.

Without asking, though his answer would have been yes, it took him out into an alley, hid with him in the shadows and drained him. It sucked every parcel and pain of his human experience right out of his flesh, then made him drink of its own. A few months later, it abandoned him, perhaps sick of his books, perhaps simply heeding another distant call. Now, he thought of it fondly, like some wild black storm so grand and hurried, it could only be witnessed once. But he never knew his dark mother's name.

Wife and children no longer a concern, he decided to continue his practice, mostly for the sake of the aforementioned fascination with medication. Then one day, an unusual patient was recommended, because of some vague, accidental success Eberhardt once had in quelling the delusions of schizophrenics. Minutes into their first session, the man realized what he was and tried to kill him. He was strong, adamantine in intent, but Thorazine had slowed him enough for the doctor to prevail. Stuart Eberhardt had encountered his first hunter.

According to the police, it was clearly self-defense. Others in the psychiatric community rallied about him with sympathy most sincere. Eberhardt even feigned a bit of Post-trauma disorder during a few mandatory therapy sessions, a maneuver which earned him some respect among the more discerning practitioners of the Masquerade. It helped explain his new paleness, even his separation and subsequent divorce. In point of fact, though, he was as ecstatic as he imagined that odd back-woods cult of Christian snake-handlers were when they danced and whirled with the poison reptiles. In death, he had finally come alive.

When he found himself delighted when hearing more and more tales of such attacks upon the Kindred, he decided on his new calling. He would study, catalogue, and ultimately eliminate these strange creatures, this odd threat to his newfound immortality. Having a live specimen was rare, but he collected data, did research and soon managed to deliver reports to the primogen, pages and pages filled with his various theories regarding hunter strengths, their weaknesses, the limits of their abilities and the extent of their flaws. With every presentation, no matter how accurate the information, his stock in the eyes of the city's masters rose. Months ago, Garth had even suggested he take part in a blood hunt, diablerize a particularly heinous offender, to make his own blood stronger. Eberhardt's standing was such that Garth was certain the prince would look the other way. Eberhardt refused. The problem then would be that he would have a clan, which meant alienating one or another of his wide-eyed supporters. In a sense, he thought himself more powerful being powerless.

Tonight, he was realizing for the first time how wrong he was. He was feeling fragile, mortal for the first time in years. During his final session with Jessica he could barely bring himself to speak. If she noticed anything different about him, she said nothing, and instead, seemed so bored by the silence that she finally curled up on the sofa and seemed ready to drift off to sleep.

For days he'd managed to resist the requests Garth brought, but they would soon become orders, then threats. He had to kill her. He had to. Clearly, for his own preservation. Quickly and carefully. Right now. A pillow. A quick blow to the head. Toss her out the window and pretend she slipped while they were looking at a bird. No, even he didn't believe that. The parents, then, upon their arrival, would have to go as well. He could carry them out. Make them vanish. Hide the pieces here and there. Sloppiness he might be forgiven, even extreme sloppiness, eventually, but inaction he would not.

He hovered over her, unaware he'd even stood and stepped to the couch.

She, still awake, twisted her head and looked up at him through sleepy eyes.

"Stuart?" she said softly, as if trying not to wake herself, "Will you make a Blood Contract not to hurt me today?"

"Shh…" he said, afraid it sounded more like a hiss.

She looked at him, Yoda-eyes sucking in every detail of his face, carefully building a phantom world in her mind, probably much more ordered than the real one. What could she see? How much did she know? What could she tell him? Should he ask her how she wanted to die?

After a moment, her eyelids dropped and she fell asleep. He just stood there, ready to abandon even the notion of mobility as he watched her. The minutes ticked along.

It was cold in the office. Temperature didn't matter much to him. It kept the bills down and tended to shorten the sessions. Some adult patients would bring sweaters, but Jessica was shivering.

Without thinking, he took a green blanket he kept folded over one end of the couch, and covered her. When she smiled as she snuggled under its warmth, he suddenly realized what he was doing and snapped to attention.

What if someone had seen? Garth could be here right now. What was he doing? Immediately, he ripped the blanket off. She made a face and scrunched up her shoulders, but did not awaken. He stood there, holding the blanket, his eyes darting back and forth in his skull, trying to see the unseen.

For the first time since his death, he felt like an utter idiot, terrified by this young piece of flesh, holding a soft green blanket in fingers that had torn open countless throats. Quickly, awkwardly, he put the blanket back on her. For appearances. It was as good an explanation as any. Garth would understand that. It was part of the Masquerade.

Eberhardt failed to notice that he was no longer even thinking of killing her. When Sheila and Mark arrived he met them at the door, holding Jessica, wrapped in the blanket, in his arms.

"Poor thing," Sheila said, softly as she took her, blanket and all. "She's had a long day."

"Yes, she has," Dr. Eberhardt said, nodding. Quiet goodnights were exchanged. Mark had a question, but decided it could wait. Stiffly, Eberhardt staggered back into his office, and placed both hands on the end table to steady himself.

"Are you here?" he said. He meant to make it sound matter of fact, but it came out as a whisper full of dread.

"Yes," Garth said, taking form, "And I saw."

There was silence for the longest time.

"Could you...?" Garth began.

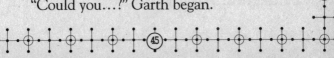

"What?" Eberhardt said hopefully.

The Keeper shook his head, "Never mind. It's too late. I was thinking perhaps that if we caught up with them before they reached home, and you killed the child, in front of me, then signed a Blood Contract, then perhaps, with much begging and pleading. But no, in the end you're Caitiff. And it's gone beyond that already. It's why I'm here. To tell you it's out of your hands – and determine what to do with you next."

"What do you mean?" Eberhardt asked as the guessed-at details sifted through his mind. "Why *before* she reached home?"

"They're coming for her tonight…"

"What?" Without another word, he bolted for the door. Garth swept in front of him, cutting him off, trying to hold him still with his great, steely arms.

"Stuart, listen carefully. It's still possible you can survive this, perhaps in some other city. Arrangements could be made. If you value your existence, go to the prince and beg. You may be allowed to simply leave the city. Elsewhere you might even continue your work, if that's still important to you," Garth said.

With a rage he didn't know he could possess, Eberhardt grabbed Garth and pushed backwards, catching him off balance only because he was more than willing to fall himself. The two tumbled onto the end table, splintering it. The photo flew into the air again. Eberhardt, oddly, rolled off of Garth and caught it. When he turned back, he saw Garth partly impaled on a leg of the table, squirming, unable to pull himself free.

"Lift me quickly you fool! It's in my back!"

Eberhardt dutifully nodded and stepped over. He started to pull Garth off the wooden shard. But then, at the last possible moment, he hesitated. Garth saw the hesitation and knew at once what it meant. A command from brain to body was already winding its way through his nervous system when Eberhardt pushed down with all his might. With a crack, the bone buckled and a bloodied wooden stump popped from the center of Garth's chest.

Eberhardt didn't look back, he simply raced out.

His vitae draining this way and that into the carpet, the pinned Garth looked around at the office and sneered. Paralyzed, but still quite conscious, the Keeper who'd once hoped to be seneschal, perhaps even prince, turned invisible – partly to keep himself hidden from unwanted visitors, partly because he'd never really liked being seen.

Down on the street, O'Malley spotted Eberhardt exiting the lobby of the building he'd seen Warburton enter. Anger welled as he watched the vampire pretend at human courtesy, by smiling and nodding at the doorman. A carnivore's nod to the cow. The creature hit the sidewalk, pivoted east, and, once out of the doorman's sight, sped off in a frantic fashion that O'Malley seldom saw in a vampire, unless it was surrounded by flames. He was moving, to O'Malley's grim amusement, like a bat out of hell.

Unwilling to lose this one the way he had Garth, O'Malley sped a block east to get ahead of it, then jumped out onto the sidewalk and began jogging west, ducking this way and that through the crowd. He'd never catch him on foot and didn't want to risk losing him to city traffic. Cars and human feet were useless in this game. Fortunately, he had a other tools.

His eyes scanned the moving pedestrians; lovers, bums and businessmen, mostly oblivious to anyone outside their immediate sphere. He could spot the vampire with a glimpse, unless it had sensed him and ducked into one of the small shops. But no, there it was, moving quickly towards him. O'Malley moved as if to get out of its way, but then, just as it passed, the imbued detective pushed to the side, letting his hand brush the thing's shoulder. Contact made O'Malley a bit nauseous, but didn't even slow the thing down. Perfect.

No thing, no person except O'Malley could see it, but a small, thin trail of smoke was leaving an echo of the monster's steps. He could follow in the car now, which would be easier than trying to carry all of his equipment.

"Got you," O'Malley whispered.

As Eberhardt raced through streets blanketed by a thin veneer of artificial light, he was utterly oblivious to the hunter. What he did know, at last, was that the breakthrough he'd felt himself so very near had nothing whatsoever to do with Jessica, Hunters or even with the Kindred. The great truth along whose edge he'd danced, mesmerized, had been about himself. As he raced to face whatever waited and whatever it was he would do when he got there, he felt so close to revelation, he could taste it.

•   •   •   •

"When we remember that we are all mad, the mysteries disappear and life stands explained."
—Mark Twain

Outside the window where Jessica slept, the motionless Eberhardt saw, or imagined, that everything around him was shining. The lean, steady fingers of rain, the rough soaked tar of the street, the colorless bricks and stone of the building, even the ribboned edges of the city haze that perpetually hid the stars — all had a glow that was either utterly new to the world, or despite its apparent glory, that Eberhardt had somehow miraculously failed to notice.

Behind a Dumpster, O'Malley waited and watched. The top joint of his index finger was hooked on the trigger of a .45 Colt Magnum, loaded with standard hollow-point rounds, which, he figured, should be more than enough stopping power for a low-level undead. If it wasn't, or if some of its pals showed, as he hoped they would — less than an arm's length away was a duffel bag stuffed with the even more interesting toys he'd been collecting since his days as a hunter began.

As long as the thing seemed to be waiting, O'Malley was content to wait as well. What he really wanted, more than its mere destruction, was what he imagined Eberhardt could lead him to: a view into the power structure behind the city's undead. That was why he'd abandoned the immediate satisfaction of avenging Padovano's death. It was a game he'd played before as a narcotics detective, letting runners or street dealers lead him to bigger game. But here there was a more immediate danger – its hunger. And so his finger remained poised on the trigger. If it made a move towards the window, he'd be sure to get its attention. Meanwhile, he ignored the moisture his shirt and pants had sucked up from the wall and floor, and practiced remaining motionless.

When, after what seemed hours, Eberhardt failed to even turn towards his hiding place, O'Malley dismissed the vampire as either incredibly dense or distracted by some undead peculiarity to the point of numbness. His impression changed immediately, though, when Eberhardt's voice suddenly called to something unseen, something even O'Malley, with his heightened sense of such things, failed to notice.

"Two Assamites for a four year old?" Eberhardt hissed as two shadows seeped into the alley entrance. Trying his very best to sound menacing, but utterly failing, he scrambled down the fire escape to all but the ground level. He thought of climbing down further, but someone had unhinged the hook that held the sliding ladder in place, leaving it dangling a foot or so above the ground, rusted and barely in place. His weight would easily pull it off the track, and a pratfall in front of the assassins would be unwise.

Instead, he leaned out into the wet air, holding the rail with one hand and glared.

"Splitting the fee? Are you afraid of her?"

As air and shade molded itself into two more undead, O'Malley held his breath and tried to soak in the details. There was a familial similarity between the new ones. They shared black hair, slim, graceful builds and slightly hooked noses, but one was nearly a foot taller than the other, taller than O'Malley himself, and the shorter one had much, much darker skin.

"Stuart Eberhardt?" the shorter one said.

Eberhardt nodded.

"You misunderstand. We're not here for the child. We're here for you."

Eberhardt smiled, feeling oddly important for a moment.

"The Keeper was to deliver your last chance. If we arrived and found you here, well, then you are to be ours. I must say, I'm very happy to see you. It's been difficult controlling ourselves during our visit to this city."

"The girl. What's to become of her?"

"Brought back to the prince. Not our concern, really. Or to our taste."

With a little growl, Eberhardt let go of the railing and leapt the ten feet to the ground, landing without a sound.

"Might I persuade you otherwise?"

The smaller one shrugged, "Do you possess anything of great value?"

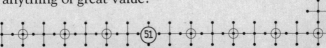

Eberhardt shook his head, "No."

"Are you much more powerful than you appear to be?"

Again, Eberhardt shook his head.

"Well then," the shorter Assamite said, stepping back. Eberhardt braced himself as the taller one came forward and tried to circle behind him.

"We heard you were an expert in the so-called imbued," the tall one sneered in a bass voice, "Are we to assume the human among the garbage is yours?"

O'Malley realized he had less than a second to react, so he fired. Eberhardt's head snapped towards the dumpster. Two rounds discharged, but before the first even reached maximum velocity, its target, the taller Assamite, vanished, leaving the hollow lead to shatter against the brick wall. Tensed and ready for combat, O'Malley lurched out into the alley, gun first, looking for another target, but seeing only Eberhardt. The two, seemingly alone, just stared at each other, each knowing exactly what, if not who, the other was.

"There's a girl," Eberhardt began, but before he could finish the sentence, the taller Assamite appeared behind him and cupped its hand over his mouth, preparing to twist his head off with one deft, well-practiced move. Again, O'Malley managed to fire twice. The second bullet hit Eberhardt in the shoulder, but the first hit the tall creature's esophagus, tearing through the bone behind it. It staggered back, shocked that it had been hurt at all, then equally surprised that its head no longer seemed properly attached.

Recognizing a scant opening, Eberhardt spun and quickly completed the bullet's work, ripping its head off. Masterless, the body slumped to its knees and pitched fell forward.

In the darkness, something screamed in utter rage. Without thinking, Eberhardt and O'Malley stood back to back, frantically trying to scan the air for any sign of the remaining predator. The scream came again, but there was no way to locate its source.

"That's blood rage, hunter," Eberhardt whispered, "We killed his childe."

When an odd shadow seemed to twist against a spot under the fire escape, O'Malley fired at it as he realized it was meant to distract him. As if caught from behind by some gargantuan machine, he was hoisted into the air, then hurled twenty feet into the dumpster. Its metal side buckled from the impact. The dent held his body aloft for a moment, then he rolled and fell the last foot to the alley floor. Through half-closed eyes, O'Malley saw the shorter Assamite clutching Eberhardt by the neck with one hand and shaking him back and forth. Eberhardt's legs and arms flapped left, then right, depending on which direction the Assamite shook him. Then, as the thought of a new pain to inflict crossed the creature's mind, he slammed Eberhardt to the ground.

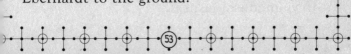

In a flash, the Assamite's heavy foot was on Eberhardt's chest, pinning him. Dizzy, bleeding badly from a scrape in his neck, not at all sure what was happening to him, Eberhardt heard the pained squeak of old metal as the Assamite ripped the dangling ladder from the fire escape. He lifted his head just in time to see the mad assassin plunge the edge of the ladder down towards him.

The bone in Eberahardt's thigh crunched as the metal edge drove through him, and deep into the concrete beneath. The Assamite leered at the pinned doctor, leaned down, and again, just screamed. Though terrified by what was happening to him, nearly unconscious from the pain, inside, Eberhardt was locked in weeping for what would happen to the girl.

Then, all at once, there was a WHOOSH! that sounded half like a strong rush of air and half like metal scraping concrete. The Assamite rocked gently forward and seemed confused. Something had hit his back. Puzzled, he twisted his long arms around, trying to dislodge it, or at least figure out what it was. As his hand made contact with the protruding edge of the incendiary grenade, it exploded. The Assamite did not have time to shout, but Eberhardt wailed as the hot white light seared his photo-sensitive flesh. Random shards of Assamite slapped into the walls, then dropped.

Two ribs in his back broken, O'Malley let go of the grenade launcher and lapsed into unconsciousness.

He wasn't sure how long he'd been out, but at some point, he woke to the feel of warmth on his cheek. Opening his eyes, he looked out of the alley. Across the street where some shorter townhouses stood, the sky had cleared and the sun was rising. A low moan brought his growing attention back to the alley, where he saw Eberhardt weakly pushing against the metal that held him fast.

Reaching into his duffel bag, O'Malley picked up a machete and crawled towards Eberhardt. Eberhardt, his face a mask of peeled skin, tried to twist his head towards the hunter, but couldn't quite manage it. O'Malley leaned over him so he could look into its eyes.

"Sun's coming up. Judging from the screams, that's a painful way to go. I can make it quick for you."

Eberhardt nodded. O'Malley shook his head.

"Not yet. Give me Garth Warburton."

Somehow the doctor managed a laugh as he spat out, "No."

O'Malley didn't understand.

"You don't owe them anything."

"He's probably as good as dead anyway, and he protected me once. But, listen, there's a four year old girl living with her parents in 5B. Jessica Simon. She's a hunter."

O'Malley's eyes went wide. The pieces finally fell into place.

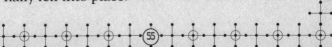

"Yes," Eberhardt said weakly, "We were all surprised. By now every vampire in the city knows about her. You'll have to try to protect her."

O'Malley nodded, "I can make arrangements."

Eberhardt squirmed as some stronger rays laced over the building-tops. Wisps of smoke curled from the burns on his exposed flesh. Feeling something akin to pity, O'Malley raised his machete and prepared to put Eberhardt out of his misery.

"No," a child's voice said.

Jessica, a Power Puff Girls bathrobe wrapped tightly over her pajamas, her bare feet covered by white bunny rabbit slippers, stood at the front of the alley looking sadly, but calmly on the scene. Oddly embarrassed, O'Malley put the machete down. Ignoring him, she walked over to Eberhardt, sat down in the blood and filth and gently shifted his head into her tiny lap.

"Do you remember?" she asked him.

Distracted by pain, confused, bemused, but happy to see her, Eberhardt looked into her Yoda eyes. On the rim of one pupil, just where the brown, green and hazel flecks gave way to white, he saw a refraction of light form a small spark. Looking closer, he saw a tiny picture. It was blurry at first, but as his strength faded, it became increasingly clear.

It was a beach, a sunny day. He was there with his wife and children. The dull ache in the back of his head that generally dogged him in those days had been melted by the giggling of the girls. As he laughed and swung his youngest in the air, he felt release and utter peace.

Eberhardt's body lurched, burning. He was again in the alley, daylight searing his flesh, a tiny hand caressing his forehead.

"Shhhh," the child said.

He saw the picture again, and this time tasted the oxygen the ocean waves churned into the air, felt the sand on the feet of the children and heard their rapid breathing. For a moment the scene reversed. He was on the beach. The alley where he lay dying was just a refraction of light on the tip of a breaking wave.

Then there was nothing.

An odd smile played across O'Malley's face, cracking the already dried blood on his lips.

"How did you know to be down here?"

A shrug, "I've known this would happen for a very long time."

"You *foresaw* this?"

Another nod, then "All of it."

O'Malley tried to get his mind around it.

"But, you're here. If you knew they were coming for you, you could have fled. I mean, if you knew he was going to die anyway, why?"

"Because," Jessica said, wiping the dust of Dr. Eberhardt from her pajama pants as she stood, "I wanted him to be happy about it."

[1] Lyric from "Calico Skies" by Paul McCartney, © 1997 MPL Communications

Two
Credo

by Eric Griffin

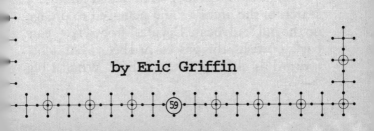

To: hunter.list@hunter-net.org
From: Xterminator306
Subject: Inherit the Earth?

So what's with this "Inherit the Earth" crap? I've been seeing this plastered all over the place here. A bunch of you folks use it in your sig line (very original, I might add). So I figured I gotta ask. You all throw the phrase around like some kind of secret password or something. So how bout letting the rest of us in on the secret? I'll let you borrow my secret decoder ring and peek at my dad's magazines…

—X

"Insert sig line. Then rotate."

To: hunter.list@hunter-net.org
From: Shogun123
Subject: Inherit the Earth?

Geez, the "Xterminator" is going to lecture us on originality… Read the FAQ, daVinci.

That stands for "Frequently Asked Questions" by the way. Didn't mean to throw you with more codespeak. Let me spell it out for you. Click Here: http:/www.hunter-net.org/faq.htm

To: hunter.list@hunter-net.org
From: Xterminator306
Subject: Thanks. For nothing.

What a bonehole. I went ahead and did a search of the archives and managed to dredge up the old "Advocate Debates" from a few years back. I ^wish^ this process had been as straight-forward as clicking a single link. What a big hairy hassle! There are some things about this siteplan that are really arcane and make no kind of sense at all.

Anyway, that thread seemed to answer most of my questions, except for the obvious one — why the heck are you guys still kicking this worn-out phrase around at all? I mean, I understand about Witness1 and his "revelation" from the Messengers. And I can appreciate what he's trying to do here. I mean, it's not his fault that this place has turned into such an asshole magnet.

But could it be that NO ONE here (coughShoguncough) even bothered to do this basic bit of homework before jumping on the Inherit the Earth bandwagon?

—X

"Insert katana. Then rotate."

To: hunter.list@hunter-net.org

From: Cabbie22

Subject: Archives

Da huh?

Xterminator, what the hell are you going on about? This site doesn't even have archives going back "a few years." The whole of hunter-net crashed last year and — well let's just say that it was thought wise not to restore the older data.

For that matter, there are damn few of ^us^ that go back more than a few years. So spill it or clear the bandwidth.

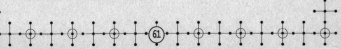

To:hunter.list@hunter-net.org
From: Xterminator306
Subject: Inherit the Earth?

Sorry, I wasn't aware I had drifted into 'codespeak.' I'm talking about the archives. A.R.C.H.I.V.E.S. That's a place where you store old documents. I don't know anything about the system crash that Cabbie is talking about. Apparently, the sysop cleaned up the corrupted files and dumped them back into the archive. Go to the search screen and type in "Advocate2." You could type "Inherit the Earth," I suppose, but you'll get a pretty high noise/signal ratio in your search results.

—X

"Tell me, Witness, how many more people have to die — before you 'inherit the earth'?"

– Advocate2

To: hunter.list@hunter-net.org
From: Cabbie22
Subject: Fool me once…

Haha. Very funny. All right, you got me. Like an idiot I go to the search page and (surprise) Advocate2 turns up… nothing. Ditto for Advocate Debates. I even went through all 2415 matching results for "Inherit the Earth" because by this time, I was pissed. Nada.

Now, you want to tell me what you're playing at?

Hell, I don't even recall any mention of who got the #2 handle. I've been around here for about as long as anybody, but that was before even my time. Witness, any help here?

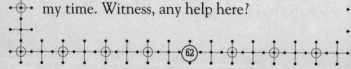

To: hunter.list@hunter-net.org
From: Witness1
Subject: Advocate and Archives

Sorry folks. I've been trying to stay out of this thread. My initial reaction was that this was just a troll trying to take a dig at me personally and get under my skin. I'm not sure of the motivation here. What I've seen here recently, however, is more disturbing.

I will restrict myself to addressing certain factual points:

1) There is no archive of messages stretching back to the early days of this site. Nor has there ever been. Hunter-net is not intended to be a permanent database, cataloging our collected knowledge of our foes. I am of the opinion that such a database would prove at least as revealing of its users as of its targets. It would, in short, be a potentially lethal liability.

2) I have no knowledge of any debates centering around the premise of "Inherit the Earth." I certainly did not participate in any "Advocate Debates."

3) Usernumber 2 is reserved under the hunter-net architecture. This is to allow me a backup signin with system admin clearance. This id has been activated only once, in an early attempt to restore the downed server during the catastrophic failure that brought down the original hunter-net. If any other user were online at the time (which was, for obvious reasons, not the case) the handle would have appeared as

Sysadmin2. There was certainly never any userid of Advocate2.

Xterminator, I don't know what your game is, but I don't like it. I think your postings to this thread are in poor taste, but so far, you haven't crossed the line. You do and I pull the plug.

—Witness1

Inherit the Earth

·   ·   ·   ·

Kim Sun pushed back from the computer, rubbing his eyes. The clock on the nightstand read 3:42 AM in oversized luminous red digits. He had a hell of a lot of work to get done tomorrow and he really didn't have the time or energy to waste on this Xterminator character tonight. *This morning*, he reminded himself ruefully.

He shouldn't let it get under his skin. This wasn't the first time this had happened — some newbie signed onto the list and decided to try to make a name for himself by creating a little friction. So he'd taken a few potshots at some of the list regulars, so what? Kim had seen it all before – someone out to prove how clever he was or just trying to rattle folks, to get them to lose their cool.

Kim knew he shouldn't get so emotionally wrapped up in what was going on online, but he couldn't help it. He hated confrontation – always had — even confrontation by electronic proxy. He knew that when he flipped on his computer tomorrow he would have a big knot in his stomach, the same big knot he had earlier today. It was stupid. He knew it was stupid.

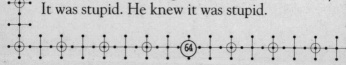

Compared to the all-too-tangible monsters he saw every day (or at least those days that he could work up the resolve to actually venture beyond the door of his apartment) the antagonists lurking online were pussycats. The real monsters still had all their claws.

But he just couldn't help it. Those folks on the list, they depended on him. They looked to him for answers — even to protect them. He provided a safe haven. A place where those like him, the Imbued, could meet, compare notes, swap war stories, share tactics – and most importantly, stay sane.

They needed him. Hell, they even liked him.

It was never like that anywhere else. Not at work (back when he could still hold down that network admin job — suits could smell a full-time employee who was only putting in a part-time effort). Not at school. Certainly not at home.

He hated being made to look foolish in front of the folks on the list. They were the only people who mattered to him now. Maybe the only people that mattered, period. And among them, he was somebody. *He* mattered. He belonged.

Yeah, I belong. I belong in a home for the clinically pathetic. Kim hit the key to pick up his email and pushed himself wearily to his feet. He headed towards the kitchen to grab a quick bite while the messages downloaded from a dozen or so different mailboxes. He picked his way over a tangle of cabling trailing from one of two floor-to-ceiling server racks that dominated the tiny apartment. Two server racks, computer desk, ergonomic chair, bed, nightstand, and trunk which doubled as both dresser and table. That was all for the furnishings. The kitchen and bathroom were little more than closets off the main room. The unflattering comparison was cleverly avoided by virtue of the fact that the apartment did not boast any closets of its own.

Kim found a pizza box wedged diagonally into the dorm-sized refrigerator. Upon inspection, the box contained a single slice, stiff as a board. Kim stuffed the business end into his mouth and tossed the box into a mounting heap of trash that dominated the far end of the kitchen, blocking access to the stove. *Need to take that out*, he thought. *Tomorrow*.

He returned to the computer and folded himself back into the chair. He cursed to find that the download had not run in its entirety. Instead, a dialog box queried, "User has requested confirmation of receipt of this message. Confirm? Yes. No."

Kim squinted at the window nestled behind the dialog box, where he could see the heading of the email in question:

To: KimSun@mindspring.com
From: Xterminator@hotmail.com
Subject: Prick

Kim lunged across the desk for the mouse. "No," he said aloud, past a mouthful of pizza. He clicked the "No" button rapidly, several times for good measure. He didn't know how Xterminator had gotten hold of his private email address – all messages to the list were anonymous, stripped of any revealing headers — but Kim was not about to confirm that address for him.

The dialog box disappeared, only to be replaced by another which read "Sending Confirmation. Click to Cancel."

Kim pounded the mouse button a half-dozen more times — to no avail. He slammed down the Ctrl-Alt-Del combo to abort the mail program and when that also proved ineffectual, he hit it again to reboot the system. Nothing.

The red status bar showed that the mail confirmation was nearly complete. Knowing he would regret it, Kim snapped down the power switch to manually kill the computer.

The image on the screen rapidly faded. Beginning at its outer edge, a bright white circle appeared and shrank inward, vanishing in a single point of light in the screen's center. Now Kim was really alarmed. That was not the way a computer monitor powered down. It reminded him more of an old-fashioned television receiver.

He counted to twenty slowly before thumbing the power switch back to life. For an instant, a message blinked in small white letters in the upper left corner of the screen. It flickered three times and then was gone, replaced by the scandisc program kicking in.

The message read simply, "You left me to die, Witness."

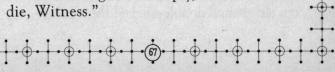

Kim sat bolt upright, as fully awake as if someone had just trickled ice water down his back. *You left me to die? What the hell?* Your computer didn't just suddenly start giving you system messages saying, "You left me to die."

That could only mean one thing, somebody had hacked into his system. But who? And more importantly, why? He needed to get in there and check the firewall. Under the guidance of the Messengers, he had done some extensive tweaking of this security program after a recent incident in which gatecrashers had barged in on the hunter-net party uninvited. So far, the newly-christened *Kerberos* program had proved itself superior even to its namesake. It stemmed incursions from either side of the Black Gate between the worlds of the living and the dead.

If someone had managed to win past the three-headed infernal watchdog program, Kim needed to know how and he needed to know fast.

He hardly noticed as the scandisc program went through its paces. Even before it had surrendered control of the system, he had already positioned the pointer over the spot where the network security icon would appear.

Kim was startled when the program terminated to find himself staring, not at the desktop, but at his email inbox. There, waiting for him, was the message from Xterminator.

Feeling the knot in his stomach, Kim reached out slowly and double-clicked the message.

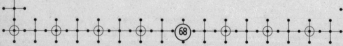

To: kimsun@mindspring.com
From: Xterminator@hotmail.com
Subject: Prick

You know what I said about it not being your fault that this place was such an asshole magnet? Well, I wrong. You're a first-class prick, you know that?

It's one thing you jumping in and dissing me on the list when I wasn't even talking to you. But I went back to the archives today, just to see what Cabbie and the others were bitching about, and (surprise) they're just not there anymore. Nothing. You scrubbed the archives. And given the timing of this little disappearing act, I think it's pretty clear that you did so just to try to make me look bad or to keep you from looking worse.

Well you know what? You weren't half clever enough or half fast enough. I've got hardcopies of the whole damned Advocate Debate thing. And just because you guys went so far out of your way to make me feel welcome, I'm going to return the favor. I'm going to repost them all for you — one by one — so everybody can see what a freaking crock you are.

Oh yeah, and just so you don't think I'm talking shit, I've attached the entire "transcript" to this message.

Sweet Dreams, Asshole,

—X

Kim felt the knot in his stomach tightening. He keyed up his best home-brew virus-protection program and turned it loose on the

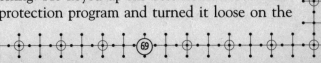

attached file. The results were pretty much as expected. Once the bomb had been effectively defused, Kim opened the file.

He scanned down the long list of email exchanges, his eyes skimming over the damning litany of subject headers:

Inherit the Earth. The Ethics of Speeding Ones Own Inheritance. Murder for Personal Profit. Patricide for Fun and Profit. Who died and left you boss? A Question of Lineage (was: Who's Bastard Are You Anyway?). Who OWNS the Earth? My Father was a Human: the Propaganda of Eugenics. Imbued as the Master Race. Enough of this Master Race crap! Everybody knows the Rots Own Everything (was: My Father was a Rot). Not Funny (was: Your Father may very well BE a Rot). You have your Father's Eyes. Consequences of being the Heir to Monsters. You only hurt the ones you love. SATAN IS THE PRINCE OF THIS WORLD. Son of Satan? Return of Son of Satan? Revenge of the Return of Son of Satan Part 3…

Kim snapped the file shut and closed down the email program. He knew those arguments, knew them well. He didn't have to read through them in all their damning detail. He had gone over them time and time again in the sleepless hours before dawn. And he had spent countless evenings — like tonight — working straight through the night to avoid facing those same haunting questions again.

And now all of his private doubts would be hung out, one by one, for everyone on the list to see. It was unbearable.

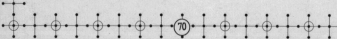

His first instinct was to run. To just snap off the computer and retreat to bed. It was late; he was tired. He could deal with this tomorrow.

But could he deal with the sleepless uncertainties that awaited him in the world outside the box? Could he deal with the fact that he was out of work, short on cash and looking at the rent coming due next week? Could he deal with the fact that his "hobby" had taken over his life? Could he deal with the fact that he was, by anybody's definition, some kind of freak? That he heard voices — voices that told him some pretty disturbing things about himself. Voices that told him to Inherit the Earth.

He wasn't sure he could cope with all that right now, on top of... everything else. Better to stay right here, on familiar ground. He had to go inside. He had to check up on the firewall program to see who or what had been in and messing with his system. If the hacker could get inside his computer, he could get inside hunternet. And there were people there who depended on him, needed him. To keep them safe.

His cursor hovered over the network security icon. Resolutely, he double clicked and felt the opening movement of the familiar ritual unfolding around him.

Deep cleansing breathe in. Hold it. Calm. Breathe out. Out. There. Emptiness.

His fingers struck a jarring contrast to his measured breathing. They were a blur on the keyboard. The userid and password were designed,

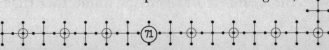

less to form coherent English words and phrases than to set up a certain rhythm of keystrokes. They were the opening notes of the fugue that would bring him into a trance-like communion with the Messengers.

The firewall program blossomed to life before him on the screen, but he hardly spared a glance for its splashy graphic intro. He could no longer see the pictures, but only the individual points of light and color. They struck responsive sparks within his consciousness. The streaming neon logodata sizzled along his optic nerve as if it were merely an extension of the computer's own circuitry. His eye was merely an i/o port in that interface — an organic i/o port, but nothing more.

Kim was already deep within the bowels of the program's datastrucure, racing along the conduits of silicon synapses. Any moment now, he should feel the presence of the Others. They did not come to him in a blaze of glory, amidst trumpet blasts and the trembling of mountains. Rather, he always sensed the Messengers as silent and invisible brooding presences — more like firm nudgings this way or that, guiding his instinctual efforts to mold the network configuration.

After a time, he began to worry. He did not feel that comforting presence. Had something gone wrong? For Kim, communing with the messengers was always accompanied by a sense of security, of everything being right in the world. It was perhaps ironic that their presence also triggered his Sight and the awareness of the monstrous all around him – an unambiguous indication that all was certainly NOT right with the world.

He rounded a corner in the circuitry diagram only to be confronted by the self-representation of the firewall. It rose before him, a daunting barrier of weathered masonry. The wall rose fifty feet into the air. From its battlements, roaring watchfires illuminated the night sky, snapping defensively at the low-hanging moon and stars.

Kim surveyed the scene before him, his every instinct screaming danger. He had expected to see only carefully marshaled columns of binary data. This was the heart of the firewall. The abrupt change from the abstract to the representational confused him.

The firewall was self-referencing. It had to be. It needed to be able to conceive of its own place within the network security system since the wall itself was most often the first target of any attack. But the program should conceive of itself as a program, as a series of sequential commands and conditional responses. The firewall should not be able to conceive of itself metaphorically— as a fire-crowned wall. Such a self-image required something more than the merely mechanical, it required imagination. A human imagination.

Could the program be taking its cues from me, from my presence here? Kim wondered. That would seem to be the only explanation for the scene before him — that he was somehow seeing the picture of the firewall painted in his own imaginings. But why, then, was its presence here so startling to him? Why wasn't it closer to the image his mind's-eye conjured up when he heard the word "firewall"? A solid wall of crackling flames?

Then, perhaps, the firewall was drawing on someone else's imaginings. Could someone else be here within the machine as he was? The thought did nothing to reassure him.

Even as this idea formed in his mind, Kim became aware of a stirring, a movement, at the base of the wall. There was the figure there, a crouched human figure in the shadows, curled in upon itself.

Against his better judgement, Kim crept closer.

As he drew near, he became aware of a sound above the roaring of the flames. It was a frail human sound, the sound of crying.

It was not the hushed sobbing of an adult, but the unselfconscious wail of an infant. Kim had trouble picturing that sound coming out of the full-grown figure hunched double beneath the wall.

At the sound of Kim's approach, the figure turned sharply. Kim found himself staring into a face that must have once been breathtakingly radiant. The skin had the luster of fine marble, but the face was smudged with ash and soot. The features looked more like something that had been liberated by a sculptor's chisel than the contours of mere flesh and bone.

Kim stopped dead in his tracks. From the shoulders of the bedraggled figure, a pair of blazing white wings unfolded. For a moment, their light eclipsed that of the watchfires above. Kim had to shield his eyes against it.

As his eyes adjusted, however, he could clearly see that the wings were tattered about the edges and singed as if, like those of Icarus, they had ventured too near the sun. Further, they were befouled with mud and muck. Kim wondered at the presence of this downtrodden angel. He pressed forward cautiously, more than half afraid that his footsteps crunching through the rubble here might be enough to set the battered figure to flight.

But already it had turned away. Not only was the angel not afraid of him, it acted as if he were of no account whatsoever. Just another small frightened thing scuttling among the detritus of the old wall.

Here, within the shadow of that wall, the hulking edifice had taken on a very different appearance. Kim could see the cracks in the masonry and the gaps where siege engines had taken their toll. Not far to his left, an entire section of stone blocks had collapsed inward, weeds springing up between the scattered stones

The flames atop the battlements no longer bore the appearance of watchfires, but rather seemed to be the smoldering remains of bodies left to burn at their posts.

Kim was aware that a significant shift had taken place around him, but could not say for certain

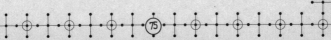

when he had crossed the threshold. His every instinct screamed for him to turn around now. To try to find his way back. To put as much distance as he could between himself and the site of this massacre. But something compelled him forward.

That something crouched just a few yards ahead of him, wearing the form of a fallen angel.

Kim was close enough that he could hear the voice of the angel now, crooning softly to itself. And always the unmistakable sound of a baby crying.

"One day," the whispered voice promised softly and intently. "One day, all of this will be yours."

Kim could now make out the bundle that the angel cradled in its arms. It was wrapped in blood-stained bandages and old newspapers. The bundle squirmed incessantly and cried. He could barely make out the baby's smudged face nestled among the layers of soiled wrappings.

He was close enough now that, if he dared, he might reach out a hand and wipe the dirt from the infants face. He instinctively bent closer, but his attention was diverted by the baby's newspaper bunting. There, at the infant's breast, an off-center headline proudly proclaimed, "Inherit the Earth."

Kim reeled. Uncomprehendingly, he looked up into the angel's face as if he might find the answers he sought written there. The angel turned on him a look that was filled with pity. Its eyes were as deep and as wide and as devoid of life as the gulfs between the stars. Kim felt himself reeling, falling.

He felt a great circle of blazing darkness opening up before him. It began with a pinprick. A singularity of infinitely dense blackness that swelled, expanding outward in concentric circles. Soon it was past him, washing over and enveloping him. Pressing on unchecked. Soon, its leading edge would swallow the horizon. He may have screamed.

Kim came to himself, forehead pressed against the monitor screen. A blazing white circle of light narrowed to a pinprick directly between his eyes. His thumb still rested against the power switch after having manually killed the computer for the second time this evening.

This morning, Kim corrected himself with a groan. He pushed himself back upright and glanced over at the bedside clock. 7:14 AM. *Not good.*

His head ached as if he had been hit in the forehead with a hammer. He extricated himself from the chair and staggered off the kitchen, stumbling over a knot of cable. He found a clean-looking mug on the counter and poured himself a cup of last-night's coffee.

The cold and bitterness helped. The caffeine didn't hurt either. After a few minutes, the pounding in his head receded a pace.

He wasn't entirely sure what had happened to him at the firewall, but he knew he had been given a great gift. A vision. He knew now what he had to do.

Returning to the computer, he logged onto the list.

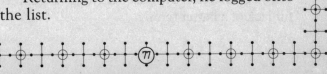

To: hunter.list@hunter-net.org
From: Witness1
Subject: Credo (long)

I have just posted the transcripts of the so-called Advocate Debates in their entirety. I must tell you that do so with some trepidation. I cannot say for certain how Xterminator may have come across these postings, but I will not denounce either him or them. On the contrary, I assure you that they are quite authentic.

That said, you should know that these "debates" do not reflect any conversations that took place here on hunters-net. Rather, they are transcripts of internal dialogs. These are the things that keep me up nights.

I have grappled with the Messenger's imperative – Inherit the Earth — each night since my imbuing. To me, these postings read like an indictment, a litany of my own inner doubts and fears.

Now I do have a theory as to how Xterminator may have become privy to these nocturnal tossing and turnings of mine. When his first posts appeared, I commented that I thought he was just some kind of troll – trying to bait me, to get under my skin. At you read this, some of you, no doubt, are thinking that I spoke truer than I knew. Some of us have had first-hand experience with creatures who ride our dreams, stealing our nocturnal thoughts or worse, visiting upon us our worst fears. I have even heard them called 'trolls' or 'goblins' for lack of a better term.

Let me say that I do not believe Xterminator to be such a creature. He is a troll, certainly, but in the metaphorical sense only. I think that it would be more accurate to say that his discovery comes from another source. You see, we serve the same patron, he and I – a being or beings who have proven themselves not above a bit of kicking down the doors of our cherished self-delusions to deliver their imperative call-to-arms. *Inherit the Earth.*

I can't say that I particularly like Xterminator, or that I approve of his approach or methodology. But I guess, in the long run, my personal likes and dislikes are just that – personal. They don't – and shouldn't — really figure into it. The Messengers chose me to deliver an ultimatum for them. Why? I don't know. If there is something special about me, I for one can't imagine what that might be. So who am I to say that they cannot chose somebody else – somebody like Xterminator — to carry the message the next leg of the journey.

I do believe that it is time (perhaps long past time) that we got some of this out in the open and that more able minds than mine were brought to bear on the question of our quest — of its meaning. Of its implications for us, our world and our future. So let's talk a little bit about *Inheriting the Earth* — about what it means and does not mean.

As "Advocate2" points out, "Inherit" is not much of a call-to-arms. Maybe that's because I'm not much of a warrior. But still you have to won-

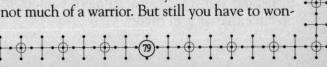

der. Are we being summoned to sit idly by and wait for our inheritance to come to us? Are we not imbued with these terrifying gifts in order to use them – to bring them to bear upon our foes?

The call to "inherit" is far too patient for many of us. It implies a generations-long approach to the problem. And frankly, we have not been around for generations. All evidence suggests that the Imbued are a very recent solution to an age-old problem.

But is this really our calling? Milton tells us "They also serve who stand and wait." A noble sentiment, but is this the kind of service the Imbued are called to? I do not think that it is.

Unfortunately, the alternative is even less appealing. Perhaps, as Advocate points out, we are called upon to speed the course of our inheritance. To cut away the dead wood of the previous generation that we might bring about the new world which is our birthright. To my mind, this argument amounts to little more than a call to murder, if not to patricide. Who must die so that we, the Imbued, may Inherit the Earth?

Is it our biological parents? I am afraid that any argument that we will Inherit the Earth from our human forebears boils down to a rather distasteful eugenics. The Imbued have been gifted with powers that set us above normal humans and thus it is our destiny to supplant them. To become the Master Race. We have heard this type of propaganda before. I know I do not have to remind you that it is even more heinous in practice than it is in theory.

From whom, then, are we to Inherit the Earth? From the monsters? The rots, for example, seem to have insinuated themselves into every strata of human society. Sometimes it appears as if they must surely rule the world by puppet strings. But are we the heirs of the walking dead? And can we deal with the consequences of such an assertion? My gut turns to think that we are ourselves no better than the monsters that we fight. But what if it's worse than that, what if we *are* monsters. Just another form of sociopathic predator? Another threat to humankind?

Or what if (a wicked thought) we are merely the creations of the undying? Their constructs, their offspring, their pawns. We flatter ourselves to think that we can see the "truth" of their exist-ence – or that we could ever do anything about it. Anything that they did not chose for us to do…

In the debate transcripts you will see further suggestions, insinuations that we are something more monstrous still. From a biblical point of view, this world – and all material things — is the domain of the Devil. Are the Imbued truly heirs to that kingdom? Are we the sons and daughters of the infernal powers?

I, for one, do not think so. I will tell you what I think. My credo. You may take it for what it's worth.

I had a revelation tonight. I saw a world in which the hunt had run its course, played itself out to its logical conclusion. It was a world where our strongest defenses had been tested — and overcome. I walked through the remnants of a vast battlefield, making my way through a landscape of rubble and ashes. From atop the last ruined battlement, our burning bodies sent an oily black smoke heavenwards, like stillborn prayers.

I came upon a figure there, huddled in the shadow of the ruined wall. It was a downtrodden angel – fallen, wounded, dying. In its arms, it held a small bundle – a child — wrapped in bloodstained bandages and old newspapers. "Someday," the angel whispered, "all of this will be yours."

And as I peered more closely at the frail shivering child, I saw what the angel had wrapped it in, to protect it against the cold and the worse ravages of the aftermath. The headline of its makeshift blanket read, *Inherit the Earth*.

I know now that I am not the child of my human parents. At least, I no longer am. They do not belong here with me in this world, the world of the breached walls and burning bodies. I would not wish this on them – not for all the world.

I am not the child of the monsters — the rots, the ghosts, the restless dead. I see them for what they are and I judge them by their actions and the suffering and carnage that follows their every move.

I am not the child of Satan or the devil or the powers of darkness or whatever you would call them. I will stand firm against the darkness. I will cry against the dying of the light. I will resist the infernal world, the world that I know must come, with every ounce of strength remaining to me.

I know what I am. I am the child of that one, fallen, bedraggled angel. I call them, the Messengers, you may know them by another name. These angels do not own this earth; they do not rule over it. That is not at all the sense in which we are called to Inherit it.

Rather, we are called to inherit their responsibility for the earth —for its protection. I believe we are called to live here in the midst of the carnage and to comb through the wreckage of the field of battle. I believe it is our appointed task to search out that which has fallen in the midst of the massacre, but is not *of* the massacre.

We are not given these gifts to slay monsters. Any idiot with a gun can slay monsters. Rather, we are called upon to gather together a remnant, a core of all that is good or strong or pure or just or beautiful or true or stubborn — and to pull it up out of the muck. To make sure it is not crushed underfoot. To ensure that it endures. Whatever else might happen, whatever the cost, we must see that the essential outlives us.

For me, hunter-net has always been the sieve with which I sift through the ashes. Please know that I am fiercely proud of each and every one of you that I have found here.

Inherit the Earth,
—Witness1

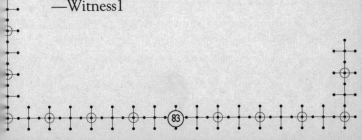

Three
The Names of the Dead

by James Stewart

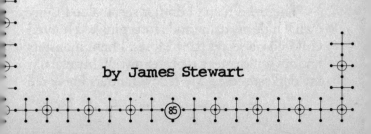

In my dream, I was a monster. Though my crimes are hazy, I leave three bodies in a burning wood but save an infant to devour later. Then imaginary pains awaken me, a tidal wave of boiling kitchen grease launched by a nightmare. My body dodges into reality, and I open my eyes on the floor. My elbow bleeds. I run my hands over the scars on my face and neck.

The lights are off in my bedroom, and the sun is setting. The heater exploded three days ago. Snow covers New York — twelve inches in Central Park. I crawl through the room, feeling for the rug. My fingers collect bunches of shag as I pull it toward me and wrap myself in its warmth. Soon I'm dreaming again.

There are three names I never say out loud. The first is the name of the man who shot John Lennon outside the Dakota apartments. He wanted to add his name to the Beatles' legend, so he deserves to disappear into anonymity. The second I call "The Pig," though I have known his true name most of my life. He was a butcher from my town. In the prison camps, he raped my sister, my mother and me. He raped all the girls from my neighborhood. From his neighborhood. Goran scarred my body, but the Pig scarred my soul. For that, he should be obliterated along with John Lennon's assassin.

The third name I do not speak aloud is my own. I hide my name and protect it like a hunted child, like a secret baby Moses. I hunt monsters and am sometimes a monster myself. My name is my darkest secret. My fellow hunters know me as Dictatrix11. A few, the trusted and the dead, know that my first name is Anna.

When I wake up again, on the floor, wrapped in the rug from my parent's home in Yugoslavia, it is night. My apartment has only gotten colder, but I am covered in sweat. My elbow has begun to heal. The blood is dry and a sore stiffness has set in. I hope that the healing leaves a scar to remind me that, on New Year's Eve in the year 2000, while the rest of the world toasted the next thousand years with lovers and friends, I had a fitful sleep. I lift myself up and feel my way through the darkness to the shower.

Hot water rains down on me. Hot water undiluted by cold. Other people might find it uncomfortable to move from freezing to burning so fast, but certain regions of my body are impervious to pain. Scars mark these places. Still wet, I turn off the water and brush my teeth. I dry my hair and comb it as best I can. There are no mirrors in my bathroom, no mirrors anywhere in my apartment. I get dressed, grab the heaviest of my fifteen coats, and lock my door.

The parking garage beneath my building is almost as dark as my apartment. The lights that haven't been broken have yet to come on. The spaces between the cars, and the unlit corners and stairwells, could conceal every rapist, mugger and car-jacker in the city, but I am too well armed to be scared. I find my Audi on the second level. I open the unlocked door.

New York City celebrates. I hear illegal fireworks in Little Italy, a few blocks away. Though the sidewalks are slushy and the air rolls off the ocean like an icy wall, revelers — bundled up and mittened and red-nosed — move through the city with the anticipation that something great is about to happen, that some moment is about to be checked off the schedule of the universe. But my car is a cryogenic tomb. I turn up the heater full-blast, hoping that the tiny heating coil will soon produce warmth. Outside they shout. I shiver.

The New York Public Library is closed when I pull into one of the employee parking spots. I swipe my security card and unlock the door. The library, at least, is warm, but no scholars come to explore the stacks, no bums huddle in the periodical section. I turn on the first-floor lights and head for the computer banks.

A flashlight winds its way down the stairs. It shines in my face.

"No parties tonight, Ms. Suljic?"

"I'll just be a minute, Mr. Chapman."

The Titles and Claims index comes up with 27 buildings owned by Julius Hathaway. I'm not sure that Julius Hathaway exists, and I don't care. He is the name behind the shell company Hathaway Realty, the public face of the creature I will destroy tonight. Though its sins demand that its name be erased from human memory, that is not the reason I do not speak the name. I do not know it, so I have invented a handle for the fiend. I call it Lord Chernobyl, for the vast scope of its feeding. I have hunted it through Staten

Island and the Bronx. I watched as it disposed of bodies in a junkyard in New Jersey. In Providence, the only place we ever met face-to-face, it called me a deformed whore. I called it an endangered species.

The list of buildings owned by Julius Hathaway is familiar to me. I have studied it many times. I have been to many of them. Lord Chernobyl was there at the shotgun house on Mulberry Street, and at the abandoned White Castle on 75th, and he drank from the pit of blood in the warehouse near the Brooklyn Waterfront — three places with only Julius Hathaway in common. I remember the tenement in Queens and the removals company near Hell's Kitchen. Those, I burned down myself. Lord Chernobyl must think I am a creature of its ilk, the way I appear at its resting places and storehouses as soon as it relocates them. Though I sometimes feel more in common with the fiend than with mankind — especially on nights like New Year's Eve at the turn of the millennium — my comprehensive knowledge of its warrens isn't some gift from the Messengers. Rather, it is an object lesson for all bloodsuckers: Don't fuck with a researcher for the New York Public Library.

But one entry on the Hathaway list is new to me — a space in a strip mall in East Harlem, a pizza place with upstairs office space, lost in bankruptcy and acquired immediately after the foreclosure by Hathaway. A great place to ring in the new year.

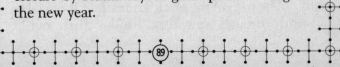

As soon as the lights go out in the office above Ola's Pizzeria, a blue 1983 Chevrolet Caprice Classic peels out of a parking space in reverse and speeds out of the parking lot. I think Lord Chernobyl has gotten the drop on me, but then I see its two servants walk outside and lock down the cages that protect the windows. I've seen them before — one is a man, early 30s, with dark hair down to his shoulders, and turtleshell glasses with round lenses. He carries a bulky gym bag in his right hand. Judging by his uneven shoulders and the way he supports the bag with his leg, it is heavy.

The other servant is much younger, a girl, an apparent teenager. She's wrapped up in a trenchcoat and a scarf, with huge glasses and black gloves, wearing a colorful chapeau that was perhaps designed for Rastafarians. She carries numerous smaller bags — a purse, an overstuffed pillowcase, a square box for storing files. Another gym bag slung is over her shoulder. Though the strip mall is dark, it looks like the girl's concealing something under her coat as well.

They hurry through the parking lot and get into a black late-model Taurus. They throw their luggage into the trunk and get in the car — the man driving, the woman sitting in an uncomfortable position with her seat leaned back all the way. They head south, toward the freeway. I follow.

The path of the black Taurus describes a labyrinth through New York. I follow them out of

Harlem and then to Sixth Avenue, then the Avenue of the Americas. A left on Canal Street, a right on Hudson. Through the Holland Tunnel. A left onto 14th Street, then on to I-78 West. I follow them through the New Jersey Turnpike to I-295 South. The East Coast is snowed in. The maze runs slick.

After we leave New Jersey, the black Taurus leaves the interstate. I kill my headlights and follow. The driver takes to the back roads, the secret byways around the beaten path, the hidden roads that America celebrates but rarely travels. I follow them along rural routes, down bootlegger roads, down the unpaved stretches awash in sleet and snow. A few times, the Taurus planes across a patch of ice, but the driver is a pro. Rather than slam on the brakes like the denizens of the city are apt to do, he glides over them, letting the ice dictate his path, until he can regain control of his vehicle.

He always turns in to the skid. I follow him all night long.

Just before six in the morning, the driver stops at an Exxon station. He pulls around to the far side of the convenience store, into the darkness near a dumpster. I think he has spotted me, but my car's almost out of gas. I turn my back to the store and pump gas, watching the reflection in my window for signs of my prey. My tank is barely half full when the car drives off again. Though their side of the parking lot is dark, and the snow falls even harder now, I see the driver. I don't see his passenger. I replace the nozzle and speed off, my bill unpaid.

The driver of the black Taurus zips back on to the interstate, then off on another rural route. I think we're somewhere in North Carolina, maybe near Charlotte. It will be light soon. Though the driver has made good time all through the night, he's driving way too fast now. I'm doing 95 and my Audi can't keep up with him. I scream as my car slides across ice in the blackness.

The shotgun in my jacket digs into my armpit. For a second, my stomach seems suspended in nothingness, unaffected by gravity. Then the car isn't moving anymore. I regain my orientation on the side of the road. I can barely make out his rear lights in the distance. As I turn around to pull back onto the road, my car quakes. Another car, headlights off just like mine, rockets past me. My Audi whines as I gun it back to the road.

I catch up with the other cars — the black Taurus and the blue boat of a car that roared past me right behind it. The driver of the Taurus slams on his brakes, but the blue car keeps going.

The rear of the Taurus crumples under the weight of the Chevy Caprice Classic that slams into it. The passenger-side rear light shatters and the wheel buckles under. The Taurus spins around twice, still moving at full speed over the ice. It flips when it hits the guardrail. I hear the car as it tumbles down the embankment and smashes into the trees below. The Chevy, after this mighty bump, veers to the left, meeting a similar fate on the opposite side of the road. When it crashes against the trees, one gives under the frost. Tons of Chevy chop at its frozen base. The tree shudders and falls across the road. That's how I stop — by slamming into this fallen tree.

I've survived too many encounters with dead things that speak, with fiends that would drain the life from a vein in my throat or man-wolves that rather tear out my jugular. Some call me a martyr, but I won't meet my end catapulting through my own front window. The seat belt rips into the flesh below chin, pinches at my waist and steals my breath. The airbag deploys. I am alive.

I unbuckle myself, pivot in my seat, and kick the door off its remaining hinge. Snow welcomes me out of the car. The headlines of the Taurus beam up from the trees below, but I see nothing of the other car. I run to the right of the road. I run to the Taurus. To my prey.

The driver hasn't gotten out of the car, but he already has his gun ready. His window is down about a third of the way, his pistol dangling out at an odd angle. He takes an awkward shot at me. I crouch and move down the embankment, approaching his car from the front. I slither through the snow, over the shards of shattered trees. I grab the gun, break the driver's wrist on the window and steal his weapon. He pulls his hand into the car and begins to cry. The first rays of the sun appear from the east.

I stand up and try to open the door. It's stuck. Inside, the driver, holding his broken hand, inches away from my door to the other side. I yell at him through the window.

"I won't hurt you. Get out of the car."

"Meshugannah cunt!"

The door won't budge, but I demand that it open. I grip the door's handle and the frame above the window. Pain erupts in my chest, my lungs strain to keep enough oxygen in my system, my eyes threaten to close and surrender to the snow. Though my arms are sore and my chest hurts, I pry the door off its hinges.

I reach in the car and pull the flailing driver out by his feet. Tears stream from his eyes. He still clutches his hand. I stare at him as he screams insults at me.

I have the second sight. Something is wrong about him. I pick him up by his coat like a kitten grabbed by the scruff of the neck. I lean him up against the car and search him for weapons.

Then I hear a banging, a hollow sound of someone pounding on metal. I look around, unable to locate the source. Then I hear the muffled voice, from the trunk: "John! Let me out! It's happening!"

The driver — John — shouts back. "Calm down! It's okay! I'm okay!"

"Right now, John. It's coming right now!"

"Shut up!" John bangs on the side of the car for emphasis. "Be quiet! The sun's coming up!"

"Forget the sun! Open the trunk! Right! Now!"

A bullet zooms past John and me. It passes through the broken front windshield and shatters the glass in the rear. I turn and see the shape of a man silhouetted in the headlights. I see the shadow of the gun and his shaky hand as it wavers in the headlights. He makes his way down the embankment. His gait is slow and awkward — he drags his left leg and clutches at his shoulder. He advances toward us, pulling the trigger as he approaches. He's screaming.

"Kill it! Kill it before it gives birth!"

The future, as it reveals itself to me, can go one of two ways — either I shoot this guy in the head right now or he kills John, the thing in the trunk, and me. I raise John's gun, wrap my hands around it, and squeeze the trigger. He falls to the snow and does not stir again. I trust my foresight, and hope that I have not just killed a fellow hunter.

At first, I think John has pissed himself, but as he moves across the headlights I see that the wet patches are blood. The driver of the blue Caprice did not miss us both. The banging from the trunk resumes, frantic this time — "It's here, John! Right now!"

John springs to the top of the Taurus, plants his good hand and turns. He lands on me, bowling me into a smashed tree. His injuries do not hinder him. His eyes are shot with blood. He picks up the gun I took from him, at the same moment towering over me. He points the barrel at my head.

"You're not opening that trunk," he says.

A long, slow scream escapes the well of the trunk. Quiet at first, an elusive hum, it crescendos into a muffled wail. At the same moment, I fire my shotgun through my coat. A flap of John's

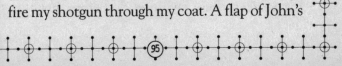

scalp flutters as he wheezes and dies. His body falls against the Taurus and slides to the ground.

The snow is bright under the rising sun. John's blood looks all the more red as it pools on blinding white. This shining snow burns me. It melts inside the sleeve of my coat, under my turtleneck, in the crevices of my ear and in the space between my fingers. The sensation reminds me of Goran's greasy fire.

I pick myself up and pry open the trunk, once again finding strength for the price of a little pain.

In the trunk, surrounded by luggage, a woman is giving birth. She rears back from the sun as her skin begins to sizzle. Next to her, in the dark-ened space behind the back seat, a half-opened gym bag holds the staked torso of a dry corpse. Two red rivulets, and two black punctures, give Lord Chernobyl its only color.

Looking at this bloodthirsty amputee, and the bags in the trunk, I realize where the rest of its limbs are.

I know from a glance that neither of these creatures is alive. After the instant revulsion I see more. In some dark room in the past, I see John drink from the wrist of Lord Chernobyl — unstaked, feral, vital though it does not breathe. I see Chernobyl scream as its servant rises up, full of his master's blood, and shoves a sharpened chair leg through its ancient chest.

The woman giving birth shares the fiend's blood. Though she does not burst into flames, as I have seen these creatures do before, her skin simmers under the first rays of the sun. Her teeth are pointed, and red from a recent feeding. Yet she goes through the motions of a birthing — her blood has already broken.

I do not know the future, but I know what I must do.

•   •   •   •

The blue Caprice is battered and windowless, but at least it runs. After I push the car free of the tree (and earn a new scar when the car slips down the hill), I head north toward the interstate on the icy road.

A baby cries in the back seat. She is a child of a new era's first sunrise. She is a living thing that crawled into the world from between dead legs. The possibility of her existence reminds me that I understand nothing. I am too weak to solve her mystery. I will not name her, and I will not keep her, but I have brought her to the world.

I have redeemed the sacrifice of her parents, of two servants who rose against their master to save their child. I have negated the sacrifice of their anonymous hunter. I cannot tell this child their names. For that reason, I cannot tell her about the four corpses I left in the woods. I cannot tell her the names of the dead.

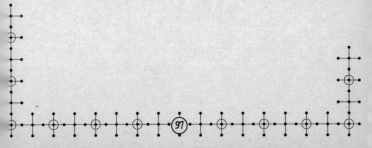

Four
Closure

by Andrew Bates

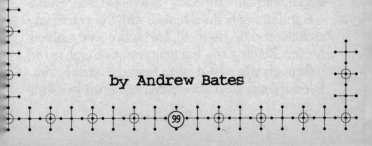

Carpenter sat up with a jerk, bobbing from the momentum like a jack-in-the-box on a tight spring. He looked around the room, trying to orient himself. Something wasn't right. The room looked the same; at least, he assumed it did. It was one of those rooms utterly lacking in character, giving no indication of where you were, what it was meant for — really, of being anything more than a space with four walls, a ceiling and a floor. It was sparse, completely forgettable, with nothing on the walls and only a minimum of furniture. A metal desk encompassed most of Carpenter's view, looming over him like some large, gray, blocky beast. Like a minimalist elephant.

That was the first clue things were off: he was looking *up* at the desk. Then there was the blocky office swivel chair next to it. Carpenter figured it was significant that the chair was lying on its side. Considering he vaguely remembered he'd last been sitting in the chair (at the aforementioned desk, in fact), he felt it was reasonable to assume that he'd fallen out of the chair recently.

Carpenter nodded. That would certainly explain why he was sitting on the filthy concrete floor.

Frowning in distaste, he rose to his feet to brush the grime from his tailored suit. Something dark dangled on the periphery of his vision when he stood. Startled, Carpenter snatched at whatever it was and almost brained himself with the worn hammer clutched in his hand. He hadn't even realized he was holding the hammer; must've grabbed it reflexively when he'd fallen from the chair before. Even though he'd almost cracked open his skull with the thing, Carpenter felt absolutely no desire to put the hammer down. In fact, a small but seemingly lucid part of him felt that doing so would be a very, very bad idea right now.

Something definitely still felt off, but he had enough immediate strangeness to deal with so he left the larger unease alone for the moment.

Using his off hand, Carpenter plucked away the thing that was hanging from his head. Holding it up, he saw that it was some kind of... earmuffs? No, like the headphones a radio announcer used, except looked like it only had one earpiece. And it was really compact, like you stuck it in your ear instead of around it. Plus, it had a curved piece extending from it with a fuzzy black bit on the end, like a really small boom mic. A cord dangled from the thing, too, the other end a metal plug that swung lazily a few inches above the floor.

Looking down as he was, Carpenter glanced around to see what the headphone thing might've been attached to. On the other side of the overturned chair he saw a rectangle of black plastic, folded in a V like a thin, half—open briefcase. What looked like a couple keys from a typewriter keyboard lay scattered around it. There was a word embossed on one side of the object, but Carpenter had trouble reading it. He realized it was because the word was upside down from where he stood, so he shifted position and crooked his neck to get a better look. That did the trick. Carpenter saw the word said COMPAQ.

He frowned. He didn't recognize the name. Sounded Spanish or something, and Carpenter didn't know any spics.

Still not quite getting it, Carpenter nudged the briefcase thing with a spotless wingtip. It tipped over (the whatsit, not the wingtip), knocking loose a few more scattered bits of itself. One half of the thing was a keyboard, the other half was a flat screen.

His thoughts finally sparked to life. Looking from the headset to the broken laptop to the overturned chair and then to the papers and photographs scattered across the desk, Carpenter finally remembered where he was.

Or, more correctly, when he was.

And, even more importantly, *what* he was.

•   •   •   •

Lupe Droin frowned at her computer screen. The message flickering before her could have been authentic, but Lupe was not about to give this bastard the benefit of the doubt. He'd proven pretty fucking sneaky in the past; she wouldn't be surprised if this was yet another trick so that she and her pals would let their guards down.

Still....

Rubbing distractedly at the smooth spot by her left eye, Lupe considered. She admitted to herself that he already had the upper hand, considering how she was allowing him to get her all pissed off like this. Hell, it'd been two days since this, his last post, and here she was looking over it again. Lupe wasn't some cringing little waif, waiting for some big he-man to protect her. She sure as shit wasn't afraid of some guy talked big and came on with industrial size attitude. Shit, she'd grown up with that all around her, and look where it'd gotten most of them. Dead, on drugs, in prison, or any combination thereof. Guys coming across so heavy were covering up for something, and Lupe had a good idea what it was.

For the most part, she let the attitude roll right off her like sweat off her back. So why did this guy push her buttons so damn easy? She'd never even actually met him. Just all this online shit. Who'd've thought a bunch of words would get her going? Not like a conversation where you can't get 'em to shut up; she could hit DELETE and be done with it. But she'd found herself scanning for his email handle every time she logged onto hunter-net.

No, it wasn't just the attitude. There was something else. Lupe knew herself well; growing up down and dirty in the big city you either faced some hard truths about yourself or ran like hell from 'em. Lupe wasn't the type to run. But this, this was some new territory. She wasn't sure what to make of it, but she knew one thing.

She couldn't get this Carpenter out of her head.

Lupe cleared away her reverie with a quick shake of her head. She moused up and clicked open the new post that shed some light on Carpenter's strange final message. She clicked the original open, too, dragging both out and arranging them side-by-side. The first started with Carpenter's usual self-satisfied comments, then switched abruptly into a disturbing "shouted" passage (as signified by being written in all capital letters) with no apparent regard for grammar or punctuation. This in itself wasn't unusual; the vast majority of Internet users thought "grammar" was a type of cracker and "punctuation" a fancy way of saying "stab."

This asshole was normally more articulate than that, though. Strange, considering he was supposed to have been some mobster back in the day. Where'd a guy like that learn to construct proper sentences? Lupe smiled, chiding herself for stereotyping somebody just like others made assumptions about her.

Anyway, the post was a wild rant, starting off with him claiming "the bitch is dead" and he was being dragged back to "the other side." The odd part was that it turned into what looked like Latin (maybe hints of Spanish, too, although it didn't make much sense to her). Well-spoken the guy might be, but fluent in Latin? That was a stretch.

The second post shed some light on things. It was from everybody's favorite researcher, Bookworm55. The kid was naive, but he knew his shit. Lupe frowned, reading Bookworm's translation of the strange text. One passage in particular caught her attention:

"The storm heralds the hour of destruction, and its winds shall fan the flames ever higher. Heaven's stepchildren wander, blind, into the kingdom of death but their sight is keen."

The words stirred something deep inside Lupe. They gave a tantalizing hint of what this was truly all about.

Of what she was, and why she was chosen.

The hammer Carpenter held was as old and well used as a sixty-year-old hooker. Its head was stained and pitted, a few brilliant lines scraping the otherwise dull metal like the canals crossing the face of Mars. The wood handle was stained almost black from years of soaking up sweat, grease, oil, and blood. A splinter was gouged out of the end, revealing a bright wedge of blond wood beneath the weathered exterior.

This was in stark contrast to Carpenter's appearance (the grime from the floor covering him notwithstanding). His black hair was combed back with a precision drill sergeants dream of for their troops, one unruly lock having tumbled forward during his fall making him look like Superman's evil twin. He wore an impeccably tailored charcoal gray double-breasted suit. His wingtips were buffed to a mirror shine, but for a few damnable scuffs from the fall. His shirt was starched with the precision of a master, firm without being too stiff. The cuffs shot from the suit sleeves precisely a half inch, showing simple silver cufflink studs. His tie was wider than the current style with a colorful pattern of swirls and loops. It was the only color to the whole ensemble. Your gaze would naturally home in on it if Carpenter's eyes didn't instantly grab you instead.

He had eyes that made Clint Eastwood at his most bad-ass look like a wounded puppy. He had a stare that would make Hannibal Lecter cough up his wallet with a whimpered apology. He had a look that made a crocodile seem like a snuggly pet in comparison. He had the eyes of a dead man.

It worked out well, since that was exactly what Carpenter was.

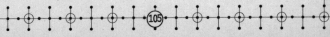

He hefted the hammer, enjoying the feel of it in his hand. It felt like a part of him, a natural extension of his body. And right now it was the only thing keeping him anchored in the living world, inside the dead body in which he dwelled.

・　　　・　　　・　　　・

Lupe stretched and took a deep breath, noting the time with faint surprise. She'd been poking at all this for too long. Time to get on the job, pick up some fares, make some money.

She powered down the computer and headed for the door, grabbing her automatic and shoving it in the pocket of a windbreaker along the way. She was on the streets a few minutes later, the sign on the roof of her taxi indicating that she was In Service. Her mind was still on the latest and possibly most unusual of monsters she'd yet encountered in the hunt.

Lupe wasn't as gung-ho as some hunters. Oh, sure, she went balls-out against a clear threat. But she agreed with some folks like Bookworm. Evil wasn't always easy to figure. Some of these walking dead were tortured souls; they might deserve her compassion instead of her anger. Most of the time that still boiled down to sending them back to the grave, but Lupe didn't normally shoot first and ask questions later unless someone was in immediate danger.

Of course, some of the bastards were so tough that you *could* shoot first and they'd still be plenty able to answer questions after.

Anyway, this Carpenter. She knew he was a zombie — a walking corpse, a rot, one of the undead. But he'd gone out of his way to give her and her fellow hunters a lot of useful information on how to take down things like him. So why would he do that? Why give your enemy a loaded gun and help him point it at your head?

And then there was that cryptic ranting message he sent just before he vanished from hunter-net. Was it a warning? A prophesy? Or one last jerk-around, a dramatic exit so they'd be appropriately awed by his mystery and power.

Lupe knew plenty of guys like that. She'd dated enough of them to recognize the type in a heartbeat. Full of themselves, had to lord it over everyone else. But insecure, too, had to keep proving how impressive they were, shoving it in your face. Men. Most were just overgrown kids with half a brain, and that was in their dicks.

She cruised up Michigan Ave, wondering idly about the sex drive of the undead. She imagined they didn't have any to speak of, being walking corpses and all. Ultimate kind of impotence, probably not even a dose of Viagra big as Texas could trigger a response. Lupe remembered this guy, Hi-Lo, she saw a little while in the days before her time in the joint. He was funny; she'd liked that he wasn't always Mister Macho bad-ass like most of the crew. But he'd changed when they were in the sack. He was urgent, almost angry. But then he couldn't get it up. He'd gotten furious. She hadn't thought it was a big deal, even laughed about it. He could always take a joke, right? But Hi-Lo had yelled, called her a cheap bitch and what did she think was so funny? He'd thrown things, ranted and raved. He'd struck her. Lupe had kicked him in the nuts and gotten the fuck out of there, pulling on her clothes as she stormed through Hi-Lo's parents' living room.

That was the end of her and Hi-Lo. He'd never said anything about it, whether embarrassed about getting nailed in the nads by a girl or fearing Lupe might spill about his little "difficulty," she didn't know. Didn't much care, either. Nobody hit Guadalupe Droin.

Didn't much matter in the long run, though. Hi-Lo got his gray matter sprayed all over the front window of a convenience store three weeks later during a hold-up.

Lupe shuddered at the memory of the life she'd been in. But think about that rage, that embarrassment. Hi-Lo was just a punk kid who couldn't get his dick up one night and he went ballistic. Think about some shambling thing out there that can never get it up again. Hell, can't do any of the normal things people take for granted, like eat and shit and maybe even sleep. That had to create some *serious* anger, especially getting out in the world and seeing everyone around you all happy and alive. Make a body mad enough to kill, you know?

•   •   •   •

Carpenter realized he had no idea what time it was — hell, not even what day it was. How long was he out? Since he'd slipped into this body he'd never been able to sleep as such. Closest he got was a kind of hazy trance state. It wasn't restful in the real sense of the word, but it did the job. It also left him aware enough to note the passage of time, at least generally.

This bizarre collapse was different. Everything was a blank for... well, he didn't know for how long. Kind of the point of why he was wondering, right? Details were slowly returning, though, the curtain slowly being pulled back to remind him who he was and what he was doing.

He called himself Maxwell Carpenter. He used to be a Chicago gangster in the Prohibition days, a thug, one with potential. Then he got killed, betrayed by the woman he loved. His body was destroyed but his soul lived on, the pain of betrayal too strong to let go of the living world completely. Then he saw that bitch marry a rival, a punk so mewling and weak he didn't even have the stones to kill Carpenter himself. Had somebody else do it; just stood there and watched. The pain inside Carpenter — the pain that *was* Carpenter — curdled to hate. That hate fed on itself, and soon it wasn't enough. Carpenter began feeding on the hate of others, the pain of betrayal making it all go down easy. Hate and pain were his fuel, they kept him going through the years in the spirit world, planning his return, planning his revenge.

And then something happened in the spirit lands. Carpenter didn't know what it was; didn't care, truth be told, except that it gave him the break he was looking for. The shroud separating the worlds of the living and dead weakened enough that he broke through, found a physical vessel as a substitute for his original, long-lost form.

He was in the living world again, and the time had long since come to exact his vengeance. Carpenter worked up to it, slowly destroying the world his former love had made for herself, letting her come to realize as those around her fell to strange "accidents" and "random attacks" that something was coming. That payback was coming. Frail and weak from the passage of years, she could do nothing but see all that she had slip through her fingers, could merely wait until the time came when she would face the specter of her own death.

Then the bitch had to go and die of natural fucking causes before he was ready!

Carpenter gripped the hammer so tightly the wood creaked, almost snapping. His memories were clear now. He'd been online, trying to manipulate those simple-minded "monster hunters" into helping him advance his agenda. Been going fairly well, too. They found out what he really was, but he'd had enough honesty on the hook that they were willing to listen while he reeled them with the lie. He looked at the headset. Used, whaddayacallit? Voice-recognition software? So he wouldn't have to type. Hated typing. Pain in the ass.

Anyway, getting ready to bring the whole plan home when he'd felt a spiritual earthquake. At the same time, a surge went through him, like grabbing the third rail and mainlining the juice. The combined pain and pleasure of it all was impossible to describe. But he knew the source, knew it as intimately as he knew his own thoughts: The bitch was dead.

Annabelle Sforza was dead.

•   •   •

Lupe made the rounds on autopilot. Working the cab was pretty easy, for the most part. Being a woman could've been a problem but she wasn't some naive soccer mom or anything. She knew the supernatural weren't the only monsters out there; growing up on the streets in Chicago had made her tough and foolish and her time in the joint had smartened her up considerably. Most recently, her time on the hunt had tempered her resolve, giving Lupe the inner strength to stand up to most any threat. Some punk figuring she was an easy mark for robbery or rape had only to be on the receiving end of her cold stare to make alternate plans.

That kind of excitement didn't happen often, though. Today was proving to be pretty quiet, which was fine by her. She knew her subconscious was trying to unearth something important about this Carpenter. She had to decide whether she should hunt him down or not, and whatever was scurrying around under the floorboards of her mind was more than likely the key to that decision.

While her subconscious went about its work, Lupe continued pondering the motives of the undead in general, with Carpenter as a representative sample. Were the dead pissed about being dead? Lupe figured more than likely. From what she'd seen, most of them just wanted to rest. They couldn't in their current conditions, though, and that drove them to do some pretty fucked-up things.

She wasn't one of those bleeding heart hunters willing to excuse the monsters because they weren't responsible for their condition. That was bullshit, far as Lupe was concerned. They might not have planned to be what they were, but they had no right to prey on the living, terrorizing normal folks for God only knew what kind of fucked-up agenda.

Lupe wondered what Carpenter's agenda was. Specifically, why had he contacted the hunters? Given them so much information on how to destroy zombies and ghosts and vampires and the like? Because he was stuck here maybe, couldn't go to his final rest unless someone sent him on his way?

No, that didn't ring true.

Lupe wasn't a psychologist, but Carpenter didn't seem like the type to suicide, which is essentially what that kind of approach amounted to. So what did that leave?

Her thoughts were interrupted as she pulled the taxi up to a funeral home. She'd nodded distractedly when her fare, an older couple, gave her the address. It was seeing all the outrageously expensive black sedans around the place that roused her from her reverie. Must've been at least two dozen automobiles — it seemed insulting to call them something as crass as "cars" — of the foreign and domestic variety. Made her road-weary taxi embarrassed to be there.

Lupe shot a look in the rear-view. The old couple seemed a little out of place, too. Their clothes were well cared-for but obviously very old, years out of style. The couple was Italian, which if

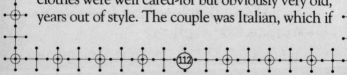

Lupe was prone to stereotypes would make her think maybe the whole funeral was mobbed up. Watching a couple head in from some German roadster in the funeral home parking lot, she figured she might not be out of line with that assumption. If that guy's sedan was worth more than Lupe'd make in two years, the suit he had on had to cost what she'd bring home in six months. The cost of the jewelry glinting on his wrist and fingers wasn't even worth calculating. Then there was his dolled-up trophy wife, looking more like she was ready for a night on the town than a funeral.

She took another look at her fare, he digging his wallet out of threadbare pants to pony up the $12 for the trip. Maybe they were distant relatives, outside the business. Explain why they took a cab instead of riding in style. Lupe chided herself. Italians were a close-knit bunch, much like her own people were. Didn't make them all Mafia.

Then she remembered who sure as hell was Mafia, back in the day. On a hunch, Lupe asked the old woman, "Excuse me, who is the service for?"

The woman smiled, a world-weary grimace that conveyed sorrow and polite warmth and made Lupe feel unaccountably guilty. It was a knack grandmothers had; Lupe figured she might learn the trick if she ever made it that far. "My cousin. Annabelle Sforza," the Italian lady said.

* * * *

Carpenter flicked his left wrist to reveal the Rolex he wore. He was less concerned about the time (just after noon) than he was the date.

Checking the little window in the watch's face, Carpenter saw it was Saturday, almost two full days later than he last remembered.

He'd been dead a long time, and had picked up quite a bit on how the whole life after death angle played. Now that his thoughts were finally clearing, Carpenter had a good idea what'd happened to him.

Annabelle Sforza was his strongest link to the living world, his anchor to reality. The strength of his feelings toward her was the main thing that kept him going. When she'd up and died on her own, it'd shattered Carpenter's ties to the physical world. He'd been in danger of plunging into the shadowlands, dragged down by his ties to the bitch just like some poor bastard in cement boots tossed into Lake Michigan.

The bitch might've been his strongest link to reality, but she wasn't his only one. Carpenter had held onto the physical world thanks to his old, worn hammer.

The tool had started out as a handy chance implement on an enforcement job early in his career. Danny Emilio was nobody special, just one of those lower-level guys always around to lend a hand. Problem was, being around like that he saw a lot. Emilio was trusted — as much as anybody ever was in the Syndicate, anyway — so there was nothing to worry about. Then came the word that Emilio was giving the squeal to Ness and his crew. Johnny Sforza had been sent over to find out what Emilio was really up to; Carpenter went along to help jog Danny's memory. He wasn't "Carpenter" yet back then, though. No, that was the early days, when he was plain Dennis Maxwell.

Carpenter scowled, remembering the good old days and his pal Johnny the Stick. Fucker helped bump him off and took his woman as his wife. If he hadn't already been dead by the time Carpenter returned — killed by another made guy for putting it to his underaged daughter — Carpenter would've loved to have worked good ol' Johnny for a week or two.

The shitbird never had the guts to do any rough stuff himself. When Emilio wouldn't give it up easy, Sforza gave the word for Carpenter — still Maxwell then — to give him an incentive. Sweating a snitch was tough work; you'd think it'd be easy since they squealed so quick to begin with. A lot of them went and got stubborn on you, though, thinking they could dodge the bullet if they clammed up.

The usual stuff wasn't working, so Carpenter had cast about for a new tactic. They were in the workshop in Emilio's garage, and Carpenter grabbed the first thing that caught his eye: an old hammer and a handful of sheetrock nails. He'd gone to work, hammering a nail into the flesh in between the bones of Emilio's hand each time the squealer lied or played dumb. Had to give him credit; he was a tough little bastard, Carpenter remembered. He put in three nails on Emilio's left hand and was two into his right before Danny gave it up.

After they found out what they needed to and took care of Emilio for good, Dennis Maxwell kept the hammer. It was a stupid thing to do, even if there was no way to tell how Danny Emilio finally bought it (if the body ever got found in the first place). Carpenter was about to throw it down the well after Emilio's body, but something stopped him. There was something strangely comforting about the hammer, its heft, its balance. It felt... *right* that he should keep it. So he slipped it into his jacket pocket when Johnny the Stick was puking. The guy had no stomach for the rough stuff.

Work out of the way, they hit one of the local joints for a late dinner and drinks. They were great buddies back then, Johnny the Stick regaling the other fellas about Dennis Maxwell's performance. "Like a fuckin' carpenter he was, y'know? Holding fresh nails in his mouth while he brought the hammer down! Just missin' the pencil behind his ear, y'know? Shoulda seen him, boys!" The nickname was a foregone conclusion at that point.

So along with the nickname, Carpenter kept the hammer. He'd used it a time or two since, but it really wasn't an effective weapon. Not unless the other guy was willing to hold still and let you get a good, solid swing at his melon. Carpenter kept it as a trophy, an indication of his status in the Syndicate.

By the time he was killed, he'd felt more comfortable being called "Carpenter" than he ever had "Dennis" or even "Maxwell." He'd been transformed, and the hammer symbolized the change. When he'd returned from the grave, it was the first thing Carpenter hunted down. He would've been surprised the thing still existed if he hadn't always known it, had protected it as best he could during his years as a ghost.

Next to Annabelle Sforza, the hammer was Carpenter's strongest link to the physical world. If he hadn't been able to grab it reflexively when the bitch died, he probably would've been lost. With her gone, it became his strongest anchor.

Carpenter looked at the hammer again, contemplating the significance of that thought. Annabelle Sforza was dead. He felt it in his soul, but suddenly that wasn't enough. He had to see it with his own eyes (or, more correctly, the eyes of the body he possessed). Days had passed; was she already buried? Easy enough to find out. He was intimately familiar with her burial plot.

•   •   •   •

Lupe barely heard herself thank the old guy for the meager tip and offer them both her condolences. Synapses fired as Lupe made the connection between Annabelle Sforza and the recent subject of her thoughts. After Carpenter started spouting off all his expertise on the undead, Lupe had researched him. Like the others on hunter-net, she hadn't realized what Carpenter truly was at first. Interestingly, it was another of the dead who spilled the beans on the guy. A ghost actually approached another hunter, Witness1, and revealed that Carpenter was a rot. She wasn't predisposed to believe the word of the supernatural, though, so Lupe did some digging. Using what Witness learned, along with the hints Carpenter'd already dropped in previous posts, she poked into the guy's past. It wasn't easy, but it helped that Carpenter was so full of himself. Even when he was talking about the habits of zombies and ghosts, he couldn't resist bringing the topic back around to him — his savvy, his experience, his skill — the guy was quite the egotist. It took a week or so of Internet and library searches, but Lupe finally put the puzzle together. Not a bad piece of work for an armchair detective, if she did say so herself; her time as a hunter seemed to have developed some handy sleuthing skills.

Anyway, turned out Carpenter was a goon from way back, dead now going on sixty years. He and a woman named Annabelle were lovers during the days of Capone and the Untouchables. Annabelle Sforza, the woman responsible for Carpenter's death, if Lupe remembered correctly.

She stared at the funeral home, tinted a faint amber in the rays of the lowering autumn sun. Focused on her epiphany, Lupe didn't wonder at the irregularity of having a funeral service so late in the day. Annabelle Sforza was probably the person Carpenter hated more than anything else in creation, his true love who'd become his betrayer. Powerful ties, extended beyond death, maybe? And here was her funeral. Did that mean he'd killed her? Lupe remembered his last post, the ranting he'd suddenly begun. Carpenter had said something about "She's dead, the bitch is dead," and about him being pulled to the other side.

That could've been an act. Maybe he did kill the woman, maybe the post was all part of some scheme. But what the hell for? Why bother?

Lupe tapped the steering wheel, then shrugged. No insights coming up there. But this was no coincidence, her being here. Ever since she'd been chosen for the hunt, Lupe'd faced way too many convenient circumstances to think it was chance. Take her being chosen for the hunt, for example. At the time, she thought facing down a monster was a spot of supremely bad luck. If she'd done just one thing differently that day, she never would've ended up in the situation, never would've learned of the horrors that lurk in the darkness.

Now, she was pretty sure that if it hadn't been that night, it would've been another much like it. She'd heard the word from on high, she'd had the scales torn from her eyes. She didn't think she was humanity's savior or anything, but she had been tapped by a higher power. There was a master plan, Lupe was sure, forces at work that still influenced her actions in many subtle ways. She was just one piece on the board, though; too close to the action to get a perspective on the larger deal. So while she knew there was a plan in the works, Lupe didn't have a clear idea what it was.

She had grown used to one of the aspects of it, though — namely, unhappy accidents like this, where she crossed paths with the undead. Lupe shook her head in bemusement. She should've seen this coming, in fact. Acting like an amateur, here. She'd had Carpenter on the brain ever since he'd dropped off the radar a few days ago, and now here she was outside the place where his strongest link to the living world was lying in a box.

So if that link was gone, that meant Carpenter was too, right? That last email was his swan song to the living world. Yeah, sure.

Lupe swore under her breath. From what she'd seen of the guy so far, it couldn't possibly be that easy.

. . . .

Carpenter parked up the street from the funeral home. He could just see the building through the trees. He'd already checked the bitch's grave. It was open, awaiting her arrival. That meant she was there, laid out for the wake. Early afternoon now; the lowering sun caught glints of gold in the trees, the first of the leaves changing color for approaching fall. Carpenter wouldn't be surprised if the gig was in full swing. He realized he felt nervous. No reason he should be. The big danger — that his spirit would be dragged back across the shroud after the bitch's death — had passed. He knew by now he didn't need the hammer in hand to stick around. Not for the first time he considered putting it someplace out of harm's way, like in a safe deposit box. Yeah, that was a good idea, but it could wait till after he took care of business here.

Carpenter strolled across the street and over the impeccably maintained lawn toward the home. He nodded in approval at how meticulously the area was maintained. The few leaves scattering before a breeze across the grounds, advance scouts for the rest, lent just the right amount of disorder to an otherwise pristine scene. Take pride in how you looked, he always said.

Your appearance was your calling card to the world. Looked like the Pellucci Funeral Home agreed with that sentiment.

He was about to enter through the front of the building when he paused. Being dead, Carpenter's physical senses weren't that great; sounds were muffled, colors and shapes a little dim and blurry. That was seldom a problem, though, since he had an extremely acute sense of spiritual energy. Better than any normal sense, not only for recognizing people but knowing whether they were alive, dead or somewhere in between.

It was kind of like radar, and right now he got a brief hint of something, just on the periphery of his awareness. Carpenter stood tall on the walkway, turning slowly and focusing around the area. There was... something out there. Something unusual, more than (or other than) human. Couldn't tell what, but it was approaching. Well, that was fine. After sixty years in hell, Carpenter feared no man — or anything that posed as one. If he was still here when whatever it was showed up, he'd deal with it then. Otherwise, fuck it.

He went through the front, noting the foyer was empty at present. Clean and precisely arranged the decor was, if a bit much for Carpenter's tastes. Didn't much matter to him if anyone saw him; if any of the old crew was here (and if they were they'd definitely be old), they wouldn't recognize him in his new body. Probably wouldn't matter if he was in his old flesh anyway, considering how long ago that was. Bunch of old fogies couldn't remember what they had for breakfast, let alone what somebody looked like from half a century ago.

He took a look at the scheduling board. Only two funerals today, the Waverly affair on right now, the Sforza gig not scheduled to start until four o'clock. This time of year, give them an hour or so before sunset. That'd explain why they had the lights set up around the grave; the bitch wasn't expected to go into the ground till after dark.

Carpenter would've thought this was pretty strange except he knew there were some folks who couldn't make the gig during daylight hours. The Sforza family was connected, and not just to the mob.

He didn't much give a shit about that. The important thing is he had an hour or so he could spend with Annabelle Sforza and not have to deal with a bunch of grieving relatives. Her service was in the West Room; poking his head inside, Carpenter saw it was set up but her coffin hadn't been wheeled out yet.

"May I help you, sir?"

Carpenter spun swiftly, checking himself before he drew his pistols. Damn, he was keyed up more than he'd thought. Carpenter gave the guy a quick once over. Nothing special about him far as Carpenter could tell. Just your typical seasoned funeral director, skilled at sneaking up on visitors like a friggin' ghost.

Slapping a slight smile on his face, Carpenter said, "I'm here for the Sforza funeral."

The guy nodded in commiseration, hands clasped before him in a traditional mourning pose. He was a chubby bastard, not the body type Carpenter would've expected for a guy running a funeral home. He was good, though. "I am Arthur Pellucci, director of the home. I am personally handling Mrs. Sforza's service," he said, conveying just the right sense of sympathy and respect. "I am sorry, sir, but we are not scheduled to begin for a short while yet. You are welcome to wait, of course, but—"

"I've been waiting long enough, believe me," Carpenter replied. "What say you just take me back to where you got her stored?"

One of the more useful talents Carpenter got when he died was the ability to force his will on another. Could make somebody want something so bad all other considerations fell by the wayside. Carpenter's eye flared with an eerie green fire as he focused his will on the guy's mind. Pellucci's look of faint surprise crumbled, replaced by a gentle smile. Without another word, the smile fixed to his face, the funeral director walked through the West Room toward a door in the back. Carpenter strolled after, anticipation growing within him.

. . . .

Lupe steered the taxi through the funeral home parking lot. She was heading around to the back of the building, hunch in play. When she saw the back door, her suspicions were confirmed.

The heavy metal fire door was wide open, the section around the lock plate peeled back and the lock itself torn out entirely. As if that

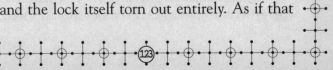

wasn't a good enough danger sign, there were also some bloody fingerprints on the wall.

Lupe thumped her forehead lightly against the steering wheel. She wasn't prepared for a confrontation, not with something had the strength to rip tempered steel out of bolted metal plating. No choice though, really. What if Carpenter was rampaging through the funeral home? She didn't much care if a bunch of mobsters got taken down, but what about her fare? They were clearly just a nice old couple, never did anyone any harm. They didn't deserve to die at the hands of a monster.

A quick check of her pistol and she was heading for the back door. Lupe considered finding a phone and calling for backup. Get some of her south side pals here or maybe that crew handled Chicago's north side. Wasn't really any time, though, not if lives were in danger in there. Plus, by the time anybody got here it'd all be over.

Swallowing a gulp of fear, Lupe focused the sight and stepped inside.

• • • •

Carpenter stood before Annabelle Sforza's coffin for over an hour, oblivious to everything but her. Her body had lost the full curves and porcelain beauty Carpenter remembered. It was old, thick and sagging. Her face was etched with wrinkles, her hair a steely gray, her pallor equal to Carpenter's own.

Carpenter thought she was stunning.

His emotions surprised him. The hate was there, of course, strong as ever. But so was… well,

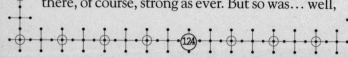

he wasn't going to name it. He refused to admit, even to himself, the feelings he still had for this woman. The woman who turned on him, who handed him over without a second thought, the woman who signed his death warrant.

Annabelle Sforza filled the entirety of his awareness. He didn't register the murmur beyond the wall as people showed up for the service. He didn't notice as the sunlight coming through the narrow windows along the top of the wall slanted ever more laterally. He didn't catch the occasional frustrated voices as people argued with Pellucci on the other side of the door about why the casket wasn't already on view. He didn't sense when the thing stinking of the grave and long decay entered the room through the other door and stumbled toward him.

●   ●   ●   ●

The corridor extended to the left for about ten feet before turning right. It was pretty wide, probably to accommodate moving caskets around the place. Lupe paused just inside, reflexively breathing through her mouth as a stench rolled through the corridor. Either this place didn't know how to embalm for shit or one of the walking dead was inside. Lupe was willing to bet the latter.

Having confirmed that there wasn't some monster about to jump her, Lupe turned her gaze to the two symbols she'd noticed on the wall opposite the back door:

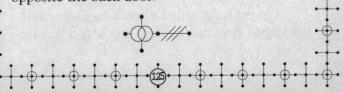

They were hunter shorthand, representing hope and corruption. Lupe's brow furrowed in consternation. The symbols were scrawled in blood; not something hunters normally did. So was a fellow hunter already here? Lupe didn't think so. Carpenter appeared to have a pretty good understanding of how the whole thing worked, if his posts to hunter-net were any indication. So did he draw these symbols? What for? Did he know she was here? That would change things, if he was ready for her. Maybe she should back off and call some people.

Another look at the bloody scrawl and she shook her head. No, it was too late for that. She had to make sure the living were all right inside. If Carpenter proved too tough for her to take on, she'd try to draw him outside and then retreat.

Moving forward cautiously, Lupe rounded the corner. The hall went another twenty feet, hugging the building's exterior wall to the left and revealing two doors on the right. There was a third door at the end of the hall. The second door down was ajar, and Lupe heard someone talking in there. Might've been on the phone, since she didn't hear anyone replying.

The stench grew stronger as she moved forward, and Lupe saw there were more bloody fingerprints on the wall next to the open door. Flexing her grip on her gun, Lupe spun into the room. The tableau revealed inside was not quite what she expected.

* * * *

Carpenter recoiled when a rasping groan escaped Annabelle Sforza's mouth. Then he

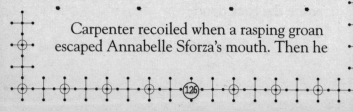

realized it hadn't come from her, but from the thing standing on the other side of the casket.

"Jesus fucking Christ!" Carpenter exclaimed in equal parts surprise and irritation. Where the hell had this guy come from? Carpenter must've been more into his little reunion than he'd thought.

The thing groaned again, hands extended over the closed half of the coffin in entreaty. It was a zombie, though one nowhere near in as good a shape as Carpenter was. Carpenter looked human, pale but could easily pass for living. This poor bastard was in an advanced state of decay, its flesh sagging, putrid and gray, maggots squirming inside gaping cavities that revealed a torso well-cleaned out by a thorough embalmer. One eye had rolled halfway back into the cranium, and rats must've gotten to the body since half the thing's face was peeled away, the attached hair and skin flopping away from the bone as it moved.

A third time it groaned, gesturing toward Carpenter with bony fingers crusted with blood.

"Not this crap again," Carpenter said. Ever since he'd returned from the dead, he'd been accosted from time to time by other walking corpses. They weren't in anywhere near the kind of shape he was; the vast majority was even more fucked-up than this guy. They didn't appear to have any malevolent intent toward him. Instead, they did just what this one was doing. For all the world, it looked like it was asking him for help.

He didn't know what they wanted from him, frankly didn't care. He'd blown the first one away out of disgust, and the next couple he'd just left after trying to start up ultimately futile conversations. They only seemed able to track him down when he stayed in one spot for a while, so he kept on the move. This wasn't too difficult since Carpenter had a few different safe houses in the area anyway.

The whole thing was a pain in the ass, though, and Carpenter wanted nothing to do with any of it. Whatever they wanted from him they weren't going to get. He was never much of a team player even in life, and he certainly didn't want to deal with a bunch of mindless corpses decaying before his very eyes. Phobic about cleanliness and order, Carpenter found simply being in the same room with something like this was an affront to his senses.

"Listen," he said, "if you didn't have the fucking brains to grab a body in some kind of decent shape, why bother even getting out of the fucking ground to begin with, huh?"

The thing groaned again, a bit of its tongue spraying out and landing on the closed half of the casket lid. It gestured toward the door, the sound of its tendons creaking causing Carpenter's lip to curl in distaste.

He couldn't believe this. What, did the thing want to take him to some fucking zombie slumber party?

Then some dame with a gun stepped into the room.

Two figures stood on either side of an open casket. The coffin was at an oblique angle, so the near one was turned almost completely away from Lupe. The other man faced her almost directly, catching sight of her the second she stepped into the room. The stench of death was almost overpowering, and emanated from the figure closest to her. One arm reached over the casket, the other reaching back as if preparing to take a swing. The man on the other side was leaning away, his hands raised as if in a warding off gesture and a look of revulsion clear on his face. His eyes flicked to her, registering surprise and something else.

Lupe didn't hesitate. "Game's up, Carpenter!" she yelled, firing a double-tap into the decayed thing's back. She'd been aiming for the base of Carpenter's neck, hoping a couple well-placed rounds might sever its head. The rot was fast, though, already ducking to the left the instant Lupe spoke. The bullets hit to the side, tearing out chunks of Carpenter's right shoulder and splattering the casket with gore.

"Get out of here!" Lupe yelled at the man on the other side of the coffin, but he seemed frozen in place. She'd seen it happen before; normal folks faced with monsters typically got hysterical and ran or locked up with fear. Just great. She had to hope Carpenter would be focused on her and not go for any bystanders.

That seemed to be exactly what he was doing, although Lupe had to admit she wasn't exactly overjoyed about it. The rot used the momentum from the bullets' impact to swing around and lunge at her. Carpenter's fingers were talons of exposed bone that came at her in a raking swipe.

As one of the chosen, Lupe had weapons other than a bad attitude and a pistol. One of these was a kind of barrier that protected her from the supernatural. It wasn't some impenetrable force field or anything; still the aura was useful enough that blows like the one Carpenter aimed at her glanced away before striking. There was a strange crackling spark and the monster's claws recoiled inches from Lupe's face.

With Carpenter looming before her, Lupe didn't have much room to maneuver. She couldn't safely back off and lead him outside. She'd have to take him down right here. It wasn't going to be easy; the two rounds she'd fired rendered his right arm useless, dangling from his shoulder by pieces of muscle and ligament, but he wasn't slowed down any. She shoved the automatic forward, angling it up under the rot's jaw, and fired off another round.

Carpenter's speed saved him a second time. His head jerked to the side, the bullet tearing through his jaw and blasting out the opposite side of his mouth but leaving his head mostly intact. He screamed an inarticulate cry of pain and outrage and sprang forward again, this time throwing his whole body at her. Lupe knew she'd be in serious trouble if the rot got her in even a one-armed bear hug. She took advantage of his useless right arm and threw herself to her left. Instead of getting caught in a clinch, Lupe ricocheted off Carpenter's shoulder. The monster moved like a freight train, the blow knocking the wind from her lungs and smashing her into the wall.

Lupe fell to the ground, desperately trying to shake off the blow. She was dead if Carpenter finished her off while she lay there. The room spun crazily despite her efforts to regain control. She felt for sure she was done for, but luck was with her. Still groggy, she saw the hazy image of Carpenter's rotting feet pound through the doorway and down the hall. She realized his lunge hadn't been to grab her, but to escape. The injuries she'd inflicted must have been enough to knock the fight out of him.

The room started settling down. Seemed like she'd only gotten the wind knocked out of her, nothing more. Good; she had to get after him, finish him off before he could go to ground. She moved to hoist herself to her feet, then two strong hands grabbed her under each arm and lifted. Steadying herself against the wall, Lupe turned to face the man from the other side of the casket. He was tall and thin, dressed impeccably in a dark suit. The tie seemed strangely jovial for someone at a funeral. Then her gaze continued up to his eyes.

In the instant before the man looked away, Lupe saw darkness, secrets, and pain. The blow must have rattled her brain a little; after blinking hard a couple times Lupe looked at the stranger again. He stepped back, his hands clasped before him and head tilted down slightly in an attitude of respect and commiseration. He looked the very picture of a somber funeral director.

Whatever. She had to get going. First, best to make sure everything was all right here, though. "You okay, mister…?"

"Pellucci," the man replied. One hand came up as if to shake her hand, then trembled slightly and moved to rub at his forehead. He was holding up surprisingly well, considering, but obviously still shaken by what had happened. "Arthur Pellucci… I'm the, ah, funeral director here. Yes, thank you, I'm fine. What, ah…"

Lupe nodded. "I bet you're really confused. Sorry, sir, but I just can't tell you what's going on right now. You know if anyone in the building was injured?"

He turned, offering her his striking profile as he contemplated the door at the other end of the room. Faint cries of confusion and shouts carried through the wood. "No, everyone's fine. Though I suppose they're all upset about the sound of gunshots."

"Wouldn't be surprised." There was something about this guy Lupe couldn't quite figure. Spare and dark, he was almost the stereotype of a funeral director. But there was a vibe to him, something more she couldn't… hell, now wasn't the time. The adrenaline rush was wearing off, leaving her feeling sluggish. She had to get on Carpenter's trail. If only she'd had a chance to mark him! "Look, Mr. Pellucci, I gotta run. I—"

"Please; I need you to do something for me first," Pellucci said. "It's very important."

Lupe was already moving to the doorway and glanced over her shoulder. "What's that, Mr. Pellucci?" she asked in irritation.

The man's eyes captured her. Lupe could've sworn she saw one eye flare green as he said, "Forget me."

• • • •

Carpenter would've found the whole thing hilarious if it wasn't so bizarre. A hunter bursts in and mistakes a rotting zombie for *him*! The woman obviously knew who Maxwell Carpenter was, but not well enough to know what he looked like. The piece of shit monster might serve as a distraction for the moment, but Carpenter knew these hunters were too good to buy the error for long. It'd be best if he'd take himself out of the equation entirely.

During the distraction of the ensuing scuffle, Carpenter readied his play. A sudden shove at the woman's mind at just the right moment of distraction and she was on her way.

• • • •

Lupe burst out the back door, looking around frantically. If she was quick, she could catch up to C— to… what the hell? Lupe took a few tentative steps toward her taxi. She had a name on the tip of her tongue, something… she was looking for someone. But who? She turned and saw the gaping doorway, a pair of hunter symbols scrawled on the interior wall. Suddenly, details returned. There was a rot out there, had been by here. Not inside; she felt sure of that. Well, not sure, exactly; the funeral home was a dead end, though. No pun intended. Why would she—

Okay, this wasn't good. She felt winded, and her memory had obviously blanked on a few minutes. She wasn't sure if this was the result of physical stress or some whammy thrown on her by… well, whatever she'd been hunting. Whatever the case, if she tried hunting while all distracted like this, she'd end up dead or worse. After some rest she could gather a few others and check out this area. They'd find the whatever-it-was sooner or later and send it back to the hell it crawled from.

•   •   •   •

Carpenter followed the woman, moving down the hall seconds before someone kicked in the other door (which he'd locked after taking Pellucci's key when he first got there). He ignored the shouts of anger and confusion, his attention on the hunter who wandered, obviously a little confused, toward a taxicab parked in the lot. He'd just cleared the circle of illumination cast by the light over the back door when she spun around and looked at the back door. Moving quietly back into the darkness, Carpenter considered the next step.

He was surprised at himself for not taking the hunter down when he had the chance. That decayed fucker hadn't hurt her much before it ran, it seemed, but she'd been defenseless for plenty long enough for Carpenter to have finished her off. So why hadn't he?

Annabelle. It offended him that violence had occurred while he was saying his farewells to the woman he once loved. And, much as he hated to admit it to himself, he still did. Hated her too, but the two emotions weren't much different. They had a powerful hold on him, even now, after six decades and counting.

Standing in the dark behind the funeral home, watching the taxi's taillights recede, Carpenter knew he couldn't leave, not yet.

He hadn't given Annabelle Sforza a proper goodbye.

•   •   •   •

Lupe pulled out of the funeral home lot, something nagging at the back of her mind. Like trying to remember song lyrics or the capital of Delaware, it hugged the shadows of her memory. She knew it was there, just couldn't see it clearly enough to bring it out. The best thing was to not think about it; focus on something else, let it come on its own—

Carpenter

She slammed on the brakes, jerking against the seat belt as the momentum carried her forward. Luckily there was no one behind her.

She'd come around looking for Carpenter. The rot. The zombie. The dead guy. Her mind's eye recalled a tall, slim figure, as if glimpsed from a distance. Must've seen him on the cemetery grounds or something. Enough to notice his build but nothing else. Full realization seemed so close. If she could only confirm... Inspiration struck. She had something in the glove box that should answer her questions.

She clicked on the interior light rooted through piles of notes, receipts, and assorted crap. After a minute of searching, she found a wrinkled photocopy of the *Chicago Tribune* from 1934. She'd come across it during her research, kept it with her on patrols, just in case she got lucky. It showed a grainy photograph of a burly, almost brutish man — almost a stereotypical mob thug, a gorilla in a suit — being led out of a building by a pair of Chicago's finest. It had a caption at the bottom: "Dennis Maxwell, questioned in the disappearance of Walter D'Amato" — as in Dennis "The Carpenter" Maxwell, aka Maxwell Carpenter.

The image wasn't the sharpest quality, but that stocky build was pretty distinctive. The rot she was after looked completely different. Slumping back with relief, she put the cab back in gear.

•   •   •   •

Carpenter waited a good half hour in the dark until the mourners settled down from the mystery of the gunshots. What with the Sforzas' mob ties, no one bothered calling the authorities to investigate. When he felt the time was right, he came around to the front. A couple of goons were checking people, but a mild push of will was all it took for one of them to declare Carpenter was okay by him.

The funeral home was packed this time around, which made it easier for him to hide from Pellucci should he pop up. Carpenter saw they'd wheeled out Annabelle's coffin and the half lid was open for viewing. He joined the line of mourners paying their respects, noting that the other half of the casket lid gleamed warmly in the lights. Guess they'd wiped up the gore from the top before they brought it out. It was only a passing thought; his mind had locked back onto Annabelle.

He'd had time alone with her, but now was the time to say goodbye. It was a big deal; he wanted to do something suitable for the occasion. Despite having plenty of time waiting outside and now in the mourning line to think about what to say or do, Carpenter was at a loss when he stood before the coffin again. It was different from looking at her in the back room; that was more personal, more intimate. This was more somber. He saw that it was finally over. She truly was dead, passed beyond to a fate that he had yet to face himself.

Carpenter remembered the hammer stuck through his belt. On impulse, he slipped it out and leaned over the casket as if in prayer. He slid the hammer under Annabelle Sforza's black gown so that it rested between her large old woman's breasts, a parody of the silver crucifix that hung around her neck. Smoothing the fabric back in place, he couldn't even tell it was there. He straightened and made the sign of the cross — except for him, it was the sign of the hammer.

He fought back a smile as he turned from the coffin and made his way outside. He'd considered placing the hammer in a safe deposit box. But it seemed suitable that it should be buried with Annabelle. Each had influenced his life in profound ways, after all.

It was fitting that they spend eternity together.

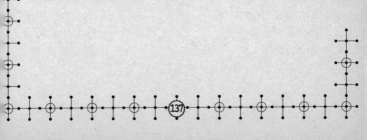

Five
Antibody

by Michael Lee

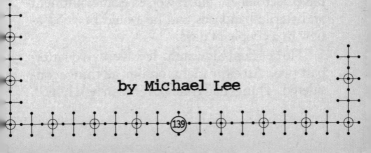

The second-story windows along the front of the old building blew out at the same time, showering the sidewalk below with jagged shards that flashed red and orange as they fell. A scream went up from the crowd of onlookers across the street; one of the girls who'd gotten out the front door in time staggered to her feet and tried to run back to the blazing building, sobbing hysterically. A young man raced after her and wrestled her to the ground, shouting for help to drag her back to the curb. Over the roar of the blaze came the distant wail of sirens, but the fire engines wouldn't arrive in time. The frantic cries of those trapped inside had died out long ago.

Joshua watched from the mouth of an alley half a block away, wiping smoke stains from his dark-skinned face with an old, faded handkerchief. He studied the writhing columns of fire boiling from the upper-story windows and allowed himself to relax. Tension ebbed, letting in a tide of weariness and pain. His right shoulder and knee throbbed in dull counterpoint to the sharp, searing pain of the burns on his face and wrist. The hunter pulled off his gloves and probed gingerly at his cheek. The burns weren't bad, no more than second-degree at most; had any of the napalm actually hit him, things would have been much, much worse. Some ointment and sterile bandages and he would be good as new in a couple of days.

He checked his watch. It was only a quarter-past two. An early night for him, all things considered. Things had gone better than he'd hoped, but now he found himself with time on his hands. Joshua toyed with the idea of simply going back to the apartment and getting some rest, but he knew that he'd just toss and turn until the sun came up.

After a moment, he reached a decision. Joshua pulled a cell phone from his pocket and dialed one of a half-dozen numbers he'd committed to memory. It picked up on the first ring. The voice on the line was that of a young man, perhaps in his early twenties. He sounded wide-awake, despite the hour.

"Hello?"

"This is God45," Joshua said quietly. "What do you have for me?"

"How did you get this number?"

"That's not really important right now, John," the hunter replied. "I was on a job that wrapped up quicker than I'd planned, and I'm looking for more work. Do you have any leads for me?"

"No. Not any more," John said harshly. "Goddamn it, I told you to leave me alone!"

Down the street the hysterical girl was struggling to break free, her outstretched arms silhouetted by the firelight as she fought to reach the burning building. "This isn't about what you or I want, John," he said evenly. "It's about doing the work we were chosen to do. You told me that yourself once upon a time."

"That's *not* what this is about!" John cried. For a moment, the line was silent. Then: "There's something on the scanner about a nightclub fire downtown. Whoever called it in said the place's fire exits had been jammed shut. You didn't have anything to do with that, did you?"

There was a grinding crash as the club's ceiling collapsed. Joshua could just hear the girl's despairing wail over the noise. "I've been hunting bloodsuckers, John. That's it."

"That doesn't answer my question."

"It does as far as I'm concerned," the hunter replied.

Silence stretched between them. John sighed. "You don't understand what you're asking. I can't be a party to the things you're doing. I *can't*."

Joshua gritted his teeth. "John, I'm not asking you to be my assistant. I'm just looking for information. If you're concerned about the way I handle a problem, then give me a lead on something that your conscience *can* handle. It's that simple."

"If only that were the truth," John said bitterly. "All right, goddamn it. Take this down." He read off an address. "It's a warehouse. Look for the Sign."

Joshua committed the information to memory. "What then?"

"I'll tell you more when you get there," John said, and the line went dead.

The sirens were much closer now. Joshua hesitated, his thumb hovering over the redial button. He wasn't in the habit of being strung along.

Then the first police cars came howling around the corner. Joshua watched them pull up to the crowd of onlookers and knew it was time to go. He slipped from the alley and kept close to the shadows, making his way back to his car.

If there were complications when he got to the warehouse, he'd find a way to deal with it. He always did.

• • • •

The address was near the docks, in an older part of the warehouse district that the city had long since washed its hands of. Joshua nosed the beat-up old Pontiac down the trash-strewn lanes, carefully eyeing every broken-out window and open doorway. Nothing moved in the early-morning darkness; even junkies and thieves had to sleep sometime, he mused.

He found the building quickly enough. The symbol for "monster" was painted in bright crimson on one of the rusting metal doors. To a normal person, the Signs were just more meaningless graffiti scrawled on city walls, while monsters couldn't seem to see them at all, much less read them. The symbols were an invaluable tool for hunters, who could leave inconspicuous warnings or even identify themselves to one another. Many of the chosen wore the symbol for "hunter" tattooed somewhere on their body, proclaiming their mission to a blind and uncaring world.

There was a Ford Explorer pulled up outside the warehouse, and a man in a dark blue

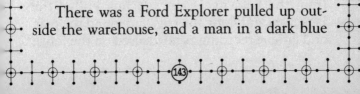

jacket stood by the passenger door, smoking a cigarette. He gave Joshua a hard look as the Pontiac cruised by, and the hunter noticed at once that the Ford's passenger window was rolled down, giving the smoker easy access to anything resting across the front seat. Like a shotgun, or worse.

There was something wrong with the man, Joshua saw at once. His face was like a death mask, pale and withered as if a fever had rendered away the soft flesh and left nothing but bone and sinew behind. The eyes were sunken and fever-bright, like polished marbles. He might have been a bloodsucker or one of their slaves, but the thought seemed wrong, somehow. He might have been a rot. Ultimately the details were unimportant — he was one of *them*, and that was all that mattered.

Joshua drove on past the warehouse and continued on to the end of the lane before turning and circuitously doubling back. He parked the Pontiac several blocks away in a narrow alley, then got out and opened the trunk. He pulled out a canvas shoulder bag and then reached into the spare tire well and retrieved a semiautomatic pistol sealed in a plastic bag. The hunter pulled on a pair of gloves, took out the pistol, and slid it into his back waistband. He closed the trunk lid carefully, then stepped around the car and pulled an army-surplus jacket from the passenger seat. Joshua pulled the jacket on and slung the bag, and found the pain and fatigue receding as he focused on the job at hand. Just like old times, he thought to himself, back when the world made sense.

It took him almost twenty minutes to make his way back to the building. He approached the old warehouse from the opposite side and paused at the corner of a burnt-out building across the street. He scanned the shadows of the surrounding buildings carefully, taking his time, but there were no telltale signs of ambush. Then he turned his attention to the warehouse itself. The building was at least a hundred years old, made of solid red brick and granite, with a row of windows running along the walls near the roof. Joshua noticed that someone had gone to the trouble to cover the windows with some kind of heavy felt, although thin shafts of light seeped through in places where chinks showed in the window frame. They had been careful, but not completely so; a tall stack of crates were set against the wall, reaching up to the level of the windows. Joshua smiled grimly and jogged quickly and quietly across the street.

On close inspection he realized why no one had tried to move them — they were decades old, and so rotted that they looked ready to fall apart in a stiff wind. Joshua tested one crate carefully, then another. Rotten wood flaked away in his hands, but the core still seemed solid. Moving slowly, his burnt arm aching with every move, the hunter levered himself onto the first crate and started to climb.

As he'd hoped, the window itself had been broken out years ago. All he had to do was reach inside and gently move the felt back to make a tiny opening. After all his careful labor, Joshua was disappointed with what he saw: dust and trash stood ankle deep across the warehouse floor. At the far end of the building there were lights on in the foreman's office, but the glass-walled room was empty even of furniture. The only individual in sight was a man who stood on the rusting stair that climbed the wall to the office, cradling a shotgun in his arms and smoking a cigarette. Like the man standing watch outside, he too, had pale, shrunken features and cruel eyes.

Joshua checked his watch. It was three-thirty. Two-and-a-half hours until dawn. The hunter rubbed at the stubble on his chin. If it wasn't for the obvious signs of corruption on the two men, he could have been eavesdropping on a drug buy.

Somewhere, far off, came the sound of a truck engine. It sounded like a big rig, probably an eighteen-wheeler, working its way in low gear amid the close-set buildings. The hunter frowned and pulled out his phone. John picked up immediately.

"I'm here," Joshua said without preamble. "What the hell is going on?"

"A business transaction," John replied. "Is the truck there yet?"

"Almost. I can hear it coming down the street now."

He listened as the semi pulled up on the other side of the building, then heard the dragon's-hiss of its airbrakes. Doors slammed, then he heard

voices shouting harshly to one another. Whoever they were, they were in a hurry, Joshua
noted. Then a trailer door banged open and the
voices began barking orders.

Movement inside the warehouse caught
his eye. The man on the stairwell tossed away
his cigarette and readied his shotgun as a rolling metal door rattled upwards and a line of
scrawny figures came stumbling inside. They
staggered weakly across the trash-strewn floor,
kicking up clouds of dust that swirled in the
shafts of harsh overhead light. Joshua
watched men, women and children driven
into the room by more skull-faced men. Some
of the skull-faces carried shotguns. Others
had cattle prods dangling loosely from their
hands. They drove their charges into the
center of the room and forced them to sit or
kneel in the refuse, getting their message
across with swipes of a shotgun butt or a brandished shock stick.

"Who the hell are these people?" Joshua
scanned the rows of terrified faces. His eyes
settled on one girl in particular who hugged her
knees to her chest and studied her surroundings
warily with dark, almond-shaped eyes.

"Illegal immigrants. Mostly Vietnamese,
some Cambodians. They sold everything they
owned and used the money to pay for a ninety-
day trip in a cargo container. They lived in darkness and ate nothing but a handful of rice a day.
Maybe half of them, the most fit and the most

determined, survive the voyage. And their nightmare is only beginning."

Two of the skull-faces were walking among the immigrants, segregating them into discrete groups: the few elderly men and women went into one group, then the young men and finally the women and children. The girl moved quickly and quietly when the skull-faces gestured; most of the others were becoming uneasy, but she seemed calm. Joshua shook his head in disbelief. "What do the monsters want them for? Don't they have enough food here?"

"They're not food. They're a commodity," John said grimly. "Think about it. As far as the good old U.S.A is concerned, these people don't exist. *Anything* could happen to them here, and no one would notice, much less care. You can work them day and night, pimp them to any sick bastard with a torture fetish or put 'em in snuff films if that's how you get your kicks. And make a hell of a lot of money in the bargain. What do you think a slave goes for in America these days?"

Down below, one of the skull-faces caught the girl eyeing one of the exits. He came up behind her in a silent rush and brought his cattle prod down between her shoulders. She collapsed into a ball and the skull-face struck her twice more, shouting something furiously. Joshua felt his guts turn to ice. "My God," he said in a choked whisper, "My God…"

"I know." The edge was suddenly gone from John's voice. "Just when I think I've learned how bad things really are, I realize that I've just scratched the surface. You know what I think? I think we only *guess* at how deep the evil runs in this world. I think the Angels are so cryptic because they know if we were told straight up what we were signing on for we'd put a gun to our heads the first night."

Joshua tasted bile. He felt a wave of despair rise sluggishly in his chest, lapping at his heart. "What does the monster get out of this?"

"Money. Influence in the local flesh trade, I suppose. Beyond that, I don't know." John hesitated. "Maybe he just took the idea of 'humans as cattle' to the next logical step."

The skull-face moved away from the girl, who continued to lie on her side, hugging her bruised ribs. There were tears on her cheeks, but her eyes were still determined. She glanced up at the line of windows and Joshua thought she looked directly at him, but her eyes slid past his without any sign of realization.

"When will the monster arrive?" he asked.

"An hour and a half, maybe a little less. Depends on the amount of 'product' to be moved. He doesn't get involved with auctioning off the old folks or the men. He only turns up later, to take bids on the top commodities — the women and children. I figure you've got about half and hour before the first person goes on the block."

"That only leaves about an hour or so until dawn," Joshua mused. "That's cutting it pretty fine for a bloodsucker."

"I didn't say he was a bloodsucker."

"Well, what is he, then?"

"Does it matter?"

"If I'm going to eliminate him it sure as hell does," Joshua said.

The line fell silent. Then, after a moment, John said, "What about the immigrants?"

Joshua frowned. "What about them?"

"Aren't you going to do something?"

"Yes I am," the hunter replied. "When that son of a bitch shows up, I'm going to destroy him."

The silence stretched longer than before. Joshua thought he heard John sigh. Then the voice on the line said, "Fifty-three people died in that nightclub fire."

"I'm sorry to hear that," Joshua replied.

"Yeah. Me, too," John said, and the line went dead.

A commotion down on the warehouse floor caught Joshua's eye. One of the elderly men had risen to his feet and was addressing one of the skull-faces. He couldn't hear what the old man was saying, but the fellow's shoulders were straight and his expression was one of stern dignity. Many of the other immigrants watched the elder with looks of reverence and growing resolve.

The man was still talking when one of the skull faces stepped forward and shot him in the chest. The elder's body collapsed in a heap, and an older woman reached for it with a shrill, anguished scream. Others took up the heartbroken cry and the skull-faces waded in with their shock sticks to beat them back into silence.

Joshua put away his phone and settled down to wait.

*   *   *   *

It started to rain at a quarter-past four. Joshua was soaked through in minutes, but he was grateful for the extra cover. Rain meant that visibility would be lower and any sentries outside would be less alert. Occasionally the hunter turned his face up to the darkness and let the cold raindrops wash over his tired eyes and the burn on his cheek. It felt like a gift from God.

The skull-faces knew their business well. They kept the immigrants in line with a methodical, emotionless application of force, and by the time the first bidders arrived, even the children sat in stunned silence, eyes fixed on the floor. Some of the men and women rocked slightly back and forth, their faces blank with shock. From time to time Joshua looked to see how the girl was holding up. She kept her eyes downcast like all the others, but the hunter noticed that she had pulled a necklace of some kind from a pocket and was rubbing it between thumb and forefinger. Perhaps they were prayer beads, or a family heirloom she'd kept out of all the possessions she'd been forced to sell. As she took strength from the necklace, he found himself taking strength from her, beating back the despair that sapped at his resolve. If she could hold together in the face of such horror, he could stay the course and do what had to be done.

The bidders were brought in groups of two to five, escorted up the rusting steel stairs to the foreman's office where they could look down on the assembled immigrants and make their offers to one of the skull-faces. Occasionally the skull-face taking the bid would call down to the floor and have one person stand up so the bidders could get a better look. The deals were conducted quickly; the winning bidder handed the skull-face in charge an envelope and then went downstairs to claim his property. As John described, the elderly went first, then the men; the first time the skull-faces began separating the purchased individuals from the crowd the immigrants went into a panic, but the thugs savagely put the crowd in its place again. Joshua watched young men separated from their wives and children, their eyes full of silent entreaties not to give up hope. By the time the last of the men were gone those entreaties had all been forgotten.

The monster arrived without warning. Joshua had grown accustomed to the brisk, heartless routine, and at first took the creature to be just another bidder. He wore an expensive black overcoat tailored to his broad shoulders and slim waist, and his dark hair and eyes further emphasized the chalky pallor of his face. He was handsome in the same way a hawk was, regal and sharp-featured, his expression cruel and aloof. The creature paused at the entrance and took everything in with a single, sweeping glance, and the whole echoing space went still. A small group of bidders trailed in the monster's wake, appearing small in the shadow of the creature's sheer presence.

Joshua watched the monster intently as he moved gracefully up the office stair. The creature was not gaunt or feverish like his servants, instead radiating an aura of icy vitality. He was very much alive, the hunter realized, yet the look in his eyes was anything but human. The creature's stare hinted at an intelligence older and more alien than anything Joshua had ever seen before, and the realization sent a chill down his spine. He remembered what John had said to him, little more than an hour before: *we only guess at how deep the evil runs in this world.*

As the monster led the bidders into the foreman's office Joshua carefully eased himself down the pile of crates. He hugged the wall of the warehouse and worked his way around the building to the front. Peering carefully around the corner he saw the same Ford Explorer he'd seen before, as well as a couple of vans and a Mercedes sedan. The hunter noticed the driver's side window of the sedan was cracked open and a thin stream of cigarette smoke curled into the cold, rainy air. Joshua nodded thoughtfully to himself, and the pieces of a plan fell into place.

He made his way back to the Pontiac, resisting the urge to break into a run. When he got to the car he popped open the trunk and reached for a small styrofoam cooler buried under a moth-eaten blanket. Inside the cooler was a lump of gray, clay-like explosive. He'd stolen the C-3 from a construction site months ago and saved it for just such an eventuality. Joshua set the ex-

plosive on the cooler's lid and pulled out a plastic baggie containing the detonators.

His hands shook while he worked. Joshua's mind kept drifting back to the girl, her slim fingers worrying at the beads and refusing to give in. He wondered what would become of her. Had she seen him when she'd looked at the windows? Was she pinning her hopes on him, praying he would come to the rescue?

Joshua was pressing a radio detonator into the C-3 when his cell phone rang. He jumped. For a wild second his blood turned to ice until he realized that if the detonator had been armed he wouldn't still be alive to worry about it.

He set down the bomb and pulled out the phone, biting back a stream of curses. "What?"

"You didn't even try to get those people out, did you?" John said, his voice cold. "How could you sit there and watch, and not do anything?"

Joshua leaned against the trunk, running a hand over his shaved head and trying to focus his thoughts. "I'm doing what's necessary, John. Surely you see that."

"Since when is it necessary to sacrifice people wholesale for the sake of one monster? The police at the nightclub said that someone had used a torch to weld the fire doors' hinges shut. You *expected* that people would die in that fire, but you didn't give a damn. What is the point of fighting if we become just like them?"

"We aren't like *them*, John, and we never will be," Joshua snapped. "They are a cancer on the

face of mankind, corrupting it from within. Someone has to cut out the tumor, and occasionally that means sacrificing a little healthy tissue in order to save the patient. People die all the time, John. We are expected to do whatever is necessary in order to ensure that humanity as a whole survives."

"How can you be so sure?"

"Because we've been made immune to the disease," Joshua said, as if explaining something to a child. "Don't you see? Humans can become bloodsuckers, or blood slaves, but we can't. A werewolf can infect any victim with his bite except us. When we die, we stay in our graves. We're antibodies. We've been created to make humanity healthy again."

"Bullshit!" John cried. "No one came down from heaven and gave you that story on a stone tablet. You're fumbling in the dark like everyone else. The fact is, we don't know who did this to us, or why. What if it isn't heaven that's doing this to us, but *hell*?"

Joshua hung up on him. Then for good measure he turned off the phone. The vision of the girl still hung in his mind's eye. And the rain beat down, but where he'd thought it a blessing before, now it made him shiver, and he couldn't stop no matter how hard he tried.

⋅　　⋅　　⋅　　⋅

He took the bomb and a shotgun from the trunk and took a circuitous route back to the warehouse, running the entire way. His lungs ached and his calves burned, and he focused on the pain, driving all else from his mind.

One of the vans was gone by the time he got back. The driver of the Mercedes still sat inside the car, out of the rain, and the earlier sentry was nowhere to be seen. Joshua left the shotgun in the shadow of a nearby alley and crept up in the sedan's blind spot. It was reckless, but at that moment he didn't care.

The hunter lay on the rain-soaked asphalt and wriggled underneath the car, pressing the plastic explosive against the sedan's gas tank. At the last moment he remembered to arm the detonator, then he clambered free and dashed back into the darkness.

He reached the alley and recovered the shotgun, and then there was nothing to do except wait. Joshua thought about the girl. Part of him hoped that she left on the first van. He wasn't sure he wanted to see her again.

We only guess at how deep the evil in this world runs. What if it isn't heaven that's doing this to us, but hell?

"We aren't like them," he told himself, holding the shotgun in a white-knuckled grip. "We can't be. We're immune."

Or are we just a different strain of the disease?

Joshua heard a door open, and then someone gave a muted order. He peered around the corner and saw a small group of women being herded by the skull-faces to the remaining van. Then came the bidders, and, finally, the monster.

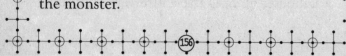

The creature moved with fluid precision, haughty as a god. The sheer force of his presence flowed around him like a cloud of ice. If the rain even touched him, he gave no sign.

The girl walked in the creature's wake. She moved as though in a dream, almost gliding along the ground. The necklace dangled uselessly from her hand, and her eyes were wide with terror.

Joshua fumbled the detonator from his pocket. The sedan's driver was already rushing out to open the door for the monster.

The hunter glanced at the women being forced into the van. The bidders stood to one side, watching the skull-faces work. The sight made Joshua's guts turn to ice.

He hit the detonator.

The plastic explosive went off with a thunderous bang, and the street lit up as the sedan's gas tank went off in a huge ball of fire. The concussion hit him like a hot wind, but the corner of the alley protected him from the worst of it, and Joshua was running towards the center of the blast within seconds, shotgun at the ready.

The car was gone. Nothing remained except burning pieces of rubber and charred metal. There were bodies and body parts everywhere. Joshua saw two skull-faces struggling to their feet, covered in blood. The hunter fired two blasts, and both creatures fell.

The monster had been less than two yards from the car when it exploded. His body was thrown back nearly to the warehouse wall, and lay in a blazing heap. The girl had fallen where she stood. The monster's body had shielded her from the fire and shrapnel, and there wasn't a single mark on her. The concussion of the blast had killed her instantly.

Joshua knelt by her side. He reached out with a gloved hand and stroked her dark hair. Her face was peaceful, as though she were asleep. "Forgive me," he said softly. "He was a monster, and he had to die."

A sudden gust of warm air was his only warning. Joshua threw himself backwards as the blazing form of the beast reared over him. His clothes had mostly burned away and his flesh was torn by shrapnel, but the fire didn't seem to touch him at all. His lips pulled back in a snarl, revealing teeth like obsidian knives.

The hunter fired the shotgun again and again, emptying the weapon into the thing's chest. It collapsed nearly on top of him, one hand closing spasmodically around Joshua's throat. He nearly blacked out before he could pry himself free.

That was when he saw it. He stared at the creature's arm, and for a moment the world seemed to spin. A fist of ice closed around his heart.

With a strangled cry of anger and pain Joshua pushed away from the body. He pulled the phone from his pocket and forced his trembling hands to dial John's number. It picked up on the first ring.

"You son of a bitch," Joshua said bleakly. "You son of a bitch. You knew. You knew all along!"

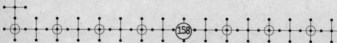

"I'm sorry," a recorded voice told him, *"but the number you have dialed has been disconnected."*

The body of the monster lay outstretched beside the young girl, one hand seeming to reach for her gentle face. The shifting glow of the fire picked out the dark lines of a tattoo on the creature's forearm. It was an arcane symbol known only to a select few.

Hunter, it proclaimed.

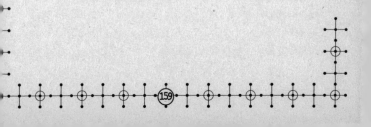

Six
Some Faerie Tales are Real

by David Niall Wilson

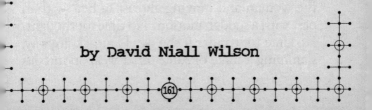

Two things caught Jake's attention as he thumbed through a worn copy of Ambrose Bierce's "*The Monk and the Hangman's Daughter*," distracting him from the novelty of holding that excessively rare volume for the first time. The first was that there was something odd about the young, too-pretty man three tables away. Without understanding exactly how he knew – maybe flashbacks to Phaedre — he knew he was watching a vampire.

The man was scanning a large leather-bound book, older and finer than most of the other works up for auction. The vampire stared at the old book with a blend of fascination and intense concentration, his head cocked to one side as if listening for some far-away voice to read to him aloud.

The second thing was that a woman was moving stealthily up behind the vampire, eyes blazing with crazy light and one hand pressed firmly down into a purse large enough to conceal a watermelon. Her stealth was forced – her gait uncomfortably tight. Jake could sense her terror – and her anger – from across the room.

Placing the Bierce back among its fellows on the auction pre-viewing table as quickly as he could without drawing attention to himself, Jake moved to the end of the table and strode quickly around the corner, darting into the aisle behind the woman and moving abreast of her — then past with a sudden motion. No time for thought. No time to wonder if she would attack anyway, slamming a stake or some other weapon into *his* back for interfering. No time to wonder if the vampire would kill them both.

Jake stepped forward, jostling the vampire from his reverie and at the same time placing himself directly between the would-be stalker and her prey. The woman's eyes grew wide and all color drained from her features. Jake watched her, assessing the danger of the moment before shifting his attention to the more imminent danger of his sudden companion.

"Sorry," Jake muttered, moving slightly away from the man along the table.

There was no immediate answer. The vampire watched with cold, distant eyes that saw through more layers than Jake could erect.

"I knew she was there," the vampire said at last. "She loves me."

Jake glanced down at the volume the man held. It was bound in deep brown leather, reinforced at the spine and corners. The pages were gilt-edged, and the single page Jake could see past the vampire's tight grip was yellowed and covered in tight, even script. Hand-scribed. Older even than Jake had thought.

A sudden sound from behind, books tumbling to the floor amid audible gaps, and Jake turned. He saw the woman, abandoning all attempts to conceal her agitation, turning gracelessly and lurching toward the door, banging into tables and pushing people out of her way in frantic haste. Security guards were already converging, uncertain whether to recover the valuable books from underfoot, or give chase. Jake shot a final glance at the slender undead, then pushed away from the table and hurried toward the door. He was careful to avoid both the books on the floor and the hands reaching to recover them.

The auction house fronted a large brownstone building on the corner of an alley, just two blocks from the main streets of the city. Streetlights glowed dimly, competing with the fading illumination of twilight. The shadows were long and weak, shifting with the motion of the clouds and the distant passing of the last of the city's day-workers dragging home. Too late for business, and too early for the night.

The woman was disappearing around the corner into the alley as Jake slid out the front door and gave chase. She was moving more quickly now, and it was all that Jake could do not to lose sight of her as he dodged into the alley. There was no moon, and with the streetlights left behind the darkness of the alley was sudden and complete. The sharp clatter of footsteps and heavy breathing echoed, then grew silent, and Jake cursed. There were garbage cans and small dumpsters lining the alley, dark alcoves and doorways. The woman could be anywhere.

"Where are you?" he called out softly. "I'm not here to hurt you."

There was no answer. Jake hesitated. He didn't even know for certain why he was following the woman. He knew nothing about her, or about the vampire he'd left at his back, and very suddenly the folly of that last act crept into his mind. He knew he could pro-tect himself – or he believed that he could – but what if he had no warning? What if this vampire was different somehow? What if the vampire just shot him? No reason they couldn't do that.

"Okay," he called out a little more loudly. "I don't know if he followed me. I don't know why you were going to kill him, but I saw him too. I don't like the idea of wandering around in this alley without knowing where he is, or even why I'm here, so I'll give you a choice."

As he spoke, Jake moved cautiously forward.

"I'll come in and you talk to me, tell me why you were going to kill him, who you are, and I'll tell you who I am, and how I know what he was. Then we'll get out of the darkness, and out of this alley, and into somewhere with more light and a crowd before he decides to come looking for us."

There was a soft scrape of leather on gravel and Jake tensed. No way to know how she would react. Then his mind juxtaposed the sounds and directions and his heart began slamming harder. Had the sound been behind him? Was it her, or was it him?

"Damn," he muttered, shifting so his back pressed to the nearest wall of the alley.

Shadows wavered and he saw a dark form melt from the deeper darkness beside a dumpster.

"You know what he is?" she asked.

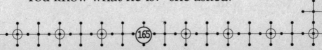

It was the first time that Jake had heard her voice. Light, wavering, but with an intensity backing her words. Jake sensed her strength, and as she drew nearer, very slowly – cautiously – he sensed her anger as well.

"You know what he is, and you stopped me?"

"I don't know you," Jake answered flatly. "I don't know him. I know what he is, but I don't consider that enough of a reason to kill him. He says you love him — maybe you could change my mind."

The woman hesitated. It was obvious that what Jake was saying was not registering as he'd expected.

"Love him? How could I . . .I was going to kill him," she said, leaning heavily against the metal side of the dumpster. "I was so close . . ."

"He knew you were there," Jake replied. "He knew you were coming for him. Who is he?"

"How could he have known?" she asked. "He didn't see me. Two more steps, and I'd have ended it all."

"He saw you," Jake repeated, taking another step forward. "He told me he saw you, just after you turned and ran away."

Now the anger flared in her eyes.

"You stayed and *talked* to him? You stood there and you knew what he was, what he can do, and you TALKED to him?"

She was moving very suddenly, stalking him, and Jake found himself backpedaling into the nearest wall.

"I don't know you," he repeated. "I don't make it a practice to stand by and watch when another person is killed.

Her syllables were clear and staccato. "That. Was. Not. A. Person. He is already dead."

"I know that as well as you do," Jake replied, inching away along the wall as she continued to step closer. "Probably better."

Taking a leap of faith, he stopped backing away and stretched out a hand in greeting. "I'm Jake – they call me Bookworm."

She hesitated. She did not take his hand, but she looked a little less inclined to stick the stake through *Jake's* heart.

"Bookworm?" she said softly. "Bookworm55?"

It was Jake's turn to hesitate – and blink. "Yes, he said, managing a small smile. On line, I am Bookworm55."

"I know you," she said. "I've seen your posts. I should have known."

Without a word, the woman turned away and began walking toward the entrance to the alley, leaving Jake to stare after her receding back.

"Wait!" he called out. "Wait, what did you . . ."

What happened next happened so quickly that Jake wasn't certain, later, of any particular detail. One moment the woman was walking away from him, the next a dark form melted from the shadows, closing on her with astonishing speed. The vampire moved so swiftly that by the time Jake registered that something was wrong, the woman had been struck across the back of the head, tossed over one shoulder like a child, and the two were steadily ascending the sheer brick face of the alley wall.

With a curse, Jake launched himself forward, but he knew he was too late, too slow, and at the moment was wondering if he was too stupid as well.

"Wait!"

His words had no more effect on the vampire than they'd been having on the woman. The vampire reached the roof above, tossed the woman over the ledge and disappeared behind her without a backward glance. Jake raced to the mouth of the alley and sprinted along the street, watching the rooftops, but there was nothing to see, and the only light available was the mellow, too-dim brilliance of the street lamps.

A moment later, he stopped. Nothing. There was nothing he could do – they were gone.

It was one of those moments. Stunned, silent, Jake turned away from the world. He wanted to scream. He wanted to reason with faces he barely knew and names he couldn't even guess at. He wanted them to come back and explain to him what had just happened, and why. He wanted to die.

"It's my fault," he whispered. "She was going to kill him, and I stopped her."

Jake turned back to the auction house suddenly. The one link he had to what had just transpired was beyond those doors. The streets

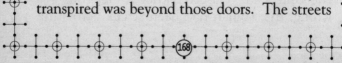

were seldom kind to him. Outside he felt vulnerable, particularly out of his own territory – but inside were the books. Jake hurried inside, letting the doors close him off from the shadowed darkness once again.

The auction had begun, and Jake nearly panicked. He had to know the exact volume the vampire had held. The viewing was over, and he felt sweat suddenly trickling down the back of his neck. The crowd had slipped into the rows of folding, leather-upholstered chairs and only the few suited attendants moved from table to table, gathering each piece to be held for the perusal of those gathered.

Book auctions catered to a sedate, but intense crowd. There was a competitive nature to it all, a hunt. Jake wondered for a moment why everything in his life had suddenly been relegated to variations on that theme.

He glanced across the room and breathed a little easier. They hadn't auctioned the items on the vampire's table of choice, having started with a small lot of Victorian romances. Ignoring the few annoyed glances that shot his way as he re-entered the room, Jake took a seat near the back and watched carefully.

He tried to concentrate, but the woman's eyes haunted him. Her words rang in his ears. "I should have known."

Known what? That he would get her killed? That seemed to be the fear they all had – Jake had heard the words often enough – and seemed

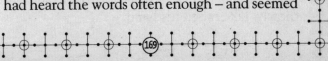

to be the reality of the moment. Why had the vampire said she loved him?

"Sold to number 510 for three hundred and fifty dollars," the auctioneer's voice rang out.

Jake watched carefully, and slowly the attendants worked their way from table to table, drawing ever nearer to the faded leather volume the vampire had held. Jake had managed to narrow it from those surrounding it by the color of the binding. It was lighter than most leather, and despite the volume's obvious age, in remarkable condition. Finally his moment came.

"This next volume," the auctioneer began slowly – almost hesitantly – "is a very unique antiquity. Hand-scribed and bound, we have dated it to the mid 1700's. I have to say, I have never seen its like for workmanship, or content. The author, Benjamin Scyther, is not known to me. He writes of life on a plantation in California, but no California I have seen nor heard of. This is either a very finely crafted fantasy, or the ravings of a madman. In either case, it is a fine specimen of early craftsmanship, and elegantly hand-lettered. I will ask that we start the bidding at $100."

Jake hesitated. He knew his funds were limited, and he didn't want to appear to eager and send some other collector into a feeding frenzy. The room was silent. Jake scanned the others quickly. Nothing. Something was making this obviously rare book un-appealing to the crowd. Even the auctioneer seemed loath to touch it. Slowly, Jake raised his hand.

"Number?" the auctioneer's voice rang out – too loud, suddenly – difficult to make out over the pounding in Jake's head. His pulse. The sudden rush of blood nearly toppled him, but somehow he managed to scrabble in his pocket and fish out the printed square with his number on it. 316. He raised the card silently.

"We have one hundred dollars," the auctioneer droned. "Am I bid a hundred and fifty?

Jake listened, but somehow he had detached from the moment. He listened, but had another bid, he could not have raised his hand again. Images rushed about his mind, whirling away before he could pin them in place and create a pattern that made sense. He saw dark figures slipping up the alley wall, and behind those, watching him, the vampire's eyes. He heard her words, echoing, "I should have known."

"Sold for one hundred dollars to the gentleman holding 316. Next we will move on to a beautiful five volume set of *The Life of George Washington*, By Washington Irving . . ."
Jake staggered to his feet, shaking his head and pressing the palm of one hand to his forehead. For a moment, he nearly lost his balance, but he managed to catch himself on the back of his chair.

Without a word he turned and exited the hall, moving to the foyer beyond where the cashier's window waited. It would be a few moments before the attendants got his auction record to them. He needed the time to catch his breath.

Thinking back, he realized that it was the auctioneer's words that had sparked the strange sensations. The story behind the book – the name. Scyther. Benjamin Scyther. Fantasy? Somehow Jake doubted that – at least not fantasy when your world had already shifted into an alternate side of life – not when the monsters surrounded you and there was no escape.

Jake took a deep breath and stepped up to the counter. The woman took his number card without a word, glanced at it and then at her records.

"Cash or credit?" she asked.

Jake fumbled the wallet from his pocket and tugged it open. Inside was all he had to his name, for the moment, Two hundred forty dollars.

"Cash," he answered.

The girl nodded again and slid a receipt book toward him for a signature. "That will be one hundred and six dollars," she said, smiling.

Jake signed the paper with a shaking hand and slid the pad back across to her. The girl took the money, rose, and moments later she returned with the book in hand, wrapped carefully in tissue and brown paper. Jake stared. There was something about that book, something more than what he'd seen when the vampire held it. There was something – emanating – from beneath the wrapping.

"Are you okay?" the girl asked.

Jake realized with a start that he'd been staring at the book, watching her approach,

The first thing that bothered Jake was the price. For what he paid, he knew he might have expected to buy a few pages of hand-illuminated manuscript. He might also have found an older first edition, or a leather bound reprint of one of the classics. For a book like this the price should have been higher. So much higher, that something had to be wrong. Of course, he'd known that since the auction, but with more time to think about it, he could almost feel a line, reeling him in. Still the pages called out to him.

Benjamin Scyther. The name was penned beneath the frontispiece, a hand-drawn ink rendering of slender young man with almost girlish features, dressed royally, but darkly, turned just so – peering out at the reader over one shoulder, as though obscuring something from sight. It was hard to tell if the name was a stylish illumination, or the signature of the artist. There was something haunting in that illustration, something in the man's expression, or the turn of his lip... the depth of the eyes.

The book was a journal, of sorts – or a history. The language was archaic and overly formal, but flowed with an odd clarity at the same time. The various "chapters" of the volume covered separate incidents of life on or around a plantation near the Mexican border. Though written in the first person, the incidents involved all manner of strange depravity and odd creatures. The dead, come back to haunt the living, who were not always truly alive – magic, romance spanning centuries – all in the same, uncannily beautiful script. If it had not been for the age of the book, Jake would have sworn the lettering could only have come from a laser printer with some amazing fonts.

On the desk across the room, the screen on his laptop flickered, endless three-dimensional pipes, sliding in and around one another, forming pattern after pattern, doing and undoing impossible phosphor knots. Complicated, and yet simple. Jake dragged his gaze back to the book.

"Juanita has come to call for the weekend," he read. "She arrived in fine fashion, drawn by horse-and-buggy across the land like so much fancy luggage, her *boys* much too pretty to be real watching over her and shielding the sun like the wanton slaves they are. No worries there, those two would shield her with their pale bodies and cry tears enough to quench any Godly blaze that tried to claim her.

"And Phaedre, alone as usual, has haunted the library. That one stalks the world as if she can read it. Perhaps she can. She read nothing she wanted to see in Juanita's arrival, to be certain, and has not removed herself from her books in a fortnight. I hope to draw her out soon, to show her how I feel, but all things in their time."

Jake's skin grew cold – clammy with sweat and awash in goose bumps. Phaedre. How could it be? Here? Now? The sensation of being drawn into something he had no control over grew stronger with each passing breath.

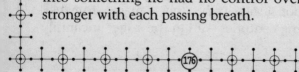

At just that moment the soft whistle of a missile crashing followed by a tinny voice calling out "Incoming!" announced new e-mail. Jake blinked, stared at the page, trying to concentrate, and failed.

"Damn," he whispered.

He moved quickly to the small desk, slipped into the chair and snapped a finger down on the space key to release the screen saver. The twining tubes disappeared and his desktop shimmered to life.

From: Thinblade17
To: Bookworm55
Subject: Danielle

You've stepped on a landmine this time my friend. I run a safe house near where you are staying, and I know the one you saw – both of them. That one had a death wish, and you may have prolonged it, not encouraged it, though why you'd stop someone trying to put away a bloodsucker is *way* beyond me.

Her name is Danielle, and she's been after that same vamp for about two years. Night and day, tracking him like he didn't know she was there. She talked about him all the time, and when she wasn't talking, you could almost hear the gears turning in her mind. We tried to help her, but she pushed us away. Hell, I tried to tell her she was crazy. He knows she is after him, and he taunts her, lets her get a little closer each time. I guess he got tired of the game.

In any case, you want to go after them, I'm up for it – and there are others. I have a pretty good idea where he'll take her – kind of a trip from here, but my 'INTEL' says he's headed down toward the border. This may not be a safe communication. I change addresses regularly – and ISP's – they're on the net too – the others. Guess you know that.

Anyway, this addy is good for about an hour after I sent this. If you don't respond by then, I'll try one more time with different credentials before I write this off. She's crazy anyway.

TB17

Jake stared at the screen. Down south. He glanced over at the book, still folded open on the bed. The border.

He reached out for his mouse and clicked on the "new message" button.

To: Thinblade17
From: Bookworm55
Subj: The Hunt is on

Agreed. More info when we meet. Back alley — Sid's on Broadway. One hour.

Pushing away from the desk, he reached out, powered down the laptop, and flipped the screen down to cover the keyboard. After taking a moment to wrap the book carefully, he headed for the door. No time to wonder if the others would show. He had just enough time to make the deadline he'd set himself. No time to think – not about the book, or Danielle – or Phaedre.

He remembered the vampire's words.

"I knew she was there. She loves me."

What else did he know? How much of what had just happened over the past few hours had been coincidence, and how much a choreographed game? He thought of the woman, Danielle, and the wild, angry stare she'd leveled at him as she spit his name back from the shadows.

The door closed behind him solidly as he slipped out to the hallway beyond.

•   •   •   •

The alley was dark, and there was no one in sight when Jake slipped off the street to scan the shadows. He clutched the book tightly to his chest, and his heart was pounding. He had no way to know if the e-mail had actually come from a friend. He knew of no Thinblade17. He knew of no Danielle. What he did know was that he'd screwed up, and he needed to find a way to make that right.'

On the bright side, if the vamp had wanted him dead in an alley, he'd probably already be there. Not like he'd never presented the chance.

Headlights sliced the darkness, angling into the alley, and Jake pressed back into the wall. It was a long, dark machine — an early Cadillac, color impossible to determine and classic lines impossible to mistake. The car slid into the alley, pulled within ten yards of where Jake pressed to the brick wall, and stopped. The lights flickered off, and the sudden darkness blinded him.

"Damn," he whispered.

The cars door opened and boots scuffed on the gravel and cement. The sound of the door closing softly was followed by the soft whisk of pants legs brushing together. Jake's heart hammered, and his breath grew short.

"Ain't got time for this," a voice cut through the silence. "If you're here, get your butt out of the shadows where I can see you. We drive all night, and tomorrow, we'll have enough sunlight left to keep us safe. We give them time, we'll never see them again, or worse — we might not make it back."

Jake closed his eyes, took a deep breath, and pushed off from the wall.

"Here," he said softly. "I'm here."

He stood and oriented himself for a moment. The shadowy figure facing him slowly grew features as his eyes adjusted to the light. A tall, lean, black man faced him, short close-packed hair and eyes so intense they nearly glowed.

"I'm Jake," he said, moving forward and extending a hand.

"Thinblade," the man replied, taking the extended greeting in stride and shaking with a steady pressure that put Jake momentarily at ease. "You can call me Thin."

"Not Blade?" Jake half-joked.

"This ain't no comic book, man," Thin replied, not really smiling. "Ain't no joke."

"I know," Jake replied.

Without another word, the man turned, heading back to the car.

"Get in back," Thin said quickly. "Brad and Northwind are there – Janey's up front with me. All of us have reasons to find this one. Just needed the right time."

Jake moved to the Caddy quickly, reaching for the back door latch. It opened before he could touch it, and he turned, just for a second, facing his companion.

"Why didn't you just go after him?" he asked. "If you knew her, and you knew him – or of him – knew she would get herself killed – or worse – why didn't you take him out?"

"I told you," Thin said softly, slipping in behind the wheel and cutting off further conversation. "I've read what you write, man. Maybe it isn't all black and white. Let's ride."

Jake nodded and slid into the back seat. As the door closed, his shoulder brushed another, and he turned. There was little light, but he caught bright, questioning eyes, and seconds later, a hand dropped onto his arm and gripped lightly.

"I'm Northwind, Man," a voice whispered in his ear. "I see them — you know? All the time.... the dead. I see them, and they talk to me."

Jake clutched the book to his chest.

He turned and faced those eyes, searching for something he couldn't even put a name to.

"Do you answer?"

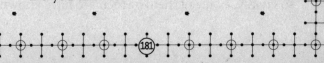

The sun was a distant glow on the rim of the Earth. Jake was dozing, arms crossed over his chest, and his head was leaning to the right. He rested on – something – then coherence invaded and he knew he was leaning on a shoulder.

"Sorry," he mumbled, lifting his head and pulling back.

"Not a problem," Northwind whispered. Jake turned. The dim light of early morning revealed a thin face with deep-set eyes. Long stringy black hair framed a face alight with purpose.

"I've been reading your book," the girl said. "Is this Phaedre the same – the one you write about on line?"

Jake blinked harder and sat up, rubbing his eyes. He saw that the girl had indeed taken the old book from his arms as he slept, and it was open over her knees. Just for a second he felt anger at the invasion – at the lack of respect for the age and quality of the book itself, then it faded.

"I don't know," he answered. "That is the book he was reading when I first saw him — when Danielle was stalking him. I went back and bought it when he took her – it was the only link I had. I hadn't read much of it when I got your e-mail."

Northwind nodded. "Some weird stuff in here, Worm, really weird stuff. Wolfmen and dudes with powers no man should have, and the dead. I can almost see them, he describes them so vividly. Some of them he seems to have known when they were alive, and then, again after they died. Like they were tied in place or something, stuck where he could watch them – or taunt them. One thing is sure. None of them liked him. None, especially not the powerful ones."

"He?" Jake asked softly, already dreading the answer.

"Scyther," she nodded. "He wrote this – didn't you know?"

"No," Jake whispered. "No, but I should have."

The illustration of the thin young man in the front of the book snapped into focus with sudden clarity. Jake shifted the clothing, and he knew. He had spoken to the author – touched him.

So, that was it then. Maybe it was a setup to catch Danielle off her guard and whisk her away, or maybe there was more to it than that. Maybe Scyther had seen her, and seen Jake, as well. Maybe Danielle would have been left alone – or taunted further – had Jake not been present. The link with Phaedre was almost too much.

"You think she's there, man?" Northwind asked, letting the book fall closed and handing it back gently. "You think she's been there?"

"Phaedre has been alive for a very long time," he answered. "It wouldn't surprise me to find out she'd spent time in the White House, if it had suited her purpose. The question is – whose purpose is being served now? If this Danielle has been his "game" for so long, why take her the moment I arrive?"

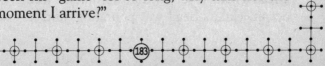

"I was wondering that too," Thin piped in from the front. "I hope I'm not reading this wrong. I'm pretty sure the blood-sucker knows you'll figure out who he is, and where he is, but I don't think he's counting on us. Danielle and I – we haven't been getting along so well. Seems she thinks we should be out killing 24/7, ridding the earth of vermin — Scyther in particular – some shit like that. Me, I'm more of a planner, like to contemplate a thing before I make it happen. Only thing I ever saw Scyther do was play cat and mouse with her. She wanted us all down there months ago. She thinks he killed her parents.

"Maybe he did. Thing is, I don't know it for a fact, and from the questions I asked, and from the answers she gave, I don't think she knows either. So I didn't go. None of us wanted any part of storming a vampire's home turf unprepared."

"I haven't spoken with Danielle in nearly a month. Until I saw your post, I thought maybe she was already dead."

"Maybe she is," Jake replied, glancing out the window at the passing countryside. "Maybe I managed to get her killed."

"More likely," Thin said, frowning, "she's about to do that for us all."

They grew silent, and the miles rolled away beneath them as the sunrise painted the road ahead a golden yellow that shimmered like a flat ocean. Jake's head was pounding, and he was hungry. Vampires might not be much good in the light, but neither was he at the moment. Could be an even fight. They drove in relative silence for most of the day. Nightwind read on in the book, and when her eyes grew tired, Jake thumbed through the pages himself, trying to get a handle on what was going on. Failing.

About half past four, Jake glanced up and saw a sign that said "Last U. S. Exit," Thin veered to the side. There was no road visible, at first, but moments later, it was obvious that where they had turned off into the desert was a well-traveled path.

"It smoothes out ahead," Thin said, turning to glance over his shoulder. "I cased the place once a while back. Road winds on up into those mountains," he hesitated, pointing ahead, and to the right. "The base of the mountains is as far as I've been."

Jake nodded. He opened the book again across his knees, and with Northwind leaning in to glance over his shoulder, began to read aloud.

"They arrived in droves the second night. We had a time getting enough help of a sort that could handle the animals without sending them into a frenzy. Lorenzo and Florence just let their carriage continue to move forward as they stepped free, laughing gaily as if the horses wouldn't wander off and wrap themselves and everything they towed around the nearest tree. I had to send Oswald and Puck to fetch the thing. Wolfies are SO peckish. The things I had to promise.

"By midnight the guests outnumbered the hosts four to one, and things were in full swing. Le Duc, the Frenchman – so intense, the Europeans — had taken it upon himself to bring in the entertainment. Fifty of them, fresh and untouched, chained at the neck and the ankle. He drove them like frolicking cattle, and I must say, he turned *my* head with that entrance.

"When he set them free, let them run and scream and cry out to their feeble gods— that was a moment. I remember it clearly, for I'd just come from the library. Phaedre had refused – once again – to join us, me in particular, and I wasn't in the best of moods. It is amazing what a screaming teenager with green eyes can do for a hungry man's anger."

Jake slapped the book shut.

The road had grown bumpier, and the bright sunlight streaming in through the windows was bringing a thirst that deepened Jake's headache.

"Why'd you stop?" Northwind asked quietly. "Don't you want to know?"

"Know what?" Jake asked. "Know that she didn't come out to *play* with the others? Know that she did? Know that they let humans loose in their garden and toyed with them until they felt like a midnight snack? Know that I sent Danielle into that place – albeit a century or two in the future?"

"You need to stop that," Brad spoke up for the first time. He was an intense, broad-shouldered young man with short-cropped blonde hair. The contrast he made with Thin was striking. "You need to get over yourself, man. You didn't send anyone anywhere. Danielle does what she does, always has. You didn't drag her into that auction – or that alley. You didn't drag her out, either. He did. You need to focus on what's happening and quit worrying over yourself."

Jake blinked.

Just then the road took a quick jog to the right, and they began to round the foothills of the lower of the mountains. Thin turned again.

"This is as far as I've been," he said. "Beyond here, I don't know exactly what to expect.

Northwind was staring out the window across Jake's line of sight. Her eyes were far away, and her lips were set in a tight line.

"What do you see?" he asked her softly.

"They are lining the road," she replied. "Not a straight line, but more than I've seen in one place. And they are watching us. Every move."

"You think they can send the word ahead that we are coming?" Brad asked nervously.

"Not to vampires," Jake cut in. "A lot of what you read and see in movies is crap, but the sunlight thing isn't. If we can find where they are before the sun sets, we have a good chance of taking them out, or immobilizing them. If Danielle is okay, we might even save her."

"I'll settle for putting them down, man," Thin muttered. "I'm in no hurry to hear Danielle spouting psychotic 'Itoldyouso's' into my ear."

They rounded a rocky outcropping, and ahead, to the left of the road, a structure rose.

As they approached, Jake could see that the place had once been magnificent. The walls were stucco, rising three stories into the glittering sunlight. There were towers where guards might once have stood, massive wooden doors that hung askew on their hinges. There was no sign that anyone had inhabited the structure in decades, let alone the last few days.

"Jesus," Northwind said softly. "Even the building looks dead."

They spread out, Thin Blade and Janey, a shorter, a thin, dish-water blonde girl in a leather jacket that looked heavy enough to drag her to the ground started around the wall to the right. Brad headed off on his own to the left, and Northwind stood beside Jake, staring at the massive, dangling wooden door warily.

"I hate this part," Jake said, cursing under his breath. He stepped forward, ducked beneath a spider's web that dangled from the door frame and entered the old home. Northwind followed like a slender shadow, and the bright sunlight fell away instantly to gloom, evidenced only in the puddle of light that leaked in through the door.

A wide, curving stair wound to the upper stories from a parlor that must once have been truly grand. The doorways leading into a long hall, and a smaller room to the left that appeared to have been the den. Jake took it all in, concentrating on the shadows. Nothing moved, and he was starting to wonder if "Thin" had made a mistake. Then things shifted.

At first the changes were subtle, a halo of light where there should be none, the sparkle of — something — in the center of a pool of darkness. Jake blinked, backing slowly toward the door. Then the dust on the floor whirled, caught in the grip of some errant breeze, and images began to transpose themselves over the drab interior. Bodies moved in time to a soft undercurrent of music, light glowed dimly, brightening gradually and glittering off a million pinpoints of crystal — a chandelier — dangling from the center of the cathedral-height ceiling.

To his right, Northwind gasped.

Jake was still backpedaling, the door a few footsteps away. He glanced over and saw that Northwind was not moving toward the door. She was turning slowly, eyes wide, staring into each corner of the room. Jake saw her hips sway, ever so slightly, and his mind correlated that motion with the sound – the music. The lights were still brightening, and the dust had faded, all but disappearing from the furniture — more furniture than there could be.

Those moving about them paid no heed to the two intruders, but danced slowly. Peels of laughter echoed through the suddenly festive hall. Festive, but with a dark edge to it that Jake couldn't quite put a name to. Something decidedly bitter and stale permeated the air. Jake stopped his retreat and stepped toward Northwind.

"Hey," he called out softly, for some reason unwilling to disturb the music more than was necessary.

He got no response.

"Hey!" he called out more loudly, stepping close and letting his hand drop onto the girl's shoulder. She spun wildly, her arm drawing back as if she would strike him and her eyes wild. For a long moment Jake held his breath, readied to drop back, or block her arm if she swung at him. Slowly, her eyes focused, and she began to tremble, slumping. Jake managed to catch her, barely, before she hit the floor.

"What . . " her question remained unfinished. Steps sounded on the stairs, and Jake turned, the motion drawing the girl close to his side.

It was Scyther. He was stalking down the stairs like a slender cat. In his hands, he held a book — the book? The volume was clasped before him, held reverently close to his chest. His eyes shone with energy. He stared right at Jake. Right through Jake. He continued down the stairs as if no one but he, and those who'd stopped their eerie dance to witness his arrival, existed in the world. Jake drew Northwind back against the wall and held her close to his side, watching the panorama before them.

There was a disturbance along the back wall, near another doorway that led beyond the parlor. Jake turned, keeping his gaze fixed on Scyther, or whatever passed as Scyther, from the corner of one eye. The crowd was parting, and someone was entering the room from the far side. At first there was the vague sensation of motion. Then there was a scent, a certain scent that sent Jake's sense reeling — because it was hers — and then the crowd parted and deep, endless eyes stared into Jake's own, and beyond.

A crashing sound reverberated through the house, and the images crumbled. They had formed slowly, intricately — they ended in a sudden crash of silence, then the scuffle of rough footsteps.

Thinblade strode into the room, puffs of dust rising around him, Janey at his side. From the far side of the room, where Jake had seen Phaedre — Brad stepped into sight, swinging his head from side to side and searching the shadows.

Jake could only stare, and he felt Northwind trembling hard against his side. He knew she'd seen what he had seen, or something very close to it. It was equally obvious in that moment that none of the others had seen a thing.

"No sign of anyone on this side," Brad called out. "No prints, and the dust is thick enough to have been here for years. A lot of years."

"Same in back," Thin replied, nodding. They all spun to where Jake and Northwind stood, trembling, near the wall.

"What happened?" Thin asked, stepping closer. Jake felt the young man's concern slide over and off and onto Northwind.

"I — WE — saw — something," she managed at last, fighting for each breath and then exhaling it in a rush that barely formed words. "A party, they were dancing, and . . . he was there." Thin's face tightened. "You saw him? Does he know we're here?"

"Not him, exactly," Jake cut in. "What we saw wasn't — here — I think. It was like a vision. We saw what happened here a long time ago. It was Scyther, all right, but there was more. I saw Phaedre."

"How could you know that?" Brad cut in. "Maybe it was him, sending thoughts into your head."

"I've heard they can do that," Thin said, nodding and staring at Jake dubiously.

Jake grew very still, then reached beneath his shirt and pulled out the book. He turned the pages slowly, skimming in the gloom, until he found the passage he'd been looking for. Without hesitation, he read.

"Things were getting into full swing when I finally made my way into the thick of things. Monty and Belle were entertaining at the bar, several of Le Duc's charges, bound to the table, stripped of annoying human garb and squirming so prettily against the wood. Different vintage for each taste — two of the young girls had been given wine so their blood — their emotion — would bear that stain — others had been whipped, stripped, blindfolded. There was Latin blood to taste, and tender white skin. A smorgasbord and I, the maitre d', watching over it all.

"As I made my way in, Phaedre finally took leave of her tedious studies to join us. A festive night indeed, and the best still to come."

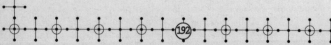

"It was just like that," Northwind breathed softly.

"You read the book," Thinblade cut in. "You read that, then your minds built it around you."

"Both of us at the same time?" Jake tried to keep the sarcasm from his voice. "I don't think that's likely. "Something happened here. A warning? A vision? A trick? I can't tell you that, only that it happened." .

A voice whispered, very softly — deep inside.

"Some fairy tales are real."

Jake shook his head and frowned, backing toward the door again.

"He drew us here," Jake said quickly. "He saw me in that auction, and he knew me. He left this damned book," he shook the old volume toward the stairs, "knowing we would find him. Maybe he even knew I'd found you."

"We were careful," Thin replied, shaking his head slowly.

"He is older than you are," Jake said slowly. "He has seen things and known things we may never even fantasize. What makes you think he couldn't get through our defenses? For that matter, if you believe he can put thoughts in people's heads, what's to keep him from taking others out?"

"Doesn't matter," Brad cut in. "We're here, for whatever reason, and he's got Danielle. We have to find him quick. Sun isn't going to last forever, and we have hunting to do."

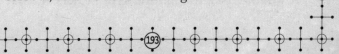

Thinblade nodded quickly and turned toward the stairs.

"I don't plan on waiting for bright-boy to wake up. He may have drawn us here, but that doesn't mean we lose. It only means we have to get smarter."

"He came from there," Jake said, pointing to the stairs. We have no way to know he sent that vision. Maybe others did. Maybe those others that Northwind sees are trying to help."

"Couldn't hurt," Janey grinned. "Let's go see if the 'Master' is in his chambers."

They turned as a group and mounted the spiraling stairway, heading upward into the shadowed gloom. The dust was thick, rising in clouds that threatened to cut off their air. Some of the clouds took shape and danced momentarily, only to fade into darkness. Jake concentrated on the steps leading upward, clutching the book to his chest like a talisman.

They reached the upper hall and stopped, staring down a seemingly endless corridor of doors. The carpet was musty and dank, the air scented with mildew and the musk of animals. Still, through it all, the building held a decadent grandeur deep within its walls. It seeped out to draw the eye to a bit of woodwork – a particularly gaudy lamp – long dead and lightless, clinging to the wall with all the grace of a skeletal arm embedded in stone.

Northwind hadn't moved far from Jake's side. It was obvious, though she kept to herself, that

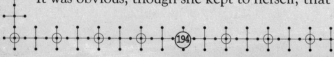

she saw more than they did. She shivered, gasping occasionally. Jake scanned the corridor, then fixed his eyes on her face. She was fixed on one door. There was no reason to pick it from the others. There must have been a dozen, but she walked straight ahead, one hand reaching out to trail along the wall, leaving trails in the dust.

Jake laid his hand gently on her shoulder.

"What do you see?" he asked.

"They litter the hall," she said softly. "Young, beautiful – young men and women. They died here. So much blood. So much. Now they are watching me – watching you."

"I don't think anyone's been here for a very long time," Brad said. He and Thinblade had nearly reached the end of the hall. Neither seemed in a hurry to push open any of the doors – as if they feared what they might find. What they might learn.

"He's here," Northwind whispered. "He's been here ever since – then."

"The party?" Jake asked.

"Yes," She replied. "Since then. Alone."

Thinblade was staring at his younger companion, a skeptical frown creasing his forehead.

"How do you know that?" he asked at last.

"They are telling me," she whispered. "In my head, all of them, dead, bleeding through the rug so it dripped to the room below, wasted – so much waste – and it wasn't enough. He was – angry."

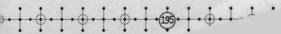

"Then why did he stay?" Jake asked quickly. "Why kill everyone – everything – even the house – and stay?"

"She left," Northwind shrugged. Her eyes were distant, and it was obvious that whatever voices whispered in her mind were distracting her from her surroundings. Her words had a disjointed rhythm, and Jake was afraid she might pass out at any moment. Extra-sensory overload?

"The voices." Janey breathed. "I've heard voices. Hell, we've all heard them. You know that Thin. Kept us alive this long – you going to give up on them now?"

"Not if they help me kill that bloodsucker," Thin scowled, turning toward the doorway that Northwind was fixated on.

They all filed in behind, Jake leading Northwind by the arm gently. The door wasn't locked, and it swung inward with a loud groan. Rust and rotted wood – and the scent of lilies. Suddenly, the air was filled with the scent of lilies. Jake stepped forward to glance over Thin's shoulder.

The floor was littered with the petals. Pots with withered plants lay in every corner and on every horizontal surface. There was a bed in one corner. It wasn't rotted, nor was it covered in dust like the rest of the old home. It was clean and the sheets were bright white. The surface of the quilt covering the mattress was littered with more of the lily petals, so many you could barely make out the material beneath, and in the center of it all, eyes closed and head listing to one side against a soft, down-filled pillow, lay Danielle.

"What the fuck is this place?" Brad whispered.

No one answered, but Jake slipped away from Northwind and over to the bed, sitting on the edge of the mattress and reaching out quickly to check her pulse. It was there, weak, but there.

"She's alive," he said, turning.

As he turned, the shadows in the furthest corner of the room rustled, and he was there. Scyther, just as he'd looked at the auction — darker — eyes blazing with an inner light that seemed to ripple and spark as his lips curled into a leering smile.

"So good of you to come," he said softly. Though the words were not spoken loudly, they carried. They echoed and whipped about a room suddenly devoid of breath, or sound.

Jake stood, turning to face the vampire. He knew he was protected, somewhat. The others he didn't know about, so he spoke.

"You left little choice."

"The world is nothing but choice," Scyther replied, stepping just a bit further from the shadows. There were no windows. There was no light. Still, it seemed remarkable to Jake that the vampire could move at all.

"Why Danielle," Jake asked. "Why me?"

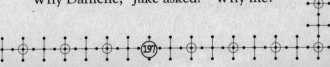

"You were an afterthought," Scyther replied with a smirk. "The woman and I have danced for years. Do you truly believe she thought she'd kill me? That this is the first time she's been here? That anything you believe is truth when everything around you fades to lies? You remind me of another – though I don't know why. You – and the books. I wanted that one back."

Scyther was pointing to where Jake still clutched the leather bound volume to his chest.

"It was mine," the vampire went on.

"Why do you want it?" Northwind asked, stepping forward suddenly. "They are gone. All of them are gone, and they aren't coming back."

Scyther's expression darkened with the swiftness of a rising storm, but Northwind appeared not to notice. She knelt slowly, reaching out to an empty space on the carpet. Jake's gaze followed her slender fingers. He knew he should not look away from the vampire. He knew, and yet – something was happening. He couldn't *not* look away.

Where there had been only dust and the withered, dried lily petals, a long, slender body was taking shape. The limbs were sprawled at odd angles. Impossible angles. It was a woman – long legs and dark hair, pooled like blood around her face, blending with what must have been blood on the carpet, lips parted in an expression close to a smile and so far from it that it defied description.

Very suddenly, and very quickly, Scyther was moving. He rushed toward Northwind, who seemed oblivious to his existence.

"She loved the flowers." Northwind's voice was clear, and something in the words struck the vampire with the force of an anvil – dropping him to his knees.

"She loved the flowers," Northwind repeated, turning toward Scyther slowly, "but she didn't love you. Never. You couldn't have her, so you took the flowers — you wrote the words, trapped the images in that book forever – and you took this one." Northwind's hand trailed along the shimmering body on the floor before her. "You took her because *she* took her first."

"She should not . . .she . ." Scyther rose suddenly, anger flaring in his eyes.

"You have no right to those memories," he grated, stepping forward again. "You have no right to see my dead. You have no rights here at all, except the right of death."

Scyther suddenly seemed taller. The room was darker, and it was hard to focus because he moved so quickly, like a flitting shadow. His voice came from all around them at once, and Jake drew Northwind back to her feet.

Thinblade, who'd been watching, and listening, had not been idle. He had a long, slender blade in his hand — polished wood, honed and balanced. He gripped Janey by her shirt and dragged her to the center of the room at his side. Brad closed in beside Janey on the

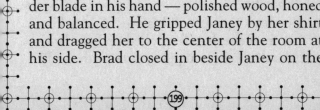

other side, and Jake, catching on quickly, backed into the circle, drawing Northwind behind him and tugging her into place between himself and Thin.

"You can stand together," Scyther taunted them, slipping around the room, more and more quickly. "You can run, and fall apart. You can watch one another's backs and curse me with your last breath. You will all die.

"I will not be stalked and mocked in my own home. I will not have you," a hand reached out of nowhere, gripping Northwind's hair and yanking her roughly off balance, only to slip away again, "and your half-truth stolen memories haunting me. You know nothing of her. You can't know the barest edge of my pain."

"She hated you," Northwind said, standing straighter. "They all hated you. No matter what you did, how extravagant, it was never enough. Danielle hated you too, and still you hope. She will hate you when she wakes, and again if you kill her and bring her back. Just like the others. You took her parents, how could she not hate you?"

There was a quick growl and Scyther shot from the darkness like a bolt from a crossbow. Jake whispered a single word as he frantically jerked Northwind aside.

"Phaedre."

Scyther's lips parted, his eyes widened, and at that moment, hands reached up from below, long slender fingers whipping through the air like lightning to grip his ankles like iron fetters. He slammed forward, crashing to the floor and whipping around. Too late. That moment was all it took for Thinblade to launch, and his stake / knife severed the vampire's heart with a clean stroke, sending a sudden cloud of choking dust whirling to the floor to settle among the dying flowers.

Northwind pulled away from Jake and knelt once more beside the body on the floor. It glowed more brightly than before, shimmering. Thinblade and the others gathered around, and Jake could tell that they now saw the woman as well, or that they saw something.

A voice slipped through the silence. Jake couldn't tell if the words were spoken, or if he somehow just heard them. They were not spoken for him alone.

"I loved him." The ghostly woman turned slowly, so that she lay flat on her back and her eyes – bright lights in a dark visage — stared at the ceiling, and beyond. "I was the only one. I loved him, and he brought me here – to a room of her flowers – to die. He killed me because she left, and he didn't bring me back.

"He once called me his Lily," she breathed. The word ended in a rasping sigh and the image broke, so much smoke in the darkness. The room, very suddenly had the empty chill of a tomb.

"Let's get out of here," Thinblade rasped. He leaned down, picking Danielle up in his arms, and turning toward the door. They filed

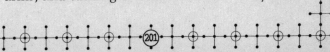

out after him, down the winding stairs and toward the world beyond slowly, each lost in his own thoughts.

Jake's thoughts were the image of the party, Phaedre, parting the crowd as she exited the library. The others slipped out the front, but Jake turned, moving quickly across the great hall and into the library beyond. The books were rotting on the shelves, some leather and older than he had ever seen, most crumbled, pages lying like the lily-petals above, scattered on the floor.

Jake reached up to the center shelf, pushed a pile of dust aside, and placed the book on the shelf.

Northwind was suddenly at his side, and he turned to her. Seeing the question in her eyes, he said simply.

"Some fairy tales are real. This one belongs here. They are his memories, and now — he is theirs."

She nodded, scanning the room slowly. Then, arm in arm, they moved toward the light.

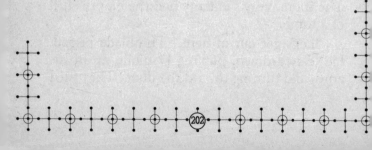

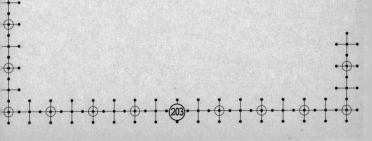

Seven
The Frailty of Humans

by Gherbod Fleming

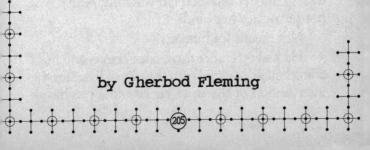

Winter-stripped boughs bent low, coated on top with freshly fallen snow like a second, crystalline bark. The evergreens, transformed into immense white-plumed birds, were the most sorely burdened. They drooped close to the ground, pressed down and denied flight by the impenetrable gray mass of clouds which seemingly clung to the treetops. The afternoon was not far advanced, but neither was darkness long to come; this time of year, at this latitude, morning was always late to arrive, and daylight never overstayed its welcome.

Kaitlin tried to weave her way through the fragile whitescape without leaving sign of her passing—tried, and failed. Stretching to make use of the drift-breaking footprints of Black Rindle, who she was following, she repeatedly lost her balance: not completely, not tumbling to the ground in full snow-angel posture, but enough that her shoulder or her arm as she flailed to regain her equilibrium brushed against a heavy-laden branch, and the snow cascaded to the ground.

There was no actual need—thank goodness—for her to pass mysterious and unseen like an Indian through the forest—no need other than her own desire to show Black Rindle that she took his admonitions seriously. The place he was taking her was secret; it was holy. And it was not meant for her kind.

Not meant for humans.

He had taken her there once before, and in so doing had jeopardized both their lives. If not for the intervention of the strangely beautiful patchwork beast, she and Black Rindle would certainly have been killed. Maybe that was why he was taking her back now-now that most of *the others* were gone.

Black Rindle was undeniably strong and, despite the humped back that made him appear stooped and forced him to limp slightly, he'd always struck Kaitlin as surprisingly graceful—preternaturally graceful. The first time she'd seen him, she'd not even noticed the hump. Of course, she'd been preoccupied by terror at the time, and the only detail that she *had* noticed, other than his glaring predatory eyes, had been the body slung over his shoulder.

Kaitlin shook her head; she gnawed the inside of her lip, willing herself not to dwell on such morbid thoughts. Slaughter was nothing new; blood was shed all across the world, every hour of every day. If she obsessed on the details, she would lose sight of the larger, broader picture. It was with a purpose that she accompanied Black Rindle; she sought equilibrium in her life, balance that could not indefinitely be maintained through isolation. But one other fact, through hard experience, she knew incontrovertibly: If she was to make her way in the world, she must choose the route carefully.

Moving through the forest, she watched Black Rindle's hunched back, tried to trace his footsteps. He was wearing an old coat that she'd bought him for seven dollars at the Salvation Army store in Winimac because he had no money. He wouldn't use a hat or gloves, said he didn't like them, they got in the way. Kaitlin's knit cap was pulled down over her ears, her fists scrunched tight inside her wool mittens. She wore a scarf, parka, her only pair of jeans, warm boots, long underwear. Still she was cold. She wondered what her ancestors would think if they could see her. Long ago sweating in the jungles or deserts of Africa, would they ever have been this cold? Had they seen snow? She didn't know the names on her family tree, but probably some forebear had been abducted and brought across the ocean in chains to experience winter frost in the American South. Kaitlin knew only the stories of her grandparents and her parents in Detroit; they had been cold. What about Clarence? Her cousin was the only family she still kept in touch with these days, and that irregularly. Was he freezing somewhere? On the street, back in prison?

Thoughts of family inevitably triggered thoughts of home-of what *used to be* home. Kaitlin had fled the city when the dead got uppity. She had already seen firsthand the inhumanity within man when she then began to see the simply inhuman: partially decayed corpses shambling down the street or sitting in a restaurant, ephemeral ghosts standing on a corner, twisted faces peering out from behind the expression of someone who used to be familiar—and no one else seemed to see. The choice had been between insanity and isolation, and so Kaitlin had fled to the rural wilds many miles from Detroit.

But ignoring the impossible had not made it go away. The spirit world had sought her out and had found her. With a vengeance.

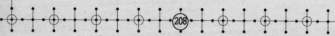

Jarred back to the here and now, Kaitlin suddenly halted her next step mid-stride. Black Rindle was so much taller that she practically had to leap to match his footsteps, and this time she looked up to see him stopped and her about to plow right into him. He bent down and examined a slight trough before them in the knee-deep snow. Then, with his bare hands, he began to shovel the snow aside.

"What are you doing?" Kaitlin asked. Her voice sounded muffled in the veritable snow cave. She ran her tongue over her cracked lips.

Black Rindle did not answer, but as he cleared away more snow she saw what he had found: a narrow strip of ice, gleaming black against the trickle of a stream that somehow managed to flow beneath.

Kaitlin looked around. She had been here before, but she never would have recognized the place. Everything out here was so completely different depending on the hour or season: day, night, summer, winter. The city wasn't like that; a building was a building, by daylight or streetlight, heat wave or blizzard.

They continued on, keeping just to the side of the trough, which was fine with Kaitlin. She had no idea how solidly the stream was frozen and no desire to test the waterproofing of her boots in sub-freezing temperatures.

When Black Rindle stopped next, Kaitlin wasn't caught off guard, but what she did not see for several seconds was the third individual standing with them near the hidden stream. He was

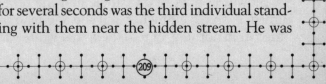

completely still, and as much a part of the forest as the trees. He was beautiful, too: in the way that a deer bounding away through the underbrush is beautiful. His long silver hair was twined with magpie feathers, and he wore furs and buckskin boots. Confusion furrowed his brow, and his pale blue eyes asked the unvoiced question: *What is she doing here?* As Black Rindle and the newcomer stared rigidly back and forth, Kaitlin could feel the tension between the two men.

Men. She kept telling herself that was what they were, though she knew it was not the truth. Not the whole truth. She wouldn't let herself look at them. Not *that* way. Yet even denying the vision, the second sight that she had tried and failed to leave behind in the city, she could sense the razor's edge that Black Rindle walked. His rage was never far beneath the surface. Kaitlin imagined that each whisker upon his pale face quivered from the strain of violence denied. He had never turned that fury on her, but she had seen what his kind was capable of. From within rather than without, the icy winter chill touched her and she shivered.

Beyond the two frozen men, Kaitlin saw a low, curving mound of snow. The miniature ridge, like the exposed stream earlier, told her where she was, and desperate to interrupt the deepening tension she pointed at the mound: "That's the shrine. I didn't recognize it...with all the snow."

Slowly, as one, Black Rindle and the other turned, each regarding her as if she had materialized from nothing, or told them that white was

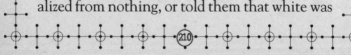

black. With difficulty, Kaitlin swallowed. Just as slowly, the two men mercifully looked away from her and resumed their stare down.

The stranger spoke first: "Evert didn't allow humans."

"Do you see Evert anywhere, moon-calf?" Black Rindle asked.

"His name is Moon-calf?" Kaitlin whispered.

"No more than his is Hunch," the stranger said, offended.

"My name might as well have been Hunch for those many years," Black Rindle said with his own refined bitterness, relenting only slightly when he told Kaitlin: "This is Barks-at-Shadows."

Nervous, Kaitlin chuckled—then realized that no one was joking. "Barks-at-Shadows" she said hesitantly. "Go figure." Then again, she reminded herself, her guy's name was Black Rindle.

"This is Kaitlin Stinnet," Black Rindle said for the benefit of Barks-at-Shadows. "She is Kinfolk."

"Kinfolk born?" Barks-at-Shadows asked.

"Kinfolk by word and deed," Black Rindle said, then added: "I put more stock in the person than in your Fang bloodlines."

Kaitlin didn't understand, but whatever Black Rindle was talking about was doing nothing to soften the mood. His words pricked Barks-at-Shadows, though still he was less angry, less bitter, than Black Rindle.

"I'm hungry," Kaitlin lied, and again the two men regarded her, almost as if they'd forgotten she was there, despite the fact that her presence was ostensibly the point of contention between them. "I haven't had anything to eat today," she said to Black Rindle. "Can you go catch something. We'll make a fire while you're gone."

Black Rindle glowered at her but, after hesitating for a few tense moments, acceded— as Kaitlin knew he would. He took pride in his hunting skills, and it was not often that Kaitlin allowed herself to ask anything of him. With barely audible throaty grumbling, he trudged off into the deepening darkness of the snow-blanketed forest.

As quite often seemed to be the case, Kaitlin began to doubt the wisdom of her actions—now that it was too late. She could feel Barks-at-Shadows watching her. They were alone except for the creaking of the heavy-laden branches. Kaitlin didn't look at him—something about direct eye contact being a challenge; it just didn't seem like a good idea. So, eyes downcast, she started rooting around in the snow, clearing a spot on the ground with her boots for the fire. Without comment, Barks-at-Shadows left her and returned a few minutes later with an armful of kindling; a second trip and a third each yielded more substantial pieces of wood.

"So," Kaitlin said, "do you guys, like, rub sticks together?"

Barks-at-Shadows reached into a pocket and produced a lighter.

"Oh." She watched as he built and lit the fire. She tried to convince herself that Black Rindle wouldn't have left her here, wouldn't have brought her, if there were danger. Not *again*.

The crackling flames were a welcome diversion, a natural focal point. Kaitlin could stare at them and didn't have to make such a constant effort not to look at Barks-at-Shadows. Besides not wanting him to feel challenged, she didn't trust herself to hold in check the second sight which would show her what she most definitely did not want to see—not right now, not while Black Rindle was gone. She had grown accustomed enough to his presence that she could see him as a *person*, not as one of those things, not as a something that *looks* human but is just waiting to reveal its true form.

She had seen Barks-at-Shadows before, when he was changed; she thought she had—when he and the others had tried to kill her. She assumed that he had been one of the snarling man-wolf creatures that had invaded her home, that would have torn her limb from limb, that Black Rindle had protected her from.

"Are the others…?" Her voice faltered. Her tongue felt thick, her lips numb.

"Gone or dead," Barks-at-Shadows said.

Kaitlin gazed at the fire for a long time, seeing in it the flaming brands of a funeral pyre. She pulled a stump closer to the fire, brushed off the snow, and sat. "You don't like me being here," she said at last, glancing furtively at Barks-at-Shadows.

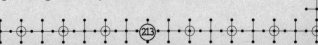

He shrugged. "Evert didn't allow humans here. But Black Rindle is Alpha now."

Alpha. But of what? Kaitlin wondered. Of one other of his kind? Of this lonely, hidden place? She felt suddenly sad for Black Rindle—and guilty herself. He had entrusted to her his greatest secrets, yet she had not revealed to him news of great importance. Despite the shared intimacy for which they both had been starved, she couldn't bring herself to tell him. She was selfishly searching out her own way.

Kaitlin glanced at Barks-at-Shadows again. He still wore his vaguely confused expression—it seemed to be a permanent state for him, as with a not-too-bright child. Kaitlin cautioned herself, however, not to underestimate him. Even a child, if he grew eight feet tall and had claws and fangs that could snap steel, could kill.

Kaitlin jumped at a sharp crack, but Barks-at-Shadows was merely snapping a stick to toss in the fire. "The others…who are gone," she said, as she tried to slow her drumming heart, "they didn't much like Black Rindle, did they?"

"He's not very likeable."

Kaitlin took a slow, deep breath. She hadn't expected Barks-at-Shadows to be so forthright. Could he be as guileless as he seemed, or was he trying to lure her in? "Then why are you still here?"

"It's my place. My tribe didn't want me."

"Why not?"

"I'm not so smart as I should be. They were embarrassed by me." Again, the blunt, unwavering directness. But without bitterness. Barks-at-Shadows seemed to accept his place; he expected no better, felt that he deserved no better.

"But you were accepted here," Kaitlin said.

"Black Rindle's mother was kind. She's dead now."

"I know. And what about Black Rindle?"

"What about him?"

"Why did the others hate him so much?" Kaitlin asked. *Did you hate him too?* she wanted to ask, *Or did you just try to kill us because they told you to?*

For a long moment, Barks-at-Shadows turned his confused-child face toward her; he seemed to pity her, that she should need to ask something so obvious. "He's metis," Barks-at-Shadows said. "Accursed in the sight of Gaia."

The words made Kaitlin's blood run cold. The matter-of-fact way in which Barks-at-Shadows uttered them, even if not dripping with vitriol and hate, bespoke indoctrination: casual acceptance of what he'd been told over and over again, more insidious than the ranting of a hate-monger. When Barks-at-Shadows said *metis*, Kaitlin might as well have heard *nigger*. The dismissal of an entire group of people as something less than human kindled her own sense of rage. Of course, in this case Black Rindle *was* something *other* than human, but so was Barks-at-Shadows, so were all the others like them. Regardless, Kaitlin had found something of humanity within Black Rindle, no matter what her second sight suggested about his state of *otherness*. She was not able to reject him out of hand, and Barks-at-Shadows' categorical judgment stuck in her craw.

But how to make Barks-at-Shadows see that? Would he ever listen to her? Was his opinion of humans any higher than of a metis? She was mulling those questions when Black Rindle returned. He would have hunted in a very different form, but there he was standing as a man, tossing a bloody hare onto the ground by the fire. The thud of the limp carcass against the melting snow struck Barks-at-Shadows like a slap across the face. Instantly, from relatively relaxed he was on edge. Kaitlin thought she could almost feel from several feet away the rumbling growl deep in his throat.

Black Rindle, too, was prepared for any challenge, any slight. As with Barks-at-Shadows's growl, Kaitlin could sense the coiled violence of Black Rindle, never too far away, but so much closer to the surface than when the two of them were alone. In that brief moment of reunion, she knew the futility of the task she had set herself. She could not reconcile these two individuals; she could not make inroads against the prejudices of their people and culture. Maybe, if she had years—but she did not have years. She couldn't wait that long.

"I'm not hungry anymore," she said morosely. "Can you take me home."

Black Rindle glared at her, but did not argue. When she did not rise from her seat, he lifted her in his arms. They did not say goodbye to

Barks-at-Shadows; they simply left. And as Black
Rindle carried her, he changed. His strides grew
larger, stronger, as he grew taller. His arms held
her as effortlessly as they might any small, insig-
nificant creature, though not so carelessly as he'd
brandished the dead hare. Steam spouted from
his lupine nostrils, and his ears lay back as he
quickened his pace and the nighttime forest of
muted white became a blur.

Kaitlin curled against his warmth. She closed
her eyes, no longer able to retrace the route she'd
taken to reach this place, and placed a gentle
hand on her belly. Even through her parka, she
could feel the life stirring within her. But she
wouldn't tell Black Rindle, she couldn't. Not
until she'd figured out what she needed to do.
She had hoped for something better from his
people; she'd let herself imagine that their sav-
agery might conceal some basic, fundamental understanding of existence. She had worried about
them not being human. As it turned out, perhaps they were all too human.

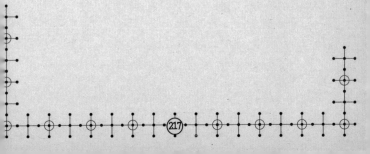

Eight
Lucimal's
Heart

by Dominic von Riedemann

". . . unfortunately, the museum is closed for the foreseeable future." Leaf Pankowski could hear the tension underlying Dr. Carleton Van Wyk's cultured tenor as he spoke from her answering machine. "I must go. Until next time." A click then silence. The machine's pre-recorded voice recited the time and day stamp. Leaf reached down and erased the message.

The heavily built woman collected her thoughts as she put away her groceries. Two packs of tofu went into the freezer, the third in the fridge. 'The museum is closed' was a code-phrase the doctor used to tell her to lie low after a mission. To act normal until any suspicion died down. But Leaf didn't want to.

After she put the groceries away, she took an apple from the crisper and picked up her copy of the newspaper lying on the floor of her apartment. Her homemade, ceramic wind chimes tinkled by the window. "Mysterious Fire Destroys Gynecology Clinic", the headline read. She shook it out and grinned. She rarely bought the tabloid, considering it right-wing patriarchal crap, but it was the only daily that had covered the fire. Leaf read the story with a satisfied smile on her wide face. *Those warlocks won't be doing any more 'experiments' on helpless women*, she thought.

Leaf wore her straight, dark hair in a boyish bob. She considered herself to be "healthy", although her GP had warned her that being twenty pounds overweight wasn't doing her heart any favors. But her doctor had bought into the beauty myth, and wasn't the ideal standard of womanhood an ideal recipe for anorexia anyway? Leaf liked her body the way it was, although she appreciated the way her figure was hardening, courtesy of her martial-arts classes.

Leaf frowned as she shifted on her futon couch. Torching the clinic had been a good thing, but she wanted to do more. Take the war to the oppressive, undead patriarchy. Dr. Van Wyk had a point; maybe she should lie low for now, pretend she was just another drone like all the others. But she felt restless, she wanted to do some more good in a world that was getting worse every day. Leaf tried not to look at the clay bust she had done of Oaken for the second anniversary of their hand fasting. Ten weeks since she had kicked him out of the apartment and he still hadn't picked up all his stuff. *Men*, she thought as she turned on her computer, *who needs them anyway?*

After half an hour searching the hunter database, Leaf found what she was looking for:

Seeking fellow Imbued in Chicago area for investigations and self-protection. No preferences but must be willing to fight the good fight.

— Cypherlou27

There was an e-mail address attached. Leaf composed a reply and sent it. By evening she had her answer.

The coffee shop was in what used to be the fashionable section of Chicago, now rapidly going to seed. Leaf bought a ginseng tea from the tattooed girl behind the cash counter and found an empty table. As she let the tea steep, she casually looked around the shop. A middle-aged stockbroker was reading the financial section while sipping his cappuccino. A gaunt, pale-skinned man with shoulder-length, black-dyed hair was looking out the window. His black-painted fingernails drummed on the tabletop. A boy and a girl were giggling together in one of the booths. Their backpacks identified them as students from the University. Leaf snorted in exasperated condescension as the girl licked fudge icing from the boy's finger.

They'll soon learn what a pile of crap love is, she thought. Briefly she thought of Oaken, the last fight they had after he had killed that vampire infant. Once again, she wondered if she had been unreasonable about kicking him out like that. *No, I did the right thing,* she thought. *He's only a man, there's no way he'd understand.* Leaf poured some tea into her cup. *I'm happy. I'm better off this way,* she told herself as she took her first sip.

"Spare some fuckin' change, bitch?" A gloved hand snapped its fingers in front of her face. Leaf recoiled, nearly spilling her tea. The hand belonged to a homeless African-American, probably in his middle twenties. He was bundled against the cold and his mouth smelled like a sewer.

"Not with that attitude, you misogynistic prick," Leaf snapped back, shock replaced by anger.

"Fuck you, ho." Only now did Leaf notice the dilated pupils and scabbed skin that

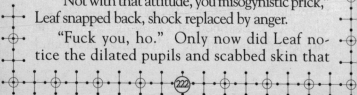

denoted crack addiction. He was shaking, his eyes wide with fury. "Gimme some fuckin' money or I cut you, bitch!"

Leaf threw her tea in the addict's face. He screamed but his left hand caught her as she tried to duck past. Leaf twisted, gripped his wrist in her left hand and slammed her right arm into his tricep the way her self-defense instructor taught her. Leaf took him down to the floor, trapping his arm across her knee and twisting his wrist so he couldn't fight back. The addict screamed curses as he struggled, his fury giving him unexpected strength. Leaf panted, barely holding onto him. He pulled an army surplus knife, the six-inch blade slashing the right shoulder of her poncho.

The homeless man's screams cut off in a horrified gurgle. Leaf looked up. The little man with black fingernails was kneeling in front of the addict, a Glock .45 rammed between the larger man's teeth.

"You wanna shut the fuck up, asshole, or shall I feed you some lead?" The little man's breath was fast in his nostrils, almost as if he was aroused. He was dressed in what Leaf supposed was the Gothic style. His charcoal overcoat was open, partially covering black Dr. Martens with white laces. "Your call."

The African-American whimpered as he stared at the pistol. His right hand released the rusted knife. The skinny man grinned, showing crooked teeth. "Let go of him, lady. Dumb fuck's got no guts."

Leaf stood up. As he stood up, the man kept the gun between the addict's teeth, forcing him onto his toes. Leaf could tell the skinny Goth was relishing the terror in the larger man's eyes. "Here's the deal, crack head," his voice shook with adrenaline. "You run real fast, real far, and maybe I won't shoot your stupid ass. Deal?"

The addict slowly backed away, his hands raised. The skinny man twitched his .45 and the addict turned, running out the door.

"Stupid niggers," he grunted as he turned around. The Glock disappeared in his coat. "You Potter116?" he asked before Leaf could make any comment.

Leaf, about to berate him for his racist language, nodded in shock.

"I guessed by the clay stains on your shirt. I'm Cypherlou27." He grabbed her arm. "We gotta get outta here before the cops show." He dragged her to the counter and slapped a fifty on the register. "You didn't know what we looked like, right?" he said to the cashier.

The tattooed girl grinned. "My memory's pretty erratic these days," she said as she smoothly slipped the money in her tank top. Cypherlou27 hustled Leaf from the coffee shop just as a siren began wailing.

●   ●   ●   ●

Leaf learned his real name was Lucimal.

"I'm a seeker of higher truths, just like you," he said as they sipped tea on his couch. Over his black t-shirt Lucimal wore a yin/yang medallion and another pendant, which Lucimal called a symbol of the Egyptian god Set. His basement apartment had garbage bags over the windows. A well-thumbed book on Aleister Crowley sat on a side table, next to a black candle and a bag of Norse runes. His Glock lay on top of a kevlar vest. Posters for bands like Deicide and Cradle of Filth lined the walls. In his sitting room, he had a large, velvet painting of a human skull with antlers. Three sixes were nestled among the points.

"You see, we approach the mystic energy from different sides," Lucimal explained between puffs on his cigarette. His colorless eyes were wide, almost embracing her with their intensity. "You worship the Goddess, the Mother, right? Well I look towards the Horned God, Pan the Destroyer, the one who brings change. And change can be painful, which is why *normal people*—" he made the phrase a curse "—think of him as the Devil, as evil, as something to be shunned."

Lucimal pointed to the yin/yang medallion on his chest. "But I'm really the other half of the same coin. The darkness to your light. And that's why I think we should work together, because we'll balance each other out; opposites allied together and being stronger for it. And I know I can trust you because I know your heart is good.

"The heart is the source, the wellspring of who we are," Lucimal continued, tapping his chest. His face was alive as he warmed to his subject. "The Egyptians believed that everything: emotion, intellect, strength, your very essence sprang from the heart. That's why, when they embalmed their dead, they placed the heart in a special jar, and just threw the brain away." Leaf nodded, smiling. His words made incredible sense to her.

Lucimal was evasive about what happened to his old team. "We raided this apartment complex, burned the place down. You probably heard about it in the news." Leaf hadn't but she nodded anyway. "I was the only one to make it out alive. It was one hell of a mess."

Leaf didn't even mind his attitude towards the undead. "Let's face it, Leaf," Lucimal said. "As much as you want to save the monsters, to *redeem* them, there's no denying that many of them have chosen to be this way, to become monsters. At that point, the only thing to do is to destroy them before they kill some poor innocent bastard."

Leaf had heard that argument many times from Oaken, during the last two months of their marriage but only now, coming from Lucimal, did it make any sense.

＊   ＊   ＊   ＊

Sander Morganfield was the second hunter who answered Lucimal's ad. He was a massive African-American albino with an easy manner that reminded Leaf of Oaken.

"My Momma put too much bleach in the bath," he chuckled, running his fingers through his tightly curled blond hair. He carried a dog-eared Webster's Dictionary with him. Sander took Leaf's and Lucimal's pictures, promising to make fake ID's for them both. Leaf didn't see

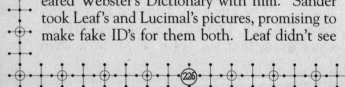

the point but Lucimal agreed enthusiastically. Sander had been in the U.S. Army and had seen "too much death" in Bosnia. It was Sander who suggested their first mission.

"Little kids have been disappearing all over the South Side. I think I know who's doin' it." Sander's affable eyes tightened in anger. He absently scratched slab-like pecs underneath his Buddy Guy's Legends Blues Bar t-shirt. "No-one's got anything on him, but I looked at him with second sight. He's corrupt all right."

Lucimal grinned. "Nice, easy job to start with. I like it."

"Do we have to kill him?" Leaf asked. "Maybe we can stop him another way. Find some evidence and give it to the police. Or maybe he's sick; he's got no choice but to kill."

Lucimal groaned. Despite her liking for Lucimal, Leaf bristled with anger. But before she could speak, Sander raised a hand.

"Mind if I have a say first?" he asked gently. Leaf nodded unwillingly. "Cops don't give two shits about the South Side. Hell, half of the cops are rots already. Call in a shooting, they show up two hours later to clean up the bodies. Now I appreciate you wanting to give this guy the benefit of the doubt. Not many of your kind will do that for a black man. But I know this asshole. He used to deal for the Italians. This makes this motherfucker worth killing, even before this shit started. And I don't care what you say, anybody who hurts little kids deserves to die."

"You say this asshole's got connections. Are we looking at tangling with organized crime?" Lucimal asked.

Sander shook his head. "Naw, no-one would miss him. No-one in this town notices if a black man goes missing, you know that."

Lucimal nodded. For a moment, Leaf wondered about the smile playing around his lips.

•　　　　•　　　　•　　　　•

Two days later, after giving them their new ID's, Sander drove them to the South Side. Leaf rode shotgun, while Lucimal reclined on the van's back bench seat. Once again, Leaf was struck by the squalor of the area. Graffiti covered one wall, above a vertical line of smeared shit reaching to the cracked sidewalk. Spilled garbage bags sat next to burned-out cars and the occasional used syringe. Sander parked the van next to an abandoned children's playground. The late afternoon sun was hidden by some clouds.

"Our man's got a place on the other side of that playground," Sander said, pointing to a low brownstone. A pack of Crips were crowded around an old Buick, hip-hop blasting out of the car's speakers. On impulse, Leaf looked at them with her second sight. They appeared normal.

Lucimal looked around the van. "I'll go check things out. Leaf could never get through and Sander, you're just too conspicuous."

Sander nodded unhappy agreement. "Luck."

Lucimal slipped out of the van, slamming the sliding door behind him. He wrapped his scarf firmly around his neck to keep away the November chill. Leaf watched him get accosted by a skinny bum as he was walking towards the playground. The bum said something in a low voice and Lucimal pushed him away.

"I'll suck your dick for some rock!" he called after Lucimal in a shaky voice. For a second, Leaf thought Lucimal was going to pull his gun and shoot him. She looked over at Sander in shock. Sander just shook his head.

"What do you think of our man Lucimal?" Sander asked after two minutes.

"He's very intense, very driven," Leaf felt an obscure need to defend Lucimal. "He has some real insight into the sacred energy."

"He's a little man," Sander growled. "He's got a little man's attitude, a little man's problems."

"I'm sure I don't understand what you're talking about," Leaf replied frostily.

Sander looked at her for a moment. "Forget I said anything," he finally muttered. "You packin'?"

Leaf, caught off-guard by the change in subject, could only gape.

"You got heat? A gun?" Sander asked. Leaf shook her head. Sander dug in his coat pocket, fished out a snub-nosed .38. "Son-of-a-bitch. Here, take this."

"I don't need it," Leaf replied, lifting her hands away from the revolver. "I've got pepper spray." She hated guns.

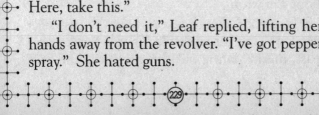

"Don't worry. There's no serial number and you're gonna need it," Sander insisted, holding it out. "Call it a feeling, intuition."

Leaf frowned as she heard a new sound, mixed with the bass thud of the Buick's speakers. She looked in the rearview mirror. Several Crips were casually kicking the flailing crack addict, between sips of malt liquor. Blood sprayed from his ruined mouth as he screamed for his mother. One Crip was making out with his girlfriend inside the Buick, his right hand busy underneath her blue top. They both looked bored.

"Don't get involved, lady," Sander commented as he watched her watching the beating. "But still think you can get by 'round here with only pepper spray?"

Leaf took the revolver. It felt warm and ugly in her hands. "Tuck it inside your pocket, like this," Sander took and slid it in her poncho. "Now no-one will see it."

"What about you?"

The sawed-off pump-action 12 gauge looked like a toy in Sander's hands. "I also got a few other surprises," Sander grinned. "But do me a favor," he suddenly became serious, "keep the gun hidden 'til it's time. Just you 'n' me, okay?"

"Why?" Leaf was puzzled.

"Like I said, call it a feeling," he replied. "I hope I'm wrong."

Leaf nodded as she looked out the passenger window. Time passed slowly. The old Buick roared past, music blaring out the open window. An empty bottle of malt liquor rolled next to the crumpled body. The sun slowly sank behind the dingy high-rises. Shadows lengthened.

Sander stiffened as they both heard a popping sound. Leaf turned to him, puzzled. Sander slipped the 12-gauge under his coat as he slammed the driver door open. His right index finger crossed his lips. Leaf opened her own door, still confused.

The winter wind caught at Leaf's poncho as she locked the van door. Sander was already looking up and down the street, making sure everything was clear. He moved quickly and silently for someone his size. Leaf scampered after him, her right hand clasping the pepper spray. They crossed the park along the left side, partially hidden by a line of sickly evergreens. The shots grew louder as they neared the brownstone. Sander hugged the wall as he moved forward, his eyes everywhere. Leaf stayed close behind him.

Sander tapped her shoulder, pointed towards an alley, hidden by darkness. Leaf nodded and he set out on a twisting run towards the alley mouth. Leaf followed, using the same random dodges. They ended up, backs to the wall, heads turned towards the alley. The shooting grew more intense.

A figure in black pelted around the corner, still firing his pistol into the alley. Lucimal started when he saw the two of them, but he slammed up against the wall, next to Leaf.

"Took you fuckers long enough," he gasped. His left hand scrubbed at his mouth.

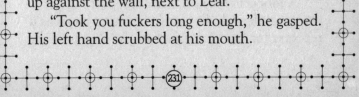

"We only heard the shots now," Sander answered. "You were supposed to case the joint, not turn into Chow-Yun motherfuckin' Fat."

"Couldn't help it." Lucimal was still rubbing the lower half of his face. His right thumb pressed the magazine release button. "There's a drug lab in the cellar, guarded by a shitload of undead. Another goddamn hunter was there, trying to trash the place." His left hand dropped from his face long enough to shove a fresh clip into his Glock. "She just bought the farm."

"So why did you start motherfuckin' World War Three back there, asshole?" Sander was steamed.

"Listen, coon," Lucimal snarled, "I've had all I can take from you—"

"Behind you!" Leaf screamed as the hulk reached for Sander's shoulder. Sander butt-stroked the hulk's chin, then whipped his shotgun around and fired, point-blank, into its face. The results weren't pretty. Leaf ducked as Lucimal fired over her head at the rot that was behind her. The rot fell back and Leaf kicked its legs out, sending it crashing down a set of stairs.

"Leaf, catch!" Sander threw a pair of objects at her. She caught the can of hairspray but missed the Zippo lighter. She dove for it as Sander's shotgun blasted apart another goon. She gripped the Zippo in her right hand as she rolled over on the scummy concrete.

A foot slammed onto her hip, pinning her to the ground. A hulk bared its rotting teeth as it reached for her. Leaf flicked the Zippo as she

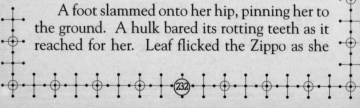

pointed the hairspray directly at it. The screaming torch stumbled back, crashing into another
zombie. They burned together.

Leaf scrambled to her feet, waving her im-
promptu flame-thrower threateningly. A bony
fist slapped it out of her hand. The canister rolled
under a dumpster and exploded, sending the
Dumpster rolling. Leaf danced back from the
grinning rot as it swiped at her. She quickly
turned her head, looking for Sander or Lucimal.
She couldn't see either of them, though at least
they weren't corpses. The rot smacked the Zippo,
sending it flying. Leaf circled away from the grinning rot, furiously thinking what to do. She
didn't even consider using the .38. It would've
been useless anyway.

Leaf screamed out a *kiai* yell as she tried a set of
percussive strikes. With snaky speed, the rot caught
her hands. Leaf saw stars as the rot's forehead
slammed her face. The zombie flung her against
the brick wall. Leaf stumbled to her feet, trying to
regain her stance as the rot advanced on her.

The rot contemptuously slapped her arms
aside. Its left hand gripped her throat, lifting
her off the ground. Her feet vainly kicked at its
knees. Once again, Leaf's back slammed against
the brick wall.

Leaf's fist bashed at the zombie's arm as his
hand strangled her. She choked, trying desperately to force air through her blocked windpipe.
In the dim light, she could barely see the rotting
Guardian Angels t-shirt on its skeletal chest.

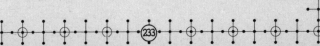

Leaf fought to control her rising panic. It was all or nothing now.

"Do you remember?" she asked in a low voice, looking deep into the rot's eyes. "Do you remember being alive?"

The grip around her throat squeezed tighter. Leaf kept eye contact with the rot, desperately trying to remain passive, non-threatening.

Leaf thought she saw something in the rot's remaining eye. The grip around her throat slackened. Leaf collapsed against the wall as the zombie backed away. It looked down at its hands, then up at her. Leaf's heart clenched at the look on its decomposed face. She had never seen such self-loathing on a face before. The rot opened its mouth as it began to moan. It turned away from her, still moaning as it stared at its hands. It stumbled away from her, the moans turning to sobs. Despite herself, Leaf's eyes filled with tears. She had never heard anything so heart-rending.

Suddenly she heard voices. Sander and Lucimal. Leaf grinned as she turned towards the sound, then stiffened as a yell split the night. Shotgun blasts reverberated through the alley. The last shot died away, and then a sudden scream, quickly cut off. Leaf froze, not sure what to do. Her reaching hand clasped the pepper spray, then moved on and gripped Sander's revolver. Three more shots echoed through the alley. Leaf stepped forward cautiously but stopped as she saw a shadow coming towards her. It was small and slender, and walked with a limp. Lucimal.

"Where's Sander, Lucimal?" Leaf asked as he limped towards her. That scream still seemed to reverberate through the alley.

Lucimal shook his head, his face still in shadow. "You don't want to know, Leaf. It got pretty nasty back there."

"What do you mean?" Leaf stared at him narrowly. Lucimal had positioned himself out of the light. Only those colorless eyes seemed to glow.

"Sander's dead, Leaf," he said. A trickle of blood along his leg caught the light. "There was one last goon. It got him. We gotta get outta here. The cops will be here soon."

"No," Leaf shook her head. "I have to see. Maybe I can save him."

"Leaf, no!" Lucimal yelled as she dodged past him. Leaf could still hear him snarling curses as she rushed down the alley. Leaf was much faster. As she ran, she pulled the snub-nose .38 from her pocket, just in case.

Leaf turned the corner and her stomach heaved. She slapped her hand to her mouth so she wouldn't bring up her lunch.

Sander was lying on his back in a pool of his own blood. His bluish-pink eyes were wide open, shocked. There was a huge, bloody hole where his chest used to be. Sander's shotgun lay by his right hand, shell casings around it. A mutilated hulk was lying almost ten feet away. It looked as if Sander had emptied every shot he had into the thing. Leaf frowned. The hulk was carrying a double-barreled 28 gauge, but the wound in Sander's chest showed no sign of powder-burn. Leaf carefully stepped closer to the dead hulk, her pistol at the ready. She slowly knelt, her left hand feeling for the gun as she kept her eyes on the corpse. The twin barrels were cool. It hadn't even been fired.

Leaf looked back at Sander's body, horrified. From her angle, she could see the albino's throat had been cut, a thick line of crimson from ear to ear. Scuff marks on his boots showed where Sander had flailed before drowning in his own blood.

"Stupid bitch," Lucimal rasped as he leaned against the wall. His Glock was pointed at her head. "You had to come back, didn't you?"

"Why did you kill Sander?" Leaf knew she couldn't get her .38 up before he fired.

"'Do what thou wilt shall be the whole of the Law'," Lucimal quoted with a twisted smile. His face, just below his nose, was a solid mass of blood. "Sander's decency and trust was his undoing. And his flesh and his power became mine."

"So why did you—" Leaf stopped, putting the pieces together herself. "Oh, Goddess. You ate his heart."

"That's right," Lucimal showed his blood-stained teeth. "The ancient Egyptians were right. The heart is the source, the strength. I get the strength, the power from his heart, their hearts. That trusting, *Christian* idiot, Joan—" Lucimal extended his left hand and a red, glowing sword appeared in it. "—she was the first. The first to die so I could gain her power. All the others followed her and I took their powers as my own. Their foolishness, their *humanity*, was their undoing, and they gave their hearts and their power so that one day I, Lucimal, could become King of Hell!"

"Don't come any closer!" Leaf warned.

"You blind, trusting, Goddess-obsessed idiot," Lucimal sneered. "I don't need your stupid heart." His index finger squeezed the trigger.

The Glock clicked on an empty chamber. Lucimal gaped. The .38 smashed the silence. Lucimal jerked with the shot, collapsing beside a dumpster. Leaf looked down at her hands in shock. She, Leaf Pankowski, a woman who had never picked up a gun in her life, had just shot another hunter.

Lucimal groaned and rolled over, his eyes glaring at her. *Oh shit, I forgot his vest,* she thought as she fired another shot. The dumpster rang like a bell. Lucimal snarled as he rose to his feet, throwing the Glock to one side. Leaf turned and ran past him, her boots slithering among the newspaper and water.

"Mine is the power! Mine is the flesh!" She heard Lucimal yell behind her. Leaf kept running, tears blurring her vision.

A sharp pain blasted her right arm. Leaf screamed as she fell into a row of trashcans. The .38 skittered away, lost in the gloom and garbage. Leaf gasped for air as she saw the empty pop can, still glowing red, roll away from her. Her arm felt like it was broken.

Lucimal was limping towards her, the glowing sword in his hands, lighting his colorless eyes with a hellish glow. Leaf scrambled to her feet, gulping back tears. She turned and ran towards the park, the blade whistling through the air just behind her, his curses seemingly in her ear.

Ahead she could see Sander's van, ahead on the street, a clean red under the yellow streetlight. She gasped for air as she ran, the whistling sword and snarled curses reminding her not to look back. She sprinted for the van, for an illusory safety.

A car screeched to a halt just in front of her, blue and red lights blazing. Leaf smacked into the right front quarter panel, rolled across the hood. The driver door opened in front of her, nearly hitting her in the head.

"Freeze, asshole!" a voice above Leaf yelled. "This is the police! Don't you fuckin' move!"

"Mine is the flesh!" Lucimal screamed, just before two pistols opened up. Leaf the sound of bullets striking flesh, and the tinkle of shell casings hitting concrete. Leaf flinched as a hot cartridge struck her hand. She was too dazed to do anything else.

Silence.

"Where's that fucking glowing sword?" one voice called out after what seemed an eternity. The smell of gunpowder was thick in her nostrils.

"I dunno," the voice above Leaf replied. "We'll find it later. We got somebody right here, though."

"Streetwalker?"

Leaf felt a strong hand grasp her collar, lifting her up. She saw a fleshy face staring at her from close range. The smell of cheap coffee and donuts hit her like a blast. "Naw," the cop holding her reported. "She's uptown. Taxpayer."

Leaf tried to find her feet and place them on the ground. She heard the first cop say something that sounded like, "Pity."

"You all right, Ma'am?" the other cop asked her, not unkindly. Leaf nodded quickly. Out of reflex, she looked at the cop with her second sight. She fought her relexive horror when she saw the corruption in his face.   "You mind telling me what's going on here?" the cop asked as she propped herself against the car.

"I was . . . I was walking home," Leaf gasped, "when—"

"Not a good neighborhood to be taking an evening stroll through, Lady," the cop holding Leaf interrupted, giving her a suspicious look.

"I was walking home when—"

"Shit, Bob, you gotta check this out," his equally-corrupt partner interrupted. He was standing over Lucimal, his flashlight illuminating the dead man's face. "This guy liked his vittles raw."

"Whaddya talking about, Vern?" Bob turned away from Leaf. Leaf held onto the Ford Crown Victoria, thinking furiously. She was grateful she wasn't wearing anything identifying her as a hunter.

"I think this guy was eating something that wasn't quite done living yet," Vern replied. "There's blood all over his teeth." He leaned down and ripped open Lucimal's coat. "Just as I thought. Body armor. Good thing I aimed for the head."

"You know anything about this, Ma'am?" Bob turned to Leaf.

"I saw— I heard shots, I went to go look and I saw. . . I saw him eating — over there—" The lies came easily to her. She pointed down the alley.

"Jesus H. Frankenchrist. Vern, go check it out," Bob ordered. "We gotta call this one in."

"Ten-four." Vern pulled out his pistol, replaced the clip. He headed down the alley, his flashlight held over his pistol, leading his eyes.

"Stay here, Ma'am," Bob ordered as he slipped back into the car. "I still got some questions for you."

Leaf leaned against the cruiser's hood, grateful she no longer had the .38. She surreptitiously tucked her knit gloves into her poncho, to conceal the powder burns. She could hear Bob talking on the car radio.

She heard the sound of running footsteps. "Her story checks out, Bob," the other cop reported between heaving breaths. "Man, it's a fucking slaughterhouse back there, and it looks like the guy we bagged was a wannabe Lecter, too."

Bob relayed the information, then stepped out of the car. He glanced over at Leaf. *He'll remember my face*, she thought, *I'm known to them all now.*

"Can I go?" Leaf called out. She saw Bob look over to the other cop. Vern shrugged.

"Sure Lady," Bob replied. "But I'm gonna have to get your name and address first." He flipped out his notebook.

Leaf gave him the name and address on her fake ID, showing it to him as corroboration. She was amazed at how easily the lies tumbled from her lips. The cop took it all down carefully, accepting the forged driver's license as genuine. *I have to disappear, go into hiding,* she realized.

"You want a ride home, Ma'am?" Bob asked when he was done.

Leaf shook her head. "I'll be fine. The cross-town bus stops about a block from here."

"Yeah, there'll be one there," he checked his watch, "in about fifteen minutes. You sure you're okay, though?"

"Yeah. I got money, too." Leaf turned away. She could see Sander's van, parked at the side of the road. Useless. She didn't have the keys.

"We'll be in touch, Ma'am," Bob promised. Leaf numbly stumbled away from the police car, carefully walking towards the other side of the street. Wailing sirens pierced the night, growing closer. Leaf crossed the road, hugging the shadows as she walked away from the scene. Nothing would ever be the same again.

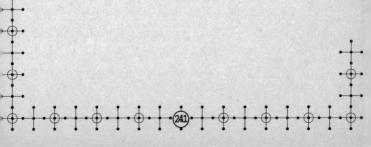

Nine
Unusual
Suspects

by Richard Lee Byers

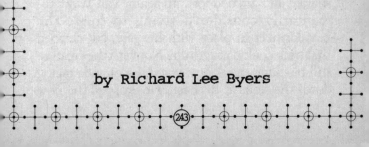

Carleton Van Wyk ran headlong down the shadowy service stairs of the old hotel, his clattering footsteps echoing in the shaft. Somewhere above him, a jovial voice called, "I'm gonna get you, old man!"

As he staggered across the landing connecting one flight of steps to the next, the slight, silver-haired physician wondered grimly how the investigation had gone wrong so quickly and completely. When one of his sources on the Net had informed him of an upcoming gathering of vampires, he had carefully planned how to conceal himself in the venue and observe them. But somehow, one of the monsters had sniffed out his hiding place almost immediately.

He hurtled off the bottom of the stairs into a crooked little corridor. To his left was an exit. He flung himself at it, threw it open, and nearly fell into the arms of the vampire waiting on the other side.

Eyes burning in his white, lean face, his grin revealing two ivory fangs, the creature reached for him. Van Wyk pointed his Sig Sauer Model 226 and fired. The bullet — his last, if he'd counted correctly — caught the monster in the chest and knocked him backward.

Blood flowing from his wound, the vampire snarled and lurched forward again. Van Wyk momentarily considered trying to freeze the blooddrinker in place with his gaze, but decided that trick couldn't save him. Not with the creature still blocking the doorway and its comrade racing down the stairs at his back. He dropped the now useless pistol, turned, and dashed back down the hallway and through the door at the other end.

Laughter rippled through the air. The doctor saw that he'd blundered into the hotel bar, and that many of the twenty or so vampires in the building had been waiting here to intercept him. He realized with a sick, sinking feeling that his pursuers probably could have caught him at any time, but had been running him around the building for fun. Until finally, when they'd had enough, they'd herded him here for the kill.

Leering, moving without haste, the vampires closed in on him from all sides. Their leisurely advance gave him a moment to concentrate, and a haze of shimmering blue light cocooned his body. Since the nimbus was invisible to others, his assailants kept on coming. When a slinking blooddrinker collided with it, the radiance sparked, crackled, and slammed the creature backward.

Wary of Van Wyk's aura, the other vampires hung back for a moment, and then a glass ashtray flew out of the shadows, missing the his head by an inch. As he'd feared would happen, one of the blooddrinkers had thrown something at him, and now the creatures knew that even if they couldn't reach him, their missiles could. They reached for whatever was handy, in some cases effortlessly hefting tables and chairs.

This was it, then. Van Wyk had watched supernatural entities of various sorts slaughter a dozen of his fellow hunters, and now, as he'd always known would happen someday, it was his turn. Dry-mouthed with fear, he felt an urge to close his eyes, but he didn't. He stood up straight, composed his features, and gazed coldly at the monsters that were about to kill him.

At that moment, two newcomers marched into the bar. One was a tall, blond vampire, his fierce scowl looking out place on his pleasant, boyish face. Judging from his tanned complexion and beefy frame, the blooddrinker's companion was a human minion. The servant looked exceedingly upset.

"Mr. Saraceno is dead!" the human cried. The vampires menacing Van Wyk jerked around in shock.

The blond creature grimaced. "I actually wanted to announce the news myself, Wilson, somewhat less abruptly."

Wilson flinched. "I'm sorry, Mr. Rand. I wasn't thinking."

"It's all right. I know you're upset." Rand looked toward the other vampires. "Well, you heard it. The prince is gone."

A short, voluptuous, black-haired vampire wearing cheap, heart-shaped sunglasses nervously turned a throwing knife in her hand. The weapon gleamed in the muted light as if it was made of silver. "Vampires don't just die," she said in a husky voice. "If Saraceno is dead, somebody had to kill him."

Rand nodded. "I'm afraid you're right. He was murdered in his suite by a person or persons unknown."

The raven-haired vampire sneered. "But I can guess who you're going to accuse."

"I'm not accusing anyone yet," Rand replied. "The facts are...peculiar."

"Whatever," she said, "you're not pinning this on us."

"I don't see why not," someone called. "You bastards are the ones with the motive. You've hated the prince for years, and now he was in a position to denounce you at the next conclave!"

"We aren't afraid of any stinking conclave," someone else retorted, "and we're not the only ones with a reason. What about the kids? They were scared shitless of what Saraceno might do to them."

"Forget the newborns," came another voice, "it was probably one of his own people. They're the ones who could get close to him and take him by surprise."

Everyone started babbling at once. To Van Wyk, it genuinely appeared that everyone had forgotten him, and he wondered if he could make a discreet exit while they bickered. It was exceedingly unlikely, but on the other hand, what did he have to lose by trying?

He quelled his aura to make himself less conspicuous—though invisible, if it brushed up against one of the vampires, it would spark—then slowly began to turn toward the door through which he'd entered. When he got all the way around, he found himself facing a youthful—and rather scruffy-looking vampire clad in a T-shirt and torn, faded jeans. Whereas many bloodsuckers appeared lean and graceful, this one seemed skinny and awkward. But if he himself wasn't impressive, the revolver he was pointing straight at Van Wyk made up for it. He gave the human an ironic, fang-baring smile.

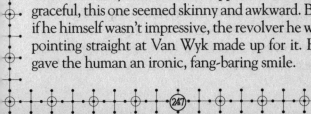

Stripped of his last forlorn hope, Van Wyk turned back around to watch the other vampires argue. He might as well go out observing the blooddrinkers like the scientist he was, if only because that objective, dispassionate mindset would help him resist the gnawing dread that threatened to break him down.

Actually, the argument seemed likely to escalate into a brawl. A number of the creatures were brandishing weapons, and they all had their retractable fangs extended. Up at the front of the room, Rand climbed up on top of the bar.

"Stop this!" he shouted, and something more than sound exploded forth from him, a palpable force of will that shocked everyone into silence. "You're all behaving like idiots. You're assuming some particular one of us is guilty, but at this point, we *don't know* who's to blame."

Suddenly, Van Wyk had a final, lunatic idea. "How do you propose to find out?" he called.

Rand peered at him as if noticing him for the first time. "Who the devil are you?"

"Besides supper," said the vampire in the heart-shaped sunglasses. A couple of the other monsters chuckled, but the room was too tense for any great outpouring of mirth.

"My name doesn't matter," said Van Wyk, knowing it might mean his death to give it, if not tonight, then in the future. With everyone now peering at him, not as prey but to hear what he had to say, he suddenly became conscious of his disheveled appearance. There was nothing to be done about the stinking,

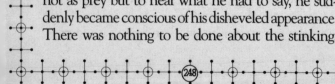

clammy sweat stains under his arms, or the tear in his slacks. But he straightened his tweed jacket, adjusted his bow tie, pushed his spectacles back up to the bridge of his nose, and ran his fingers through his hair, talking the while. "But I'm one of the new breed of humans that studies beings like you, and puts them down when necessary. Your compatriots just witnessed one of my powers."

"Yeah," someone said. "Gives us even more reason to put *you* down, van Helsing."

"Go ahead," Van Wyk replied, "if you're sure you can identify your prince's murderer by yourselves. Are you? Are any of you trained investigators? I am. I'm a pathologist, and before I became involved in your world, I sometimes worked in the coroner's office. I helped the police solve some particularly perplexing homicides."

"You may be Sherlock fucking Holmes among the donors," said the black-haired vampire, "but you couldn't catch a killer on our turf. You don't know anything about us."

"You underestimate me," the doctor replied. "I've already discerned that two very different groups of vampires are met here tonight. One faction affects a tough, blue-collar look: boots, denim, black leather, PVC, and gaudy jewelry. It's rowdy and uninhibited. The other side dresses expensively and conservatively, like corporate executives. Its representatives are polite and reserved, or at least they were until news of Mr. Saraceno's death robbed them of their composure. But the differences between the groups run deeper than taste in clothes or demeanor. As I was being chivvied about, I noticed the Blue Collars sometimes moved with superhuman speed. Here in the lounge, I've observed that they're the ones who lifted heavy furniture as if it were weightless. The Executives did neither of those things, but Mr. Rand has demonstrated a preternatural ability to impose his will on others, which I take to be characteristic of his group. Thus I infer that your two parties represent two distinct subspecies of vampire."

He gazed at the black-haired blooddrinker. "You, Miss, are clearly at least the unofficial leader of the Blue Collars. Mr. Saraceno led the Executives, and apparently had some claim to final authority over both groups. Mr. Rand was manifestly his enclave's second-in-command, and with the prince gone, he ascends to the primary position.

"Finally, your two groups have longstanding differences. Nonetheless, you arranged this meeting to resolve a problem involving certain young people, perhaps because the alternative was war."

A surprised murmuring ran through the crowd. The raven-haired vampire grinned. "I have to admit, Doc, that was pretty good. My name's Polly, by the way."

"Insightful or not, it's irrelevant," said Rand. "We aren't going to let a mortal poke around in our affairs."

"Why not?" Polly replied. "Afraid of what he might find out about you?"

"Of course not. But we protect our secrets, always."

"Your gang believes in 'always.' Mine is more flexible. Finding out who offed Saraceno is more important than keeping one mortal from learning a little bit more about us. Because if we don't find out, we might wind up fighting each other for nothing, or your side might denounce us to the old farts for breaking a truce. And the truth is, my people *don't* have a detective. You don't, either, and I wouldn't trust him to report the truth if we did. But we can count on Doc here to be impartial."

"Yes," said Van Wyk, "provided you guarantee me safe passage out of here when my task is done."

"Oh, sure," said a male Executive, "*absolutely*." Other vampires laughed.

Van Wyk's mouth tightened. Clearly, he couldn't trust their word, but there was no point in saying so. His immediate task was to survive the next few minutes. If he succeeded in that, who knew what would happen? Surely there was at least a slim chance that, if he solved the murder, they would decide to let him go. Or perhaps he could find a way to escape.

"Hey," called a Blue Collar, "how do we know the Peter Cushing wannabe didn't kill the prince himself?"

"Because, fool, we, or our servants, have been watching him pretty much every second since his arrival," an Executive with a trace of a French accent replied. "And I say his proposal has merit. He found us, didn't he? Perhaps he can find the murderer as well."

"Not a chance in hell," said a female Executive. "But it might be fun to watch him try, and maybe we could use some entertainment right about now. It'll give us time to calm down."

Other vampires jabbered in agreement.

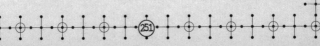

Rand glanced around the room, gauging the sentiments of the crowd. "All right. I still think this is an asinine idea, but I won't have you suspecting I vetoed it because I'm the murderer. So, Doctor, here's how it's going to work. It's ten before nine. You have until dawn to find the guilty party and earn your freedom." Laugher rippled through the room. "Otherwise, we'll kill you and try to solve our own problems." He looked at the gawky vampire who had prevented Van Wyk from sneaking out, the one creature who didn't look as if he truly belonged with either faction. "Marvin, I'm appointing you the doctor's assistant. Help him in his inquiries, and make very sure he doesn't escape."

"Sure, okay," stammered Marvin, plainly surprised at having been chosen.

Polly grinned at Van Wyk. "So, the game is afoot. What's your first move?"

"I'd like to examine the crime scene and the body," the doctor replied.

"Sounds like a plan. And maybe Rand, Wilson, and I should tag along."

Van Wyk felt a twinge of disappointment. With four of his captors accompanying him to the elevators, he would have absolutely no chance of making a break for the front door. But then, he'd known it wouldn't be that easy, anyway.

Saraceno had been staying on the top floor of the hotel. When Van Wyk stepped out into the corridor, he saw that someone had knocked the door to the prince's luxury suite off its hinges. It had fallen inward.

The doctor looked at Wilson. "I assume you did that."

The other human nodded. "I was standing guard out here in the corridor, and I was supposed to make sure Mr. Saraceno was out and about by eight. When I yelled and pounded and he didn't answer, I got a bad feeling and kicked down the door. Then I found him in the bedroom." He grimaced at the picture in his mind.

"Then evidently you didn't have a key."

"Nobody did. Mr. Saraceno was kind of paranoid about his personal security. He said that was how he'd survived this long."

They walked on into a large sitting room opulently furnished with antiques. What might well be an original Matisse hung on the wall, and a beautiful Chinese porcelain vase sat on a marble-topped stand. Tucked away in one corner in the midst of all the elegance and taste was a collection of medieval torture implements, including thumbscrews, barbed whips, and even a half-open iron maiden, the tips of the spikes brown and rusty.

Van Wyk looked about for a moment, taking in the details of the scene, and then his investigator's intuition whispered that he ought to look at the interior face of the fallen door.

He pointed. "Could someone please lift that up?"

"No problem," Polly said. She hoisted it effortlessly, with one hand.

Van Wyk's eyes narrowed. "There are locks here that can only be opened from the inside, and which were engaged when, you, Mr. Wilson, battered down the door. Is there another way in?"

"Not as far as I know," Rand replied, "and I think I would. We Ven—, that is to say, my faction built and owns the hotel."

Van Wyk walked to one of the windows. It was locked, and it, too, could only be opened from the inside. He would examine all the others, but already sensed he would find them in the same condition.

A locked room and a guard, he thought grimly. Those must be the "peculiar" features to which Rand had alluded.

"Let's inspect the bedroom," the doctor said.

The spacious sleeping room was as handsomely appointed as the rest of the suite, but with odd, heavy black drapes covering the window. Van Wyk took note of the fact as evidence that vampires truly couldn't bear sunlight. But most of his attention fixed on the gory tableau in the center of the room.

Anthony Saraceno's body lay in bed beneath blood-soaked covers. From the looks of things, his killer had crouched over him and pressed a strange blade with a wooden handle at each end into his neck. The vampire prince had grabbed hold of it, and, heedless of the cuts he was inflicting on his hands, tried to shove it away. Van Wyk knew because the dead creature was still clutching the weapon. Unfortunately, struggling hadn't done Saraceno any good. The edged steel had sheared completely through his spinal column.

His chestnut-haired, brown-eyed head had tumbled off the bed onto the floor, where it lay on one ear staring glassy-eyed at the intruders in the doorway.

Marvin made a little choking sound of revulsion.

As he moved into the room, Van Wyk kept his eyes on the floor, trying not to step on any pieces of evidence. That, of course, was assuming he would know them if he saw them. Actually, he had exaggerated his qualifications as a sleuth. He was entirely competent to perform an autopsy, but less so to evaluate every element of a crime scene. Well, he would simply have to do the best he could.

Bending down, he gazed closely at the murder weapon. "This a strange-looking implement. Has anyone ever seen it, or one like it, before?"

Evidently no one had, or at least he wasn't admitting it.

Van Wyk peered at the raw stump that had been Saraceno's neck. "This weapon could have been used to saw or chop through your prince's neck, but I can tell from the appearance of the wound that it wasn't. Someone pushed it through all at once, like a guillotine blade, while Mr. Saraceno tried vainly to hold it back."

"That would require prodigious strength," said Rand, "which, as you observed, is not an advantage we 'Executives' possess."

"I told you," Polly said, "you aren't pinning this on us."

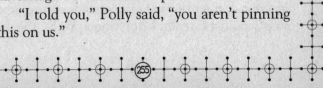

As the two squabbled, Van Wyk continued his examination of the corpse. After a while, he noticed that the blade had nearly cut Saraceno's hands in two as well. He touched the edge with the utmost gentleness and still bloodied the tip of his finger.

He cleared his throat to draw his companions' attention. "You made a reasonable inference, Mr. Rand, but in fact, the killer didn't need superhuman strength. This blade is amazingly sharp, keener than the finest Japanese katanas. Tell me, is there actually such a thing as a 'magic' weapon?"

"Yeah," Polly said. "They're rare, but they're out there. Of course, guys with a whole lot of money are the ones who can usually get their hands on them. Isn't that right, Rand?"

"You and your kind may enjoy the bohemian life," the Executive replied, "but I'm reasonably certain you have your own wealth socked away somewhere. The criminal enterprises you control must turn a healthy profit."

Van Wyk observed that Saraceno's skin was purplish, and his nails, white. The eyes in the severed head had begun to flatten. However, there was no sign as yet of rigor mortis. If a vampire corpse deteriorated in the same manner as a human one — a tenuous assumption, he realized — the prince had apparently been dead at least thirty minutes and probably less than four hours.

The doctor completed his investigation of the crime scene without turning up anything else of interest. Under normal circumstances, the next step would be to look for fingerprints, but he

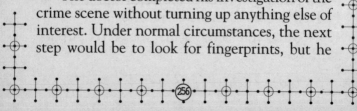

didn't have the equipment and was reasonably certain that a killer clever enough to enter and depart the suite unobtrusively would have had the sense to wear gloves anyway.

"Now I'll need to question people," he said. "I suppose there's no reason why I shouldn't conduct the interviews right here in this sitting room. Mr. Wilson, if you'll please stay, I'll begin with you."

Polly chuckled. "I can't remember the last time I let a mortal tell me to get lost. But anything for you, Doc. Send for me when you need me." She and Rand took their leave.

In the sitting room, Van Wyk settled himself in a velvet-upholstered wingchair. Marvin flopped down on a hassock. Wilson remained standing until the doctor waved him toward the couch. Then he perched on the front of the cushion, his back so straight that he might have been standing at attention.

"I need some background," said Van Wyk. "What, exactly, was the nature of your relationship with Mr. Saraceno and his kind?"

Wilson hesitated. "I'm not sure how much I'm allowed to tell you."

"I understand your dilemma. But if you had regard for Mr. Saraceno, your best hope of seeing his killer unmasked is to speak candidly."

"Besides," Marvin chimed in unexpectedly, "you know that the other vamps probably won't let the doc walk out of here alive, no matter what they promised. Got to maintain that first tradition."

Wilson's mouth tightened. "Yeah, okay, I'll answer your questions. Unless you ask about some secret that I'm sure I'm not supposed to talk about."

Van Wyk said, "Fair enough."

"I worked for Mr. Saraceno, but it was more than just a job. There's a...perk that vampires can give to their mortal helpers." To Van Wyk's surprise, he detected a hint of shame in Wilson's voice, as if the tough bodyguard were revealing an unusual sexual proclivity. "It keeps you from getting old. Believe it or not, I was born in 1923. I don't know where I'm going to get my treatments now."

Van Wyk had had no idea that individuals like Wilson existed. He was accumulating a wealth of new data, information of use to any hunter, and he hoped that he wouldn't die before he could pass it along. "You stood guard outside Mr. Saraceno's door. When did you come on duty?"

"Three o'clock. Hours before dark. Before any of the vampires should have been up and moving around."

"You're assuming another vampire killed him."

Wilson cocked his square, crewcut head. "Naturally. Trust me, no mortal has what it took to do the job, or to get into the suite without me spotting him."

"Did anyone come up to this floor while you were on duty?"

"No."

"Did you see or hear *anything* out of the ordinary?"

"No."

"I'll be frank with you, Mr. Wilson. I don't necessarily agree that only a vampire could have killed your employer. I could conjecture that you kicked down the door, did the deed, retired to some refuge to wash off and exchange your bloody clothes for clean ones, and then sought out Mr. Rand to report Mr. Saraceno's demise. Given that scenario, it's no longer necessary to explain how the murderer got in and out without disturbing the locks and without you noticing anything amiss."

"I get that," Wilson replied, "but I didn't do it. I had no reason to. Mr. Saraceno treated me okay, and like I told you, he was my ticket to eternal life. Besides, I *couldn't* do it even if I wanted. My treatments affected my mind. They made me completely, unconditionally loyal."

"I see," replied Van Wyk noncommittally. "Then who, in your opinion, would have wanted to kill Mr. Saraceno?"

Wilson snorted. "Who wouldn't? Vampires are always plotting against each other, settling old scores, jockeying for power. Sometimes it winds up with one of them dead. But my money's on one of Polly's gang. They're rebels and troublemakers by nature, and they never wanted to accept the prince's authority over the whole quadcity area, them included. And when they took the youngsters in, that was defying him outright. Maybe they figured they needed to murder him before he got around to punishing them."

"Who are these youngsters?" asked Van Wyk.

Marvin brushed a strand of his long, unruly hair out of his pale blue eyes. "Saraceno turned a lawyer named Jonathan Billings into a vampire. Afterwards,

Jonathan was supposed to obey his sire, the prince — in this case, the same dude — and the traditions — the laws — just like the rest of us. One of the rules says you can't make a new vampire without permission. But as a mortal, Jonathan had a girlfriend named Elaine, and he didn't want her to get old and kick, so he turned her without Saraceno's okay.

"When the prince found out about it," the skinny vampire continued, "Jonathan and Elaine ran away to Polly, and her people took them in. As you can guess, after Saraceno found out about *that*, he was even more pissed. The factions were going to meet her tonight to discuss if the runaways would be handed over to their elder, if the two sides would go to war, or what."

"Interesting," said Van Wyk. "That's all for now, Mr. Wilson. Please find Polly and send her up."

"You got it," Wilson said.

Once the servant had gone, Marvin said, "Do you really think you can pull this off?"

At the best of times, Van Wyk hesitated to confide his personal feelings to others. He certainly had no inclination to engage in idle chitchat with one of his captors. Despite his sad sack appearance, Marvin was a predator on humanity, just like his fellows. But the doctor hoped it would benefit him to ingratiate himself with his guard. "According to you, it doesn't matter. You people are going to kill me regardless."

The vampire blinked. "Uh, I shouldn't have said that. I mean, I just said it to convince Wilson to open up. I'm sure they'll let you go if you crack the case."

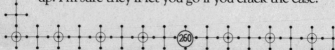

"I'm glad to hear it," said Van Wyk, pretending to believe him.

"So, do you think you can figure it out?"

"I hope so."

"I guess you don't have some weird power that will point to the killer."

'Alas, no. Or if I do, I haven't discovered it yet. The truth is, I'm only just beginning to explore these abilities. I don't fully understand their uses and limitations. Occasionally, I forget I even have them."

Marvin nodded. "Turning into a vampire is the same way. Some of it comes naturally, but a lot of it you have to learn."

"You don't seem to be quite the same sort of vampire as any of the others."

"No," the creature replied with a bitter smile. "I'm what they call a caitiff. Thin, dirty blood. No heritage. I'm lucky Saraceno even made a place for me in his family, even though I'm at the absolute bottom of the pecking order. Rand probably picked me to help you because I can't give away any of his special secrets, or because he figures a mortal doesn't deserve quality help."

Despite himself, Van Wyk felt a vague pang of empathy. As a bookish, introverted child, he had learned early on what it was like not to fit in. "Should I believe Mr. Wilson's assertion that he was constrained from harming Mr. Saraceno under any circumstances whatsoever?"

Marvin frowned as he pondered the question. "I'm pretty sure you can, but there's never anything one hundred percent certain where vampires are concerned. You've got all these different powers that can work against each other. Of course, Wilson himself *isn't* a vampire."

"Definitely not," drawled a throaty feminine voice. Startled, Van Wyk nearly jerked in his chair, but managed to maintain his composure and turn slowly. Polly was standing in the doorway.

"Didn't take you long to call me back up here," she continued, sauntering to the couch. "You got the hots for me, or am I your number one suspect?"

"Neither," said Van Wyk, automatically rising for her as he would for any woman. It cost him a twinge. At his age, he was still fit enough to dash frantically about for a while, but he stiffened up badly afterwards.

Polly half sat, half reclined on the sofa, legs akimbo, in a provocative and unladylike pose.

"I don't have a 'number one suspect' as yet," the doctor reiterated, "but according to Mr. Rand, your faction did have a good reason to kill Mr. Saraceno."

"Sure. We didn't like taking his orders."

"Then why accept his authority, even grudgingly?"

She grinned. With her fangs retracted, it was a fetching smile. "Power. He was the toughest mosquito in town, and that's how you declare yourself prince and make it stick."

"I gather that your relationship, never amicable, had deteriorated of late."

"Uh huh, because we took in those fugitives. Not the brightest move I ever made. It gave him an excuse either to declare war on us or go bitch about us to some old timers even more powerful than he was. But I sympathized with the kids, and I never was able to pass up a chance to give Saraceno the finger.

"But," she continued, "I didn't kill him. When I agreed to this meeting, I also agreed to a truce, and I don't break promises. I may not give a damn about laws or authority, but I've got honor up the wazoo. You understand the difference?"

"I do. Nonetheless, I must ask you where you were between sundown and, say, eight fifteen."

Polly chuckled. "Mostly I was playing tag with you. You almost put a bullet in me."

"Given the protracted nature of the pursuit, and the way we ranged all over the hotel, you could easily have absented yourself long enough to commit the murder."

"Maybe, but I couldn't have gotten past those locks without busting something. My 'subspecies' has disciplines — powers — that are good for beating the crap out of people. We're not big on subtlety. We're also too savvy about fighting to use a blade like the one that cut Saraceno's head off. I don't care if it is magic, I never saw such a clumsy, stupidly designed weapon in my life. A grip on each end? The killer would have been ten times better off with a machete or an ax."

"That had occurred to me as well. But leaving it aside for the moment, let's consider this. If you didn't murder Mr. Saraceno, perhaps it was someone else from your group, someone whose

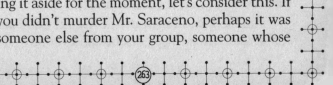

notion of honor diverges from yours. A rebel against *your* authority."

She shrugged. "I've got no problem believing that one of them would *want* to do it. But you still have to explain the locked door and the moronic weapon."

"True."

Polly smiled. "Doc, I get the feeling you're not even close to an answer. But maybe you can still survive past dawn. I could drain you but then bring you back as one of us. You're smart enough to be useful, and you're kind of cute."

Van Wyk couldn't tell if she was serious. "Please don't do that. I don't want to be a vampire." A flash of knowledge came to him then, as had occasionally happened ever since the day he discovered that the world of the supernatural was horribly real, and that he had somehow acquired uncanny abilities himself. "Even if I did, I can't *be* transformed."

"But I'll bet you can still be eaten." She grinned, and this time her glistening fangs were extended. "You might even like it. You got any other questions for me?"

"Not at this time. Could you please ask Mr. Rand to come see me."

"Sure." She exited the room, hips swaying.

"Hope she didn't get you worked up," said Marvin, a hint of laughter in his voice. "That slut routine is all an act, to lure in the prey. Vampires don't have a sex drive. Just the thirst."

Van Wyk was taken aback. Could Polly actually flaunt herself so brazenly, and yet have no

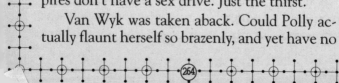

genuine erotic feelings at all? It was strange, somehow disturbing, and another piece of precious information to file away.

"Was she telling the truth about the extent of her powers?" the doctor asked. "Could she have changed into a vapor and flowed under the door, or bypassed it in some equally exotic way?"

"I doubt it."

"Could Mr. Rand, or a member of his faction?"

"No. Their powers are all about messing with your head. Like mine, as far as I even have any. Except..."

"Except what?"

"There *is* a discipline that lets vampires change form. It usually belongs to guys from one particular group, but once in a while, a power can manifest in a vamp from a bloodline that isn't supposed to have it. So there's a chance, just a tiny one but still, that Polly or Rand or one of their followers can turn to mist, and just never let anybody know."

"Wonderful," sighed Van Wyk, suddenly feeling lost and overwhelmed. He wasn't going to solve the mystery. No one could solve it, not with the supernatural involved. There were too many imponderables. Even if he somehow did, the vampires would almost certainly kill him anyway. And his escape plan was a joke.

"You okay?" Marvin asked.

"Yes. Yes, of course." He sat up straighter and did his best to push defeatism out of his head. While he still had a chance, however slim, he mustn't give way to despair.

"Hello again," said Rand from the doorway. "How's it going?"

"I'm making progress, I think," Van Wyk replied, trying to present a confident façade.

"I hope so, for your sake. Time is slipping away." Rand seated himself on the couch, then produced a silver cigarette case from inside his double-breasted jacket. "Would you like one?"

"No, thank you," said Van Wyk. "I would like to know where you were between sunset and the moment when Mr. Wilson made contact with you."

"In my room alone," said Rand, striking a teardrop of blue and yellow flame from his lighter, "pondering what my faction ought to say to Polly's in the negotiations. So I suppose I have no alibi. I also have no motive."

"I've been told that many vampires hunger for power. Perhaps you wanted to eliminate Saraceno in order to rule his principality yourself."

Rand exhaled a breath of pungent, sinuous blue smoke. "I admit that like most 'Executives,' I'm a political animal. My ambition is to rise as high as possible. But I was nowhere near ready to move against Anthony. I also have no vampiric power which would have enabled me to get at him when he was protected as he was."

"So I understand. But if there is a secret way in here, you, as Mr. Saraceno's lieutenant, are the one most likely to know about it."

"You've already searched the suite once, Doctor. Go over it again if you like. If you find a secret door, it will be news to me."

"Would any of the other Executives want to kill Mr. Saraceno?"

"It's possible that someone was harboring some sort of grudge. But like me, he couldn't have gotten in."

"How difficult would it be for someone unaffiliated with either your faction or Polly's to infiltrate the hotel?"

"Very difficult. We have sentries and security systems covering the approaches. That's how we spotted you."

Van Wyk frowned as he strained to think of a new question, something that could cast a ray of light into what seemed an impenetrable darkness.

"You're stumped, aren't you?" said Rand.

"No, I simply haven't hit on the answer yet."

"Don't bother trying," the handsome vampire said. "I knew you wouldn't get anywhere. I only agreed to let you try because it bought me time to figure a way out of this mess. And I have. I've worked out a solution that will help you and me both."

"Go on."

"If you pin the murder on Polly or one of her people, it will probably cause a war between our two factions. If you don't accuse anyone, my associates will simply assume that the someone on the other side was responsible, and we'll still have to fight. And I don't want that, not at the very beginning of my reign. I have other matters to attend to. I have to consolidate my position with the members of my family and also the elders of my kind.

"So here's the answer. Pin the murder on Wilson and let Polly's crowd off the hook. He's just a human flunky, so no one will care if he takes the fall. If you're as slick an investigator as you say, I'm sure you can work out a convincing way to frame him. And if you convince everyone, I'll make sure you walk out of this place alive. I'll have to, won't I? I can't let anyone molest you for fear that you'll shout out the truth about our arrangement."

You could try to have me attacked so suddenly and viciously that I wouldn't have time to shout, Van Wyk thought. Still, the scheme seemed to offer genuine hope of survival, far better hope than he'd had before. He sat silently for several seconds, thinking it over. At last he said, "I'm sorry. It's an interesting proposition, but I must decline."

Rand stared Van Wyk in the eyes. "You should reconsider. Otherwise you won't live out the night."

Van Wyk felt dazed. Woozy. He gave his head a vigorous shake and his thoughts snapped back into focus. Rand blinked in surprise.

"As I told Polly earlier," the doctor said, "some of your vampire powers don't work on me. Including your mesmerism, evidently. I believe we're done for now. Please send up Jonathan and his young lady."

"Think about my offer," growled Rand, his fangs extended. He stalked out.

Marvin shook his head. "He throws you a lifeline, you throw it back."

"With great reluctance. But I believe in seeking the truth, and in keeping faith with the truth by acting justly."

"Even when it's only justice for a creep who works for vampires? A guy you might wind up killing yourself for, some other night?"

"Even then."

"Weird."

A male and female vampire appeared in the doorway. Jonathan Billings was tall, with close-cropped, receding ginger hair, shrewd green eyes, and a deep cleft in his chin. Elaine was sharp-featured and petite, with a fondness for gold jewelry than shone vividly against her olive skin. Both were as expensively and conservatively dressed as the other Executives. When Van Wyk ushered them to the couch, they sat close together and held hands.

"I haven't seen either of you before," said Van Wyk.

"No," Billings replied. "When we arrived at the hotel, Polly advised us to stay in our room until someone sent for us. She was afraid that if we ran into Rand or some of his followers, there might be some sort of altercation that would make the negotiations even more difficult."

"Was anyone with you?" asked Van Wyk.

"No," Billings replied. "But I swear, we didn't sneak out and kill Anthony. Surely you understand that we couldn't."

"Why do you say that? Has someone informed you of the circumstances of his death?"

"No. But with vampires, the offspring is always weaker than the sire." Yet another nugget of information; Van Wyk tucked it away. "Anthony was

my sire, I'm Elaine's sire, so there you are." He spread his soft-looking, manicured hands.

"You will at least concede that you had reason to kill Mr. Saraceno."

"Not really. Even if he was dead, Polly might still have turned us over to his successor, depending on how the discussions went."

"But it was Mr. Saraceno you defied," said Van Wyk, "and not Mr. Rand. Perhaps you expected the latter to be less angry, and thus more lenient with regard to your punishment."

Billings smiled mirthlessly. "Evidently you don't know Rand very well."

"Perhaps not," the doctor said. "Still, you must have resented Mr. Saraceno. Killing him would have brought you a certain satisfaction, even if nothing more."

"Or course I resented him," Billings said. "Before he gave me the gift, he said he wanted me for my legal acumen. I was supposed to rise high in the councils of our kind and become a major player. But after the change, he treated me like an infant! He tried to control and restrict me in all sorts of ways, including forbidding me to make another vampire. He said I didn't know how to survive as a nightwalker myself yet, and certainly wasn't ready to be responsible for another one; ask again in a century or so. Well, Elaine didn't have a hundred years!"

"So you transformed her, and the two of you fled his retribution. I'm surprised you didn't run farther."

"I wanted to," said Elaine in a flat little voice. "But Jonathan hoped that if we stuck around,

eventually he could find a way to worm his way back into the prince's good graces. Mr. Operator. He thinks he can wheel and deal his way out of anything, and he wasn't willing to give us his chance to be a big shot. Thanks to that, we're probably going to die."

Billings looked shocked. "That wasn't the reason!" he protested. "It would have been hard and dangerous on our own."

"Yeah, well," she said, pulling her hand from his grasp and shifting away from him, "thank God we avoided any danger."

Van Wyk asked the pair a few more questions, failed to uncover any indication that either was capable of bypassing the late prince's security, and finally sent them on their way.

He turned to Marvin. "Are those two really too weak to have posed a threat to Mr. Saraceno?"

The caitiff shrugged. "What they said was right as far as it goes, but even so, plenty of vampires have taken down their sires. You build up your power until you're a match for the old bastard, or else you outsmart him somehow. But it would be very unusual for two kids as young and clueless as that pair to pull it off."

"Previously, you mentioned that vampires lack any propensity for erotic love. Mr. Billings's devotion to Elaine would seem to contradict you."

"Sometimes the young ones hang on to old, outdated habits for a while. Eventually, assuming the family doesn't kill them, those two will either develop a different kind of love, one that's got noth-

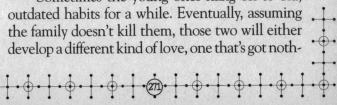

ing to do with screwing, or else wind up hating each other's guts. In this case, I'd bet on hate.

"So, boss, what now?"

Van Wyk looked at his watch and was dismayed to see that it was already twelve forty-five. "I'm going to question you." Marvin looked surprised, then grinned. "After that, I'll see everyone else, one at a time, beginning with Polly's followers."

Thus began a series of interviews no more illuminating than the ones that had gone before. Some of the vampires were arrogant, some, amused, and some, matter of fact. Some spoke freely, and some, evidently mindful of the law that forbade them to tell their secrets to humans, were closemouthed. Some eyed Van Wyk with ill-concealed bloodthirst, the tips of their fangs indenting their lower lips. None gave him any reason to believe that he or she was the regicide.

By the time he finished with them and their human servants as well, it was three thirty, long hours past an old man's accustomed bedtime. His back ached, and his eyes burned. He took off his glasses to rub them.

"What now?" Marvin asked.

"I'm going to sit and think. And would you please go downstairs to the kitchen and get me some hot coffee? I really need it."

The caitiff rose and ambled toward the door. Van Wyk held his breath, for this was his grand escape attempt, such as it was. For the last few hours, he had cultivated Marvin. Treated the vampire as a confidant and collaborator. Done his best to immerse him in the investigation, get him wrapped up in the puzzle it presented. The idea was to make the blooddrinker lose sight of their essential roles as prisoner and guard. To make him willing to leave his charge alone. Whereupon Van Wyk would make a break for the elevators or the service stairs, and, if he was very, very lucky, slip past all the guards and alarms and out of the building.

Marvin walked out into the hall. Van shivered with excitement. He'd thought it such a long shot, a ludicrous plan, even if it was the only one he could think of, but it was working! Then the vampire spun around, bared his fangs, and charged the human in the chair. Van Wyk barely had time to invoke his blue aura. The caitiff slammed into the light and rebounded in a shower of sparks. Snarling, he pulled his revolver out of the waistband of his jeans.

"You can't shoot me!" cried Van Wyk. "Rand told you to guard me, not kill me."

"I'm not stupid!" Marvin screamed. "I may be a shitty little caitiff, but I'm *not* fucking stupid!"

"I know that," said Van Wyk, as soothingly as possible. "But I had to *try* to trick you. In my place, you would have done the same thing, wouldn't you?"

Marvin hesitated, then said, "Turn off the force field."

Van Wyk complied. "Done."

Marvin groped warily in the air, confirming that the energy had disappeared, then slapped the human in the face. "Don't try to get away again."

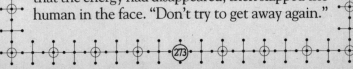

"I won't." His face stinging, his heart leaden with disappointment, Van Wyk shifted his glasses back into the proper position. "I really do need that coffee. Perhaps you could phone downstairs and have someone send some up."

With his one chance at escape gone, Van Wyk saw no alternative but to do his utmost to try to solve the mystery of Saraceno's murder and hope that, despite all indications to the contrary, the vampires would keep their promise and release him. Although probably, it would never come to that, for he had no confidence in his ability in his ability to unravel the mystery.

But against all rational expectation, an answer came to him at twenty past four. It was based on far too many probabilities and not nearly enough certainties, a product of induction rather than deduction, but it was better than nothing.

"Get Polly, Mr. Rand, and anyone else who cares to join us," he said.

Marvin, who had been watching television with the sound off, jerked around. "Do you know who did it?"

"I believe so. Make the call."

As it turned out, all the vampires and most of their human agents crowded into the sitting room of the suite. Van Wyk abandoned his chair and moved back to the window to place his entire audience in front of him.

"Good evening again, everyone," the investigator said. "Several hours ago, you gave me a commission. I am now ready to discharge it."

"You actually know who did it?" asked one of the Executives skeptically.

"I believe so."

"So spill it," said one of the Blue Collars, a bare-chested vampire with pierced nipples and a tattooed face, demanded.

"I'd prefer to review the evidence and my reasoning before stating a conclusion, so you'll know I'm not just guessing."

"That's the way Sherlock always operated," said Polly. "Do it your way, Doc. And make it good."

"Thank you," said Van Wyk. "By now, you all know the essential facts. Someone decapitated Mr. Saraceno in this suite, where he was seemingly protected both by a sentry's vigilance and by a locked door and windows which could only be opened from the inside.

"It occurred to me early on that Mr. Wilson, who was himself standing guard and who kicked down the door before anyone else knew that the prince had come to grief, might be the killer. If so, there would be no need to explain his failure to spot an intruder, or the curious fact that all the interior locks are still engaged."

Wilson's mouth fell open in horror. Rand smiled. Other vampires clamored in agreement, or pivoted toward the human with their fangs bared.

Van Wyk raised his hand to bring the assemblage back to order. "Please, you're anticipating me, and erroneously so. Even though he in some respects seems the most plausible suspect, I'm satisfied that Mr. Wilson is innocent. He was subject to a form of psychological conditioning which rendered him incapable of harming his employer, and he would be disinclined to do so in any case, given that Mr. Saraceno was the source of his longevity."

Wilson slumped with relief. Rand frowned.

"Now," Van Wyk continued, "many of the rest of you did have strong motives to eliminate the prince. Resentment, fear, and ambition, primarily. However, neither the Executives, the Blue Collars, nor their human agents would have been able to pass in and out of the door or a window without disturbing the locks. I'm told there's no secret entrance to the suite, and I certainly haven't been able to find one. I've also been assured that no vampire from another bloodline, with a different set of powers, could have slipped into the hotel tonight. So where does that leave us?"

He paused to take a breath. "I'll tell you. Mr. Saraceno killed himself."

For a moment, his audience stared at him in silence. Then they began to laugh and jeer.

"I know it sounds unlikely," said Van Wyk, raising his voice to make himself heard, "but it explains why your prince was killed with such a peculiar and unwieldy weapon: to disguise the nature of what occurred. When we saw his headless body lying with its gashed hands gripping the blade, our minds immediately conjured up a picture of someone looming over him, kneeling on his chest perhaps, and pushing the blade down while he struggled and failed to fend it off. That's what we were supposed to think. In reality, Mr.

Saraceno simply lay down and pulled the weapon through his neck with one strong jerk. An awkward maneuver, admittedly, but entirely possible with a blade as sharp as that one. This hypothesis also tells us why the killer abandoned a magical and hence valuable artifact at the crime scene."

"So Saraceno not only committed suicide," said Polly, her voice dripping disbelief, "he went to the trouble to make his death look like murder."

"Yes. Otherwise, he could have killed himself more simply and less messily. By leaving his bedroom curtains open to the morning sun, for instance. It occurred to me that he might not want to be thought a suicide because of some obscure point of pride. But I think it more likely that someone else with mental powers programmed him to destroy himself in this particular way, perhaps to divert suspicion from those possessed of hypnotic abilities onto those accustomed to work mischief with their hands."

"So what it comes down to is, you're accusing my people," said Rand, glowering.

"No," Van Wyk replied. "It *could* have been a true suicide. Or, perhaps the compulsion to kill himself at this particular time and in this particular manner was implanted in his mind some time ago, by who knows who."

Looking regretful, Polly shook her head. "I'm sorry, Doc, especially since your theory lets my gang off the hook, but it won't wash. Saraceno wasn't the suicidal type. He was also too psychically powerful and too well protected for anybody to mess with his mind to the degree you're suggesting. What's more, I don't think that any vampire, even the dumb bruiser type like my breed, would be so weak-willed that he could be mind-fucked into destroying himself."

She sighed. "It's too bad. I kind of thought you had a chance of figuring it out."

The vampires bared their fangs and glided toward him.

Van Wyk's heart hammered, and his body shook. He'd delayed the inevitable for as long as he could, but now the moment had come. The blooddrinkers truly were going to kill him, and just to make his demise even more galling, he knew it was because his solution was, if not entirely wrong, at least incomplete. Otherwise the vampires wouldn't have rejected it so quickly and unanimously.

As he summoned his aura and, despite himself, shrank backward, he suddenly had an idea, which in turn triggered another, and that, another, like a line of dominos falling down.

"Stop!" he cried. "I've just now thought of something!" The advancing vampires paid no heed. The Blue Collar with the pierced nipples reached into the shimmering blue haze, and for some reason, the radiance didn't repel him.

His white, powerful hands began to close on Van Wyk's forearm, and then Marvin grabbed his fellow vampire and spun him away. "Chill!" yelled the caitiff, and psychic energy jolted through the air. It wasn't as irresistible as Rand's effort, but it sufficed to startle the blooddrinkers and make them falter.

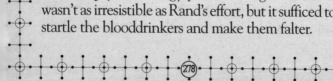

"You promised Doc he could have till dawn!" Marvin cried. "And I want to hear this. Maybe he's got the real answer now."

"All right," said Polly. Van Wyk suspected that vampires didn't actually need to breathe, but she was panting anyway. Perhaps it was a manifestation of her struggle to suppress her bloodthirst. "We'll give him one more chance, but then it's happy hour."

"One more should suffice," said Van Wyk, allowing the aura to fade away. "Let's take another pass at this problem. If Mr. Saraceno was neither suicidal nor under the psychic influence of an enemy, and no one entered this suite to effect his demise, where does that leave us?"

"Nowhere," said Rand impatiently. "You just eliminated every possibility.."

"Actually, no," said Van Wyk. "As Polly's friend Mr. Holmes would have anticipated, one improbability remains now that all the impossibilities have been eliminated." He noticed that the vampires were still bunched all round him, hemming him in. "If you'll allow me to reenter Mr. Saraceno's bedroom, I'll show you what it is."

The creatures made way for him. The crime scene was just as he'd left it, except that the remains had begun to smell. He picked up the severed head, examined it, and smiled, for until that moment, he hadn't been at all sure that his final, fear-triggered chain of inferences — guesses, really — was correct. There was satisfaction in knowing that he'd uncovered the truth at last, even though it probably wouldn't save his life. He displayed the grisly, dripping object to the watching vampires.

"Plastic surgery scars," he said, pointing to the tiny white marks at the hairline and the underside of the chin. "I missed them before because I wasn't looking for them. I imagine Mr. Saraceno's transformation into a vampire preceded the invention of cosmetic procedures. I have something even more anomalous to show you, but to do so, I'll need to borrow a knife."

Polly gave him one of her leaf-shaped silvery blades. He set the head on a little round table, pulled back the upper lip, and began to cut.

"I don't know what sort of structure serves to extrude a vampire's fangs," he said after a moment, "but notice, this specimen doesn't have it." He sliced and pried until the bloody tooth came free of the bone and gum. "In fact, as one can see from the length, this isn't a vampire fang at all, just an ordinary human canine."

"I don't understand," someone said.

"It means that the dead man isn't Mr. Saraceno. He's a human pawn, surgically altered to resemble him exactly; and no doubt psychically compelled to impersonate the prince and ultimately to destroy himself."

"But this is crazy," said one of the Executives. "We can tell who's a vampire and who's a mortal."

"Generally, that may be true," said Van Wyk. "But what if the human was the exact duplicate, in speech and manner as well as appearance, of a vampire you were expecting to see? What if the substitution only occurred very recently, so that the deception didn't need to bear scrutiny for very long?"

"It's possible," said Polly, frowning thoughtfully. "None of us is the kind of vampire with super-sharp senses. We wouldn't have heard the heartbeat. Besides, Rand and his crew *are* dumb as rocks."

Rand's mouth tightened at the gibe, but he opted not to respond in kind. "But who created the double and made the switch?" he asked Van Wyk. "And why? And where is the real Anthony?"

"I can't answer all of that," the doctor replied. "But I suspect that your prince himself was behind the deception. You say he has the power to dominate a human mind, even, I would speculate, to the extent of replacing the original personality with a false one and imposing a suicidal imperative. He was certainly the ideal trainer to prepare a dupe to impersonate himself, as well as the only vampire who would experience little difficulty effecting the substitution."

"Bravo, Doctor," came a deep, resonant voice from the back of the throng.

The vampires spun around. At first Van Wyk was unable to see through them to what they were gaping at. Then the crowd automatically gave way to let the animate counterpart of the bloody, headless form on the bed stroll forward. Presumably he had been eavesdropping out in the hall.

"And here I thought my little subterfuge would fool everyone," the real Anthony Saraceno contin-

ued. "That damn ridiculous blade. I suppose I should have killed my twin with my own hands, broken in through the window or something. But I thought it would be nice for him to die in a sealed room, with his loyal bodyguard oblivious to his plight. Murders are more disturbing when they're thoroughly mysterious. More aesthetically pleasing, as well."

"I don't understand," said Rand, "why would you do this?"

"Perhaps this will explain," said the prince, and then, in an instant, he changed.

He grew so tall that his head nearly brushed the ceiling, so gaunt that he resembled a stick insect. Every trace of hair, even his eyebrows and eyelashes, vanished, while the brown eyes turned black and sunk into his skull. His handsome suit became a dark, musty-smelling robe as dingy, ragged, and shapeless as an old shroud. He gave off a palpable feeling of both great power and extraordinary age.

The vampires gasped and cringed backward. Van Wyk resisted an impulse to do the same, his curiosity even stronger than his fear.

"I'm afraid I still don't understand," the doctor said, "at least, not entirely. How have you been creeping around spying on us undetected?"

Saraceno smiled. "I designed the alarm and sentry system."

"And exactly what manner of creature are you?"

"Ah, of course, you wouldn't know. I'm one of the oldest surviving members of my race. Perhaps you can imagine how tedious such a life span can

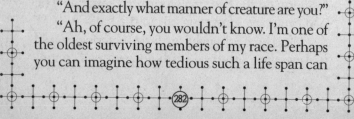

become. To pass the time, my fellows and I conceived a game, We started playing when Babylon was a village of mud huts, and are likely to be at it still when all of you are dust. It's a contest of murder, conquest, and intrigue, and our progeny, and their get, serve as our chessmen."

"You're saying that you created the identity of Anthony Saraceno, established a family and a principality, and finally faked your own murder, just so you could foment trouble between the two subspecies?"

"Not exactly," said the ancient vampire. "When I began, I didn't know how I would choose to end my tenure. However, when I discerned that circumstances would soon oblige me to move on, I assessed the current disposition of the game and decided it would be advantageous to leave the locals in a state of conflict and confusion. To that end, I created my doppelganger, transformed Billings, refused him his heart's desire, and all the rest of it. But please don't ask me to explain how hostilities here advance my overall strategy. It would take hours.

"Now you've spoiled my trick," Saraceno continued, "but perhaps all is not lost." He turned toward Rand. "I'm still your prince, and you detest Polly Donovan and her ilk. If I command you to fight them, will you do it?"

Rand had to swallow before he could find his voice. "If you had seen fit to deal fairly with us, we'd still be your loyal vassals. But you tried to trick us into fighting and risking our lives for no valid reason whatsoever. We don't owe you a damn thing now, and we'll never do your bidding again."

Saraceno chuckled. "Well, perhaps not tonight. But I created this family's policies, alliances, and portfolios. I surreptitiously sculpted your very personalities. Rest assured, in the long run, you will have no choice but to further my schemes, without ever knowing that was the true purpose of all your striving.

"But enough about that," the prince continued. "You're naughty children, but even so, I don't mean to demoralize you." He pivoted back toward Van Wyk. "I'll just chastise this meddler, then take my leave."

Backpedaling, Van Wyk wasted a second trying to summon the aura before remembering that he'd used it only a few minutes before. It wasn't available yet, hadn't recharged or whatever it was that it did. He stared Saraceno in the face and tried to freeze his bare, white feet to the floor. The ancient vampire laughed, exposing a mouthful of teeth grown long and pointed as stilettos, and advanced. His nails lengthened into black talons.

The other blooddrinkers watched huddled in the bedroom doorway, the dread in their pale faces a testament to their elder's might.

Van Wyk grimly evoked yet another of his new talents. He knew it wouldn't save him, not from this threat, but he might as well put up as good a fight as possible.

Saraceno lifted his hand to claw at him. The doctor sensed that a jump backward or to the right would mean death, but a sidestep to the left would leave him unscathed. He dodged, and the strike missed. The vampire immediately followed up

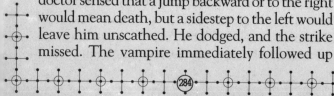

with his other hand. Now a step *into* distance, perfectly timed, was the only way to avoid being gashed from throat to groin.

Three more attacks, three more desperate evasions. Then Saraceno sucked in a deep breath and blew out streamers of darkness, which rapped themselves around Van Wyk's head.

Fortunately, the doctor's superhuman perceptions allowed him to see perfectly in the dark. He avoided the next attack, and Saraceno hissed in frustration.

Van Wyk noticed that the audience of vampires looked astonished and in some cases even excited. But if they thought he had even the slimmest chance, they were mistaken. He had nearly exhausted his preternatural ability to choose the right move, and when it stopped working, he would be at Saraceno's mercy.

At least he achieved one instant of satisfaction before the end. An evasive maneuver worked so well that he was actually able to strike back, lunging in close, pinking the vampire with Polly's knife, and jumping back again.

Saraceno roared. His clawed hands began to whirl in a complicated martial-arts pattern, blindingly fast, the way the Blue Collars could move. Van Wyk's ability to sense the right option abruptly cut out on him, and he knew that when the antediluvian vampire attacked again, it was going to be like getting caught in a threshing machine.

"Fuck it," said Polly from the other side of the room. "If Saraceno's having trouble killing a human, how tough can he be?"

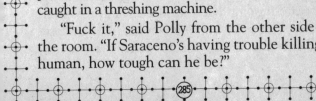

"We have him outnumbered twenty to one," replied Rand. "Let's do it."

The Executives and Blue Collars surged forward. Caught by surprise, Saraceno hadn't quite finished turning around when the attackers at the head of the pack slammed into him.

Winded, his powers ineffectual or spent, Van Wyk scrambled into a corner, then watched the battle in awe. The center of the room was a maelstrom of darting, leaping, reeling forms, of shining eyes and teeth. Vampires moved faster than the eye could follow, or struck with bone-shattering force. Psychic forces hammered through the air until the doctor's head pounded, and his nose bled. Saraceno blew out ragged sheets of darkness to blind his assailants, and conjured bursts of yellow flame to burn them.

At first, the younger vampires fell one by one, ripped to pieces, charred black, or stunned by bolts of mental energy, until Van Wyk was all but certain that Saraceno would succeed in defeating them all. But then someone — the doctor didn't see who or how — landed a telling attack. The prince reeled, fell to his knees, and at once the other creatures swarmed over him like rats.

Saraceno fought on for another three minutes, but never quite managed to shake his attackers off. At the end, he gave a long, ululating shriek and then stopped moving.

Van Wyk expected that would be the end of the frenzied struggling, but instead it continued without a pause. The surviving vampires had all had a taste of Saraceno's blood, and for some reason, they couldn't get enough of it. They madly bit and sucked at the corpse, fighting one other for the spots on the long, gaunt body from which gore could most easily be extracted. Occasionally one of the creatures lifted his crimsoned face and wailed in mindless ecstasy.

The doctor was appalled. Over the last few hours, he had imagined he had gained a new understanding of vampires, had come to know them as creatures whose intellects were largely human. But there was no humanity apparent in the rabid creatures guzzling from Saraceno's body. They were like animals, or something worse.

Van Wyk noticed the vampires' human attendants withdrawing. Evidently they didn't care to remain in their masters' presence when the blooddrinkers were in this condition. And if they were leaving, so could he, for there was no one left who appeared to be paying the slightest attention to him. He tiptoed around the feeding monsters and out into the hallway.

The elevator was the old-fashioned kind, meant to be run by an operator. Van Wyk pulled the brass lever and started down. It seemed to take the rattling cage an eternity to reach the ground floor.

When the doors opened, Polly was waiting outside. In her current condition, face twitching, fangs extended, no one would think her attractive. She was covered in blood, her own and Saraceno's, reeked of it, and swayed as if intoxicated. When she spoke, her voice was an almost unintelligible growl.

"Bet you don't know how I beat you down here," she rasped.

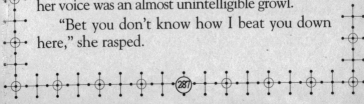

"Considering how fast you are," replied Van Wyk, "and how slow the elevator is, I imagine you simply ran down the several flights of stairs."

"Smart," she said. "That's why I like you, like you so much I chased you down here."

"I trust it was just to see me off," said Van Wyk, not believing it for a second. "You all promised to let me go if I solved your puzzle, and you told me that however your compatriots may behave, you at least are a person of honor."

"But maybe honor only applies between one vampire and another," she said, leering. "Or maybe it's just too dangerous to let you walk out of here knowing what you know. Or maybe the beast is so strong in me that I don't give a shit right now. I've been craving a taste of you all night."

Van Wyk tried to paralyze her with his stare. Nothing happened, and he wasn't surprised. He was too tired. He'd exhausted all his strengths, including the mystical ones.

"If you mean to attack me, do it now," he said. "Otherwise I'm walking out of here."

She stood and thought for a moment, then laughed. "You know, you'd taste like piss compared to what I was just drinking upstairs. So I'll tell you what. I'll give you a ten minute head start."

Van Wyk shivered with relief. If his car was still where he'd left it, ten minutes ought to be enough. He gave her a nod and walked briskly toward the exit.